DINOSAUR CAT

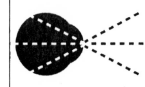

This Large Print Book carries the
Seal of Approval of N.A.V.H.

DINOSAUR CAT

Garrison Allen

WHEELER PUBLISHING

Published in 2006 by arrangement with Kensington Books, an imprint of Kensington Publishing Corp.

Wheeler Large Print Softcover.

The text of this Large Print edition is unabridged.
Other aspects of the book may vary from the original edition.

Set in 16 pt. Plantin by Al Chase.

Printed in the United States on permanent paper.

Library of Congress Cataloging-in-Publication Data

Allen, Garrison.
　　Dinosaur cat / by Garrison Allen.
　　　p. cm.
　　ISBN 1-59722-209-7 (lg. print : sc : alk. paper)
　　1. Big Mike (Fictitious character) — Fiction.　2. Warren,
Penelope (Fictitious character) — Fiction.　3. Booksellers
and bookselling — Fiction.　4. Women cat owners —
Fiction.　5. Arizona — Fiction.　6. Cats — Fiction.
7. Large type books.　I. Title.
PS3551.L39227D56 2006
　813'.54—dc22　　　　　　　　　　　　　　2006007743

For Sunshine

THE FOSSILS

More or Less in Order of Their Geological Appearance

Corny-Milly. A dinosaur who wandered away from its herd and met a bad fate during the Cretaceous period of the Mesozoic era some one hundred million (plus or minus ten million) years ago. Even a forty-ton dinosaur has enemies.

Big Mike aka Mycroft, Mikey. An Abyssinian alley cat from Abyssinia who wandered away from *his* herd somewhat more recently in search of adventure. And found it.

Penelope Warren. An attractive woman who, in her mid-thirties, is working on her third or fourth career (depending upon the manner of counting), but she had not planned on a starring role in what seems to be a bad remake of *The Third Man.*

Empty-by-God-Creek, Arizona. Established 1870. Once a quiet little desert com-

7

munity some miles to the north of Phoenix, where the somewhat eccentric residents like their lifestyle just as it is. They are unprepared for a descent of foreigners wearing trench coats and going "psst!" in alleyways.

Harris Anderson III aka Andy. Editor of the *Empty Creek News-Journal.* He took forever to work up the nerve to ask Penelope out and an eternity before kissing her for the first time. Now they are an Empty Creek item.

Millicent DeForest. An associate professor of geology with a special interest in paleontology.

Red the Rat and Daisy. A wizened desert rat who has been searching for a lost gold mine for upward of three decades. Until recently Red had an eye for the ladies, but shared his life only with a succession of mules. Daisy, despite the gender difference, was best man when Red finally married *the* "fine figger of a woman."

Mattie Bates. A striking woman in her early fifties who found true love with Red on her fourth trip to the altar. There is no truth to the rumor that Daisy lives in the guest bedroom of their double-wide.

Lonesome Bend. A huge chunk of desert scheduled for luxury homes by the Desert Development Company (DDC). It is not to be confused with Lonesome Bend Ranch.

Albert J. McCory. Vice president of the DDC and project manager for the Lonesome Bend development.

Nora Pryor. President of the Empty Creek Historical Society and Museum and author of *Empty Creek: A History and Guide.* Her dust jacket photo could make a saint think naughty thoughts.

Anthony Lyme-Regis. A tweedy Englishman who directs television commercials and, while no saint, does have a naughty thought or two when he is separated from Nora.

Storm Williams aka Stormy. Soon-to-be-famed actress in a series of B movies and mostly straight-to-video epics popular in the more Teutonic European countries. In real life, she is Cassandra Warren, Penelope's little sister.

John "Dutch" Fowler. Chief of police in Empty Creek. He is Stormy's fiancé and her biggest fan. He has turned the home they share out of wedlock into a shrine to her career, to say nothing of his office.

Elaine Henders aka Laney. Empty Creek's preeminent romance novelist, sexual guru, and best friend of Penelope's. Like the heroines she creates, Laney enjoys a good ravishing and shares her life with Wally, one of the six or seven *real* cowboys left in Empty Creek (when she is not tossing him out on his saddle sores), and two diminutive Yorkshire terriers named Alexander and Kelsey. Laney listed their occupations as security consultants when applying for Visa gold cards in their names.

Samantha Dale. When she became president of the Empty Creek National Bank, Samantha — Sam to her many friends — was a conservative, *Wall Street Journal*-reading, always stylishly clad, no-nonsense woman of business and finance. Sam still reads the *Journal* every day, but Empty Creek has had its typical impact and she now demonstrates an entirely different temperament on occasion, usually with Big Jake Petersen, the man in her life. Although delighted when Sam gets a little crazy, Penelope blames it on the local water supply.

Lora Lou Longstreet. The will-of-the-wisp owner of the Tack Shack and Art Gallery. Prior to keeping company with a younger man, an artist of considerable talent for painting nudes, Lora Lou was content to provide all the horsey things for the community. As David Macklin's main model, however, Lora Lou knocked out one wall of the Tack Shack and opened an art gallery largely devoted to her honey's work.

Kathleen Allan. A talented young lady who is working her way through college by assisting Penelope and Big Mike in the daily operations of Mycroft & Company. Even if she never graduates, Kathy is acquiring a splendid, if somewhat unusual, education just by hanging around Penelope, her number-one heroine.

Timothy Scott. A deranged poet hopelessly in love with Kathy. His verses celebrate her every feature, but he has abandoned *The Kathiad*, a twelve-book epic poem after the fashion of Homer. Encouraged by Penelope to diversify, he is contemplating "Ode to a

Lizard at Lonesome Bend."

Tweedledee and Tweedledum. Sometimes known as Larry Burke and Willie Stoner. They are longtime partners in the Empty Creek P.D. Robbery-Homicide Division. In fact, they *are* the Robbery-Homicide Division.

Sam Connors, Peggy Norton, and Sheila Tyler. Uniformed police officers.

The Double B Western Bar and Steakhouse. A famed watering hole where the locals gather for food and drink, assorted charitable events, celebrations of weddings and divorces, and the occasional rowdy episode.

Debbie Locke. An Ivy League graduate who gravitated naturally to being the best cocktail waitress in the western hemisphere. She works at the Double B Western Bar and Steakhouse, which is worthy of her talents. She also keeps company with Sam Connors.

Alyce Smith. Empty Creek's own astrologer and psychic. She was probably a witch in another life, but not a very good one because she is allergic to cats.

Harvey Curtis. A detective with the ECPD who isn't averse to arresting a certain astrologer on occasion even though he shares her boudoir on a regular basis.

Schyler Bennett. A student of paleontology.

The Mahoneys and the Hackers. Empty Creek's version of the Hatfields and the McCoys. Rival clans of trailer park trash who have been feuding so long, no one can remember why. If any of them had managed to graduate from college — or even high school — they might have been known as the Montagues and the Capulets.

Cully and Sully Mahoney. None-too-bright brothers who think the French kiss was a recent introduction to erotic interplay between the sexes.

Buxter Mahoney. The elder brother of Cully and Sully who coped with his heritage by retreating into a schizophrenic world where most of his hallucinations and the voices he hears are more pleasant than those of his immediate relatives.

Cricket. An exception and a refugee from the feud, she had her name legally changed from Sally Ann Hacker after running away to and returning from Berkeley. Her Rapunzel-like hair will come in handy if she ever meets *the* man and needs to sell it to buy a watch fob for him. She is boss lady at Lonesome Bend Ranch.

Leigh Maxwell née Kent. When "Our Leigh" assumed the directorship of the Empty Creek Public Library, circulation soared, even among the illiterate males. When she married Burton Maxwell, many a heart was broken and circulation declined drastically.

Juan-Carlos Estavillo aka Noogy. A short, fat, bald-headed, fiercely mustachioed Mexican-American (his family has been in Arizona almost as long as the rattlesnake), Noogy is a skilled reference librarian. He has a weakness for nougat-filled candies and señoritas of all persuasions.

Boris and Natasha. Fyodor Popov and Katerina Rakitin, Moscow's contribution to the bumbling detective community. Fyodor is fond of quoting from his namesake's body of literature, while Katerina, who wanted to be a ballerina but became an Olympic shotputter instead, develops a fondness for caffe latte and cowboys.

Hiroshi Ishii. A former member of the Yakuza, now seeking a more honorable position as a purveyor of fossils. His left little finger keeps falling off at inopportune moments.

Yitzhak Cohen. An Israeli fossil hunter who used to sell Dead Sea Scroll fragments to tourists in Tel Aviv. He manufactured them in a shed on his kibbutz. For a price, he can obtain a splinter from the true cross.

Hayden Chudnik, Ph.D. Chairman of the geology department at Empty Creek Community College and the city's consultant on paleontology. His rock collection has a better personality than he does.

Chester Handley, Ph.D. A rival paleontologist with a fair tolerance for pain.

Mayor Nicole Pagliero. A psychiatrist who would rather rescue animals and pursue politics than continue her practice, despite the many of her constituents who could benefit from her chosen profession. She is married to Dr. Victorio Pagliero, a practicing shrink with a penchant for home movies.

Mrs. Elaine Burnham. Empty Creek's unofficial town crier. She is susceptible to alien visitations and the occasional moment of lucidity.

Mom's Doughnut Shoppe and Coffeehouse. It used to be known simply as Mom's Do-Nuts until the coffee craze reached Empty Creek, some years after the rest of the nation.

The Rest of the Fossils. A dastardly Allosaurus, Morgan Fairchild (she would have done *Jurassic Park* for free, but what does Steven Spielberg know?), Guido, SOD, Sotheby's, Orson Welles, Joseph Cotten, Yorick, a one-armed saguaro, Michael Caine, Chesty Puller, a 1931 Ford dually, Sir Richard Burton, a retired dominatrix, Jack Webb, Dan Rather, Michael Eisner, Jane Austen, Hugh Hefner, Jack Nicholson, and a hot air balloon.

PROLOGUE

The shot echoed through the hills, disturbing the bleak landscape of the back country, silencing the chatter of birds, and freezing lizards in their tiny tracks.

A startled Satan's Lady skittered sideways at the unnatural sound. Even Daisy, a placid old mule trailing along behind the horse and her rider, swiveled her ears and looked for the danger.

Red the Rat, who had been daydreaming of a certain naked lady for the past two hours, was rudely jerked from there and then to here and now by an excruciating pain in his right leg. Instinctively, Red brought Satan's Lady under control, pulled the Winchester Model 94 from its scabbard, worked the lever action to chamber a round, and scanned his immediate surroundings for the SOB who had shot him.

The desolate hills provided a thousand hiding places for an assassin. Like the desert floor far below, the hills swallowed life, hushed sounds, and masked a teeming infrastructure of predators and prey. There was no way of telling where the shot had been fired with the sound reverberating off hillsides through canyons and back again.

Red cautiously risked a glance at his leg and found the reason for the pain. When Satan's Lady spooked at the gunshot, she had taken Red a mite too close to a jumping cholla and the vicious little cacti had retaliated, flinging a half dozen spears into Red's leg, right through the tough material of his jeans.

"Damn you, Lady, do that again and you're gonna be dog food," Red said. He unloaded his rifle by the simple expedient of cranking the round off as a warning to whoever fired the first shot. The prospect of going to the dog food factory apparently settled Lady's nerves, because she only tossed her head this time. Red replaced the rifle and reached down and pulled out the cholla spines. Those little suckers hurt.

Daisy snorted contemptuously at Red's predicament.

"You can be taco bait yourself, you old bitch," Red threatened. He urged Satan's Lady forward, trying to reclaim the image of that certain naked woman, but wondering about the lone gunshot. Poacher after an out-of-season deer, plinker, varmint hunter shooting at a coyote for no good reason? Red didn't like varmint hunters. Man didn't need much to get along — good woman, good whiskey, spirited horse, and a faithful mule. He had all four and found no reason to go around shooting creatures minding their own damned business. Coyotes had to earn a living too.

Fifteen minutes later, the little party had picked their way down the hillside to a canyon floor that had been greatly rearranged by a flash flood the week before during a horrendous thunderstorm. Red was a little nervous about the prospect of being caught by another torrent. An unseen storm miles away could trigger the rushing waters, but he was eager to get home, and they could make better time through the canyon. Satan's Lady and Daisy knew they were heading for the barn and a good meal and picked up the pace without complaint.

Approaching an outcropping, however, Lady whinnied nervously and tossed her head. Despite pushing Red into the bead of the jumping cholla, Lady was no fool and he heeded her warning. For the second time that day, he chambered a round and rode warily around the jutting rocks.

The woman was lying facedown, arms

flung out, at the wall of the canyon. Blood stained the shoulder blades of the bright yellow western shirt she wore. She didn't move. Her horse, hobbled, stood twenty yards away, looking at Red with wide, imploring eyes.

Red dismounted and patted Satan Lady's neck reassuringly. "It's okay, baby," he whispered, scanning the canyon. Rifle at the ready, he approached the woman. A small pointed pick hammer was on the ground near her hand, lying next to a paintbrush. She had obviously been working at the cliff face when she was shot in the back.

The motionless body convinced Red she was dead, but still he squatted next to her and took her wrist to search for a pulse.

"It's mine," the woman wheezed through bloody, foam-specked lips.

Red dropped her wrist and ran for his first aid kit.

CHAPTER ONE

Penelope Warren was not a joiner by nature and did not belong to the Modern Language Association, the Book-of-the-Month Club, or the Mystery Guild, despite possessing a hard-earned doctor of philosophy degree in literature and owning a bookstore called Mycroft & Company, which specialized in detective and crime fiction. Nor was she a member of the Cigar of the Month Club, the National Rifle Association, or the National Organization of Women. And when her time came, she seriously doubted that she would swell the membership roster of the American Association of Retired Persons.

This aversion to joining the ranks of various and sundry organizations went back to her appearance at the United States Marine Corps recruiting station on the day after graduating from high school. This had led to her standing at attention very early one late-summer morning at Parris Island while various people screamed that her slovenly civilian days were over, that sand fleas were her friends, and expressed doubts that she would ever be a Marine. After surviving boot camp, however, Penelope had rather enjoyed her four years in the Marine Corps, even rising to the rank of sergeant. After deciding not to ship over, Penelope vowed to be extremely cautious about joining anything ever again, a promise she broke almost immediately upon receiving her Ph.D. by joining the Peace Corps, *after* receiving assurances that this particular corps did not utilize drill instructors and that she would not have to rise in the middle of the damned night to carry out her assigned duties.

Still, Penelope supported a great many worthy charitable and service organizations with monetary contributions or volunteer labor, which explained how she came to be spending a late Saturday morning making the main street of Empty Creek, Arizona, safe for rattlesnakes.

While not a member, Penelope agreed with the primary goal of Save Our Desert, SOD for short, which was to preserve as much of the natural desert landscape in and around Empty Creek as possible and maintain the native habitat for the various critters and creepy-crawlies who lived there —

and there were a great many. Thus, Penelope volunteered, despite all Marine Corps instincts to the contrary, to lead a team of concerned citizens in erecting a Rattlesnake Crossing sign as a warning to the wild-eyed drivers who careened up and down Empty Creek Highway.

Her crew consisted of Harris Anderson III, the gangling editor of the *Empty Creek News-Journal*; Nora Pryor, local historian and a petite goddess with strawberry-blond hair and a voice that could defrost a refrigerator; Anthony Lyme-Regis, a transplanted Englishman visiting Nora from Los Angeles, where he directed television commercials; and, of course, Penelope's friend and colleague, a very large cat named Big Mike (someone had to supervise the supervisor). He was the only member of the crew not wearing a T-shirt emblazoned with the head of a mountain lion and the bold slogan SAVE LONESOME BEND.

"I've got blisters," Andy said.

"Baby," Penelope said, tossing her hair with disdain, a movement she had been practicing before the mirror ever since agreeing to let her hair grow out at Andy's request.

"I'm a journalist, not a post-hole digger," Andy grumped.

"Let me have a whack at it."

Penelope took the post-hole digger and raised it above the hole that Andy had carved into the reluctant earth. She plunged it into the hole. "Oof," Penelope said. She pulled it out, unloaded the fraction of earth she had managed to dislodge, and dropped the digger, disturbing Big Mike, who was catching rays on the Rattlesnake Crossing sign. Brushing her hands briskly after a job well done, Penelope said, "I think that's deep enough."

"Good. It's time for a pint of bitter," Tony said, shucking his accustomed rumpled tweed jacket. "Don't you agree, dearest?"

"I do," Andy said enthusiastically.

"You're not Dearest."

"Soon," Nora, who *was* Dearest, replied.

"Later," Penelope said. "First, we plant Guido."

"Guido?" her companions chorused.

"The sign has a cement shoe, so I named him Guido," Penelope said. "The representation of the rattlesnake, not the sign. It's a tribute to Mario Puzo and *The Godfather*."

"I think he called it 'sleeping with the fishes,' " Andy pointed out. "There hasn't been a fish around here for a hundred million years or so. Give or take an eon or two.

Whatever they are."

"If it's a tribute to Puzo, why not call him Mario?" Lyme-Regis asked.

"Because he looks like a Guido."

"Of course he does. My mistake."

With the sign duly named and baptized, they set about man- and woman-handling the sign and the heavy round glob of cement at the base of its metal pole into the hole. Between the four of them, it would have been a relatively easy task, except for Big Mike, who had decided to go into the hole headfirst, apparently in an effort to examine the geological time frames revealed in the layers of soil.

"Move your butt, Mikey," Penelope said.

That command had its usual impact on Big Mike, which is to say, he ignored it entirely, swishing his tail ominously.

Eventually, however, he backed out of the hole, looked up at Penelope, and said, "Meow." She took that to mean he was thirsty and ready to head for the Double B Western Bar and Steakhouse.

"Let's do it."

The Rattlesnake Crossing contingent was the first to arrive at the Double B. They were greeted by a round of drinks on the house, and settled in to await the arrival of those charged with implanting the Deer, Quail, Coyote, and Javelina Crossing signs at strategic, if more far-flung, spots around the environs of Empty Creek, in the noble effort to prevent their furry, feathered, and scaly friends from becoming road kill. Big Mike, who didn't care for noisy celebrations, hopped on his usual stool, put his front paws on the bar, and waited for Pete the bartender to pour his saucer of nonalcoholic beer with a side of lima beans.

The quail crowd stumbled in next. Samantha Dale, president of the Empty Creek National Bank, plopped down next to Penelope and said, "Well, that was fun." She looked up at the wall, blushed, quickly rose, and moved around the table to sit across from Penelope with her back to the wall.

Penelope smiled, knowing exactly why Samantha moved. Penelope planned to spend the entire month of June in bed with the covers pulled over her head. She didn't care how hot it was. Ditto for Nora Pryor when July rolled around.

Big Jake Peterson, Sam's special friend and poker-playing buddy, had no problem in looking at the calendar on the wall behind her. It was February and a gloriously nude bank president adorned the Official Sixteen-Month Women of Empty Creek Calendar. Although Samantha wore an exotic black mask to hide her face from the financial world, there was little doubt as to the owner of the pale blond hair in the stylishly rendered portrait painted by David Macklin, a youthful local artist whose number-one model was Lora Lou Longstreet (December), owner of the Tack Shack and immediate past president of the chamber of commerce.

All of Empty Creek was proud of its women, and a great many calendars were sold. After all, it was for the children. Proceeds from the calendar had provided a substantial amount of money for a local children's charity.

The deer people arrived in the form of Dutch Fowler, chief of Empty Creek's police department, and his fiancée, film star Storm Williams (April), otherwise known as Cassandra Warren, Penelope's younger sister. They were accompanied by Leigh Kent-Maxwell (the next February), the sexiest librarian in the western states, and her husband, Burt, an English instructor at the local college.

A harried Debbie Locke (January), Empty Creek's favorite cocktail waitress, struggled to keep up with the demand for drinks and burgers.

Waiting for Elaine Henders (of August fame) and her entourage, conversation degenerated from saving the local wildlife and potential solutions for many of the world's problems to staging a rematch of a memorable wet-T-shirt contest between Stormy and Debbie, the only time *ever* Debbie had relinquished her championship crown.

"Best two out of three," Big Jake proposed.

"Four out of seven."

"It's too cold," Stormy protested. In what passed for winter in Arizona, the temperature outside was a bone-numbing sixty-six degrees.

"We'll use warm water."

Debbie wavered. "That works for me," she said.

Penelope shook her head. Her efforts to keep the conversation on a higher plane had failed as usual. But Big Mike, snoozing on his bar stool, perked up an ear. His allowance was on Stormy. "There will be no T-shirt contests, wet or otherwise, ever again," Penelope announced. "Not until certain people in this group agree to the Men of Empty Creek Calendar."

"I'm too fat," Big Jake said hastily.

"I'm too skinny," Andy countered.

"I'm too ugly," Burt offered.

"You are not," Leigh protested.

"I'm English," Lyme-Regis declared. "The queen doesn't like that sort of thing."

"For God's sake, we're not sending it to Buckingham Palace," Nora said.

"I'm just right" — Dutch grinned — "but regulations forbid the police chief from posing in the nude."

"They do not," Stormy cried.

"They will by tomorrow."

"They'd better not," Penelope warned.

"Or what?"

Before Penelope could dream up a suitably horrible consequence, they were interrupted by the javelina squad. Laney, along with her significant other, an unemployed cowboy named Wally, had been placing the Javelina Crossing signs.

"What's your excuse?" Penelope demanded of Wally.

"Don't have one."

"Good. You can be January."

"Oh, no. I've got saddle sores."

"And very nice saddle sores they are, sweetie," Laney said.

"And the whole world's going to see them."

"Well, I was almost wounded in action," Laney announced dramatically, brushing at her flaming red hair, flaring her nostrils, and heaving her bosom, thereby overriding Penelope and Wally's exchange. "I hope those little porkers appreciate my contribution to their continued good health."

"You look perfectly fine," Penelope declared a little testily. She didn't like being upstaged, even by her best friend. "What happened?"

"Red the Rat was in the backseat of a tour Jeep going like hell. Kicked up a stone that whizzed right past my ear. I could have been concussed."

"That's not a word."

"It is now."

"And what in the world was Red doing in a tour Jeep?" The company specialized in taking snowbirds and tourists on explorations of the backcountry, but a denizen of Empty Creek would rather be caught in flagrante delicto with a moose than in a tour Jeep.

Three people tuned out simultaneously.

Penelope frowned. What *was* Red doing in a tour Jeep? Crime was her business, and not only as a purveyor of novels. On more than one occasion she and Big Mike had been instrumental in solving a murder. Red the Rat in a tour Jeep. . . . She glanced at Andy and then at Dutch.

Andy's suspicious reporter's mind was in high gear. He rose and headed for the pay phone, fumbling for change.

Dutch had been a cop for too many years to think that Red had suddenly decided to take advantage of a guided tour. He reached into Stormy's purse and extracted a portable phone and punched in a programmed code.

"It's Dutch. What's up?"

Penelope watched her future brother-in-law's face as he listened to the reply.

Dutch nodded grimly and said, "Call Burke and Stoner. I'm on the way."

Penelope reached for her purse. Larry Burke and Willie Stoner were the Tweedledee and Tweedledum of Empty Creek's Robbery-Homicide Division. In fact, they *were* the division.

Dutch returned the phone to Stormy's purse. "I've got to run over to the department for a minute," he said. "I'll be right back. Don't start without me."

"There is going to be no contest and I'm going to freshen up," Penelope said, understanding Dutch's ruse. He didn't want half of Empty Creek's population following them and contaminating a crime scene. She scooped Big Mike from his bar stool and intercepted Andy. They slipped

31

out the back door.

"What is it?"

"I called the hospital," Andy said. "Red brought in a woman who had been shot. She died on the operating table."

Dutch was already in his pickup when they circled around to the front of the Double B. "The emergency room," he said. "You want to come with me?"

"We'll follow," Penelope said, popping Big Mike into the backseat of her Jeep.

Red the Rat was outside the waiting room with a shaken tour driver.

"What happened?"

"Found a woman. Shot. Thought she was dead, but I went to check her pulse anyway. That's when she said, 'It's mine.' "

"What was she talking about?"

"The dinosaur bones, I reckon."

"Any identification?"

"Wasn't time to check. I bandaged her up best I could. Got her on her horse and headed for home lickety-split. This feller here was at Lonesome Bend Ranch, and I kinda commandeered his vehicle. But when we got here, it was too late. I don't know. Maybe I did the wrong thing. Moving her and all, I mean. Mighta been better to leave her and ride for help. All I could think, though, was she needed a doctor. Do you think I did the right thing?" He looked at Penelope. There were tears in his eyes.

"You did everything you could, Red," Penelope said, patting his hand reassuringly. She did not know the victim, but she felt Red's pain. She could read the grimmest accounts of murder in a novel without flinching and close a book with satisfaction when a killer had been brought to justice. But that was fiction. When real violence intruded and a life was snuffed out senselessly, sorrow filled her heart.

Burke and Stoner skidded to a halt and jumped out of their car.

"Oh, yeah, something else," Red said. "I heard the shot about fifteen, twenty minutes before I come across her."

"What's up, boss?" Burke asked.

"Woman's been murdered."

"I left my passengers out there," the driver interrupted timidly. "Can I go get 'em?"

Dutch took charge. "We have to impound your Jeep, son," he said. "Stoner, get the lab guys moving. Burke, you take him to get another vehicle and then follow us out to Lonesome Bend Ranch. We need to move fast now. How long ago did all this happen, Red?"

The desert rat squinted up at the sun.

Couple of hours now, I reckon. Least that."

"Let's get going."

"We'll go with you this time," Penelope said. "I don't want to miss anything."

On the way to Lonesome Bend Ranch, Dutch and Penelope took turns pumping Red for additional details. "She had one of them little pickaxes and a paintbrush," the prospector said. "She had found some dinosaur bones, all right. Big mother too."

Andy stopped loading film into the camera to jot that information down in the reporter's notebook he was never without. "What's the name of the dinosaur?" he asked.

"It doesn't have a name," Penelope said. "Yet."

"Always get the name of the dog. That's what Reid Bundy, my old editor, always told me."

"Mr. Dinosaur will have to do for now," Penelope said. "Or Mrs. Dinosaur. I wonder how you tell the sex of a fossil?"

At Lonesome Bend Ranch, the victim's horse shied away and kicked at Dutch. A young boarder had watered him and kept him in the shade to cool down, but she hadn't touched anything. Surrounded by strangers, blood on the saddle, and the memory of the gunshot all contributed to the gelding's nervousness.

"Let me do it," Penelope said. The horse watched her warily with wide brown eyes when Penelope walked slowly toward him, unwrapping a peppermint candy taken from the pocket of her windbreaker. Penelope's own horse, Chardonnay, was fond of peppermint candies. "Hey, babe, nothing to be afraid of, everything's okay now," Penelope crooned. She offered the peppermint, and when he took it, she stroked his neck gently, whispering, "It's okay."

Pacified by the candy, the horse stood docilely while Penelope took the saddle off and put it on the ground. She found a purse in the saddlebags, opened it, and took out a wallet. The face of Millicent DeForest smiled at Penelope from the driver's license. Surprisingly for a driver's license photograph, it was fairly good, much better than Penelope's own. Millicent DeForest had attractive features — rather short, neatly brushed hair, a thin, finely shaped nose, full lips, and a pleasant smile that revealed slightly crooked teeth, an imperfection that added rather than detracted from her pretty face.

She had been a Scorpio, born November

3, 1964. Hair: Brown. Eyes: Brown. Her height was listed as five feet seven inches and her weight was one hundred thirty-six pounds. She lived in a town house complex off Bell Road in the northern reaches of Phoenix. The license would not have expired until her first birthday in the new century and the new millennium, momentous events that someone had prevented her from celebrating.

"She kept her horse here and frequently rode on weekends," Andy said. "The horse's name is Ghostdancer. One word."

In communion with the dead woman, Penelope had not heard Andy approach. She showed him the license. "Her name was Millicent DeForest. The dinosaur's name is Milly. In her honor."

Andy nodded solemnly.

The process was repeated with Dutch when he returned from telling the tourists they would have to wait and be interviewed by uniformed officers. "They probably didn't see anything, but you never know," Dutch said. He took the purse and dropped the wallet in. "We'll go through this later."

The forces were rapidly gathering for the preliminary investigation. Two black and whites — one a four-wheel-drive Ford Bronco — had arrived. Burke was right

36

behind them. The crime lab people would be there shortly.

Dutch issued several orders and then headed for the Bronco. With Dutch, Red, Burke, Andy, Penelope, Big Mike, and Peggy Norton, one of the uniformed officers, conditions were a little crowded, but they piled into the Bronco anyway. Penelope sat on Andy's lap and held Big Mike on her lap. Andy's hand rested casually on her thigh, a comforting gesture. She hoped Millicent DeForest had known love before she died.

"Better stop here," Red said.

"You're sure?"

"Yep. Marked the spot by that one-armed saguaro up there. This is it, all right."

"You said there was a pickax and a brush. I don't see them."

"They was there when I left."

"Well, that simplifies things," Penelope said. "We just find someone with a pickax and a paintbrush that doesn't belong to them."

They climbed out of the Bronco and stood in a semicircle, surveying the scene from a distance. The site was at the very edge of the backcountry. The beautiful, desolate hills were populated by scattered saguaros, like drawings of stick people, their arms raised in mute surrender to the planned development that threatened to encroach upon their home.

"Sure looks like dinosaur bones sticking out there."

Four rock-like things resembling footstools for a giant protruded from the earth.

" 'Course they is," Red said. "I know a fossil when I see one."

"Vertebrae, maybe?" Penelope offered. She felt as if she'd been dropped onto the set of one of her sister's earlier films, *Queen of the Cave People*, where Stormy, clad only in a loincloth for seventy-six of the movie's ninety-two minutes, spent most of her time fleeing a slavering Tyrannosaurus Rex and some gourd people intent on serving her up in a family barbecue.

Big Mike started off to investigate despite knowing absolutely nothing about paleontology. But that was how a cat learned and how murders were solved — through careful and detailed investigation.

Penelope picked him up. "Stay with me this time, Mikey." Even for a cat raised in Africa, where he had fearlessly cowed everything up to and including hyenas with a fierce imitation of a bear, this was wild country. Civilization was behind them, way back in Empty Creek, and Penelope had no intention of allowing Mycroft to stray.

"Whatever it was, it was big. Ate a lot of lima beans." Big Mike's fondness for lima beans was well known.

"Who owns the land?" Burke asked.

"Let's hope it's not BLM." The backcountry belonged to the Bureau of Land Management.

"I think the BLM boundary is farther back. We're still in Empty Creek. This must belong to the Desert Development Company or Lonesome Bend Ranch," Penelope said. "In any case, it's going to put a big crimp in the DDC's plans. Now the city can demand a paleontologist," she added with satisfaction. "Declare it a city treasure or something." As her T-shirt indicated, SOD was fighting the DDC's plan to build a gaggle of luxury homes, destroying all of Lonesome Bend in the process.

"I hope you're right," Peggy Norton said. "If the feds get involved in this, they'll screw it up for sure."

"Shoot a roll of film for us, Andy. Just until the lab guys get here."

"Sure, Dutch."

Andy quickly shot a roll from different angles, zooming in for close-ups. He had just loaded a second roll, when the warning came.

"Fire in the hole!" The shout could have come from anywhere. The echo reverberated in the canyon. "Hole! Hole! Hole!"

"What the hell!" Dutch exclaimed.

Penelope's brain raced, connecting long-ago dots with the present moment. Marine demolition experts always hollered "Fire in the hole" before blowing something up or administering the ultimate hotfoot with a bit of C-4 explosive. It took no more than a second or two for the imaginary pencil to trace a route from Dot A to Dot B. There was about to be a big bang.

"Incoming!" Penelope shouted. Then she hit the deck, grabbing Mycroft on the way down, and crawled under the Bronco.

It got pretty crowded under there.

CHAPTER TWO

Penelope quickly took roll, another bit of training left over from the Marine Corps: Never leave anyone behind. Everyone was there except Andy. The damned fool was still taking pictures. Penelope tugged at his pants leg. "Get down!" she cried.

"Nothing's happening," he said.

"Well, get down anyway," Penelope replied. She was beginning to feel a little foolish. Except for some heavy breathing underneath the Bronco, it was damned quiet out there.

"Get off me, Burke, you big doofus," Peggy said.

"I'm trying to protect you."

"You're just copping a feel."

If Burke protested the accusation, Penelope didn't hear it because of the explosion.

The concussion swept over them, rocking the Bronco and bringing back memories of the range at Camp Pendleton, where the artillery regiment and the tank battalion practiced their arts, firing the big guns. Something heavy jumped on Penelope just before dirt and rocks peppered the Bronco. "Ow!" she cried.

"Just trying to be gallant," Andy said from on top of her.

"*You* can cop a feel while you're at it. I've never made love *under* a car."

The echo of the blast died, a last rock pinged off the roof, and an eerie silence descended over the backcountry.

"Stay down," Dutch ordered, immediately violating his own advice by crawling out and crouching by the front fender, service weapon at the ready.

Penelope and Big Mike quickly followed.

"I said, stay down."

"I can't hear you. My ears are ringing." She jumped up, opened the Bronco door, pulled the shotgun from the rack, and worked the slide. "I'm ready."

So was everyone else. Guns bristled in every direction. Burke and Norton had their weapons out. Red had produced an enormous .44 revolver from somewhere. Big Mike's fur was raised. With teeth and claws, he was armed better than anyone.

"I don't want to be the only one without a gun," Andy wailed.

"Here," Burke said, reaching down and pulling a snub-nosed revolver from an ankle holster.

"This is a popgun," Andy said with dismay.

"Scare him to death. Yell, 'Bang!' "

"Police!" Peggy Norton shouted. "Come out with your hands up!"

"Up, up, up."

"That did a lot of good," Burke said after the echo died.

"I don't get to say it very often. Besides, you got a better idea?"

"Nope."

"Listen," Dutch said.

"What do you hear, boss?"

"Nothing, dummy, I'm trying to." He was watching Big Mike.

"Oh."

Big Mike's ears swiveled to the right, away from the buried crime scene. If he heard the footsteps of a fleeing villain, it was there. It wasn't the most scientific approach to apprehending a murderer with a penchant for blowing up hillsides, but Dutch thought it was a pretty clever improvisation, even if it was the most likely place for a killer to take cover.

"Over there. Behind those rocks," he said. "Cover me." He dashed across the canyon floor.

Penelope was right behind him, the shotgun at high port. Stormy would never forgive her if she let Dutch get shot.

Dutch took cover and looked up the incline. "What are you doing here?" he asked when Penelope knelt beside him. Big Mike slid to a halt between them. Somebody had to protect the protector.

"Practicing house-to-house combat," she said.

"The nearest house is ten miles from here."

"That's the trouble with you, Dutch. No imagination."

The rest of the posse puffed their way over.

"Christ," Dutch said, "if you can't follow orders, at least spread out a little."

The troops reluctantly separated, putting an interval of two or three feet between them. Penelope shook her head. This crowd would never make it through Advanced Infantry Training.

"What now?" Burke wheezed, the years of jelly doughnuts exacting their toll.

"I'm going up there," Dutch said.

"I've got a plan," Penelope said. "We'll make a three-pronged attack. Like the Zulus. The head of the fighting bull buffalo."

"What Zulus?" Burke asked "What buffalo?"

"Haven't you ever seen *Zulu*, for God's sake? The Battle of Roarke's Drift? It was Michael Caine's first big movie."

"Jesus," Tweedledee said. "I never know what you're talking about."

Andy sympathized. The world according to Penelope was seen through slightly distorted rose-colored glasses. And *he* could recite whole chunks of dialogue from the film. Penelope had made him sit through it often enough.

Mycroft stared at his nemesis in disgust. They'd had several encounters over the years, always with unpleasant results for Tweedledee, who bore several scars as evidence. Big Mike too had seen *Zulu*, at least seven or eight times, along with all of Penelope's other favorite movies with an African setting.

"Never mind," Penelope said, "I'll explain later. Now, here's what we do. Dutch, you and Andy take the middle. Burke, you and Red circle around to the left. Peggy and I will take the right flank. The head and the horns of the fighting bull buffalo. See? We'll surround him."

"I got a question."

"Yes, Burke."

"This *Zulu*, how many people get killed running around like buffalo?"

"Quite a few, actually."

"I thought so."

"What's *your* plan, Chesty Puller? Sit here until the millennium?"

"I suppose it was his first movie too."

"Chesty Puller, you ignoramus, was just about the most famous Marine ever."

"Enough," Dutch said. "Left horn, move out. You too, right horn." He turned to Andy. "You ready, head?"

"I feel like Henry Morton Stanley at the Battle of Magdala. All we need are some Lordlings. That's how he described the young British officers."

"Christ, not you too?"

"Semper fi, Henry," Penelope said, scuttling away to take up her position. Peggy was right behind her.

Big Mike decided to stay with the head and went through his pre-attack checklist, lowering his head, flattening his ears, raising his butt, twitching his tail slowly, ominously. "Mewr," he said, "Mewr." He quivered with the excitement of the stalk.

Dutch looked to both horns, received a thumbs-up from each, and stood. "Charge," he yelled. *His* favorite movie (after all of Stormy's, of course) was *Rio Grande*.

46

As a re-creation of Teddy Roosevelt and the Rough Riders' charge, this military movement was singularly lacking.

First, Dutch wouldn't make a very good cat. He took off before Mycroft was ready. Several more butt twitches, a few tail swishes, and some quivering were the absolute minimum necessary for a good stalk and pounce. Good God, even a kitten knew that much.

Second, Burke slipped halfway up the incline, barked his funny bone a good crack on a rock with an attitude, and slid down the slope into a barrel cactus.

Finally, Penelope damn near scared everyone to death when she fired a round after taking the high ground. "I didn't have a hand grenade," she explained belatedly. "And I wanted him to keep his head down. A grenade would have been better though. Why don't you order a case for me, Dutch, just in case?"

"God, don't you just love a woman with hand grenades?" Andy said.

"There's no one here," Dutch pointed out, rather mildly under the circumstances.

"Good thing for him," Peggy said, overdosing on adrenaline.

"He was here," Penelope said, approaching Mycroft, who had what appeared to be a bit of string caught on his claw. "This looks just like part of a fuse for dynamite."

"Yeah," Dutch said. "And he knew what he was doing too."

The explosion had been exact, dislodging several tons of dirt and rock, creating a landslide that buried the crime scene. The one-armed saguaro stuck out of the big mound. That was another charge to add to murder and unauthorized use of explosives. It was against the law to uproot a cactus without a permit.

It was dark before all the equipment was ready. The buried crime scene was brightly illuminated, however, by lights powered by a portable generator. The Empty Creek P.D. had appropriated the entire supply of shovels and wheelbarrows from the hardware store. A number of makeshift sieves had been constructed for filtering the dirt when it was removed from the crime scene. Coffee and sandwiches were in plentiful supply for the additional police officers and lab technicians who had been called to duty. The overtime hours would go through the desert sky and put the department's budget out of kilter for the next several fiscal years.

"This is the Before," Dutch said, holding

up one of the hastily developed photographs shot by Andy. "That's the After." He pointed to the mound of dirt that covered his crime scene. "Make *that* look like *this.* And carefully."

"Jeez, boss, we'll be here forever."

"Probably."

Satisfied that there was nothing to be learned at the scene for hours, perhaps days, Penelope gathered up cat, boyfriend, weary prospector, and went to Dutch to arrange a ride back to Lonesome Bend Ranch.

"Take the Bronco," he said. "I'm going to be out here all night. I told Stormy to spend the night at your place. That all right? She's making spaghetti for you."

"Of course. It's hard being a cop's fiancée."

After Red made arrangements to board Daisy and Satan's Lady overnight and went off to tend to their needs, Penelope introduced herself to the woman who owned Lonesome Bend Ranch. "I'm Penelope Warren. This is Harris Anderson, but call him Andy, and this big guy is Mycroft."

"I'm Cricket."

"What's your last name?" Andy asked,

notebook and pen poised.

"Cricket."

"Cricket Cricket?"

"Just Cricket. Only one word. That's my legal name. Bet you folks could use a drink."

"That would be very nice."

"Come on in."

"That's what your hair will be like," Andy whispered.

Cricket's auburn hair was long. Very long. Rapunzel-like long, falling way below her waist. But her hair was not the only striking feature about Cricket. She wore a faded University of California sweatshirt that did not hide the swell of a provocative and braless bosom. Her waist was slender, but she filled her equally faded black jeans in the important places. Cricket was a definite candidate for the next Women of Empty Creek Calendar.

"I've got beer, wine, or tequila and orange juice. I used to drink scotch, but it gives me headaches now."

"Tequila and orange juice is fine," Penelope said. It never hurt to offset dissipation with a little vitamin C.

"The same for me."

"Make yourselves at home. I'll just be a minute."

Penelope went straight to the bookcases, which were plentiful and crammed. The first contained a collection of philosophers through the ages in no particular order. Rousseau was next to Aristotle. Plato was jammed in sideways on top of Descartes. Several shelves held the classics of European, English, and American literature — Thomas Mann, Chekhov, Ibsen, Dickens, Hemingway, Tolstoy, Sartre, Flaubert, Cervantes, Fitzgerald, Faulkner. There were a number of science fiction paperbacks, a little heavy on Heinlein. Other shelves were devoted to various religions. There were a great many texts on the histories of England, France, Mesopotamia, Africa, Japan, Thailand, the Americas — North, South, and Central. Astrology was well represented, as were mysticism, past life regressions, UFOs, anthropology, psychology, the history of the English language and linguistics, sociology, and a great many equine subjects.

Several shelves contained works on the history of art and coffee table books on impressionism, expressionism, romanticism, modern art, surrealism. Cricket seemed to favor individual artists like Van Gogh, Gauguin, Dali, and Munch.

Who is this person? Penelope thought,

moving to another bookcase, skipping past the science section and its works on metallurgy, soils engineering, and composting. The collection got really interesting there with the *Kama Sutra* (well thumbed with pertinent passages highlighted by a yellow marker), De Sade's *Justine* and *Juliette, Story of O* (in French and English), *The Joy of Sex* (both volumes), a tome about the art of spanking, and six paperback novels by Juliana Masters. Penelope pulled *The Education of Lady Cassandra Fairbanks* from the shelf, read a page at random, blushed, and hastily returned it to its place. How could they get in that position?

"Those financed my junior year abroad," Cricket said. Glasses clinked on the tray.

"You're Juliana Masters?"

"I was, until I couldn't think of any more variations. Then Juliana retired in Mexico."

"You went to Cal?"

Cricket nodded. "Off and on for six years."

"What did you major in anyway?"

Cricket laughed. "Whatever seemed interesting at the time. Bookstores, coffeehouses, and safe sex, mostly."

When everyone was settled, Big Mike climbed into Cricket's lap and stared up at her. Cricket scratched behind his ears and he switched his purr motor to high. Satisfied that he had a new lady friend, he curled up and gazed placidly into the mysterious place that only cats can see, content to let Penelope ask the questions.

"How well did you know Millicent De-Forest?"

"She came with the ranch. That's one of the reasons I bought the place. There was an excellent cash flow already in place with people who boarded their horses here. Milly was one of them. She came almost every Saturday and Sunday to ride. Sometimes during the week, especially during the summer. But I didn't know her well. She was a bit of a loner. Like me."

"You must have talked."

"Oh, sure, but mostly about horses, the best worm medicine to use, vitamins to mix with feed, that kind of thing. We didn't exchange intimacies."

"Did she ever bring anyone with her?"

Cricket shook her head. "Not since I bought the place, but I've been here only a year. After Juliana retired, I had the money for a down payment. Did I tell you Juliana was a dominatrix in San Francisco? She had her own dungeon."

Andy spluttered and had a coughing fit, dribbling orange juice and tequila down his chin.

"That must have been interesting," Penelope said.

"Oh, it was," Cricket said. "These men spent most of their time ruling the world. They'd come to me, I mean Juliana, and she'd make them grovel for a while, and then they went back to ruling the world. Some of them were quite distraught when Mistress Juliana announced her retirement."

"I'll bet they were. How did a nice Berkeley girl wind up a dominatrix?"

"Just lucky, I guess."

"And Empty Creek?"

"Oh, I grew up around here," Cricket said, waving vaguely in the direction of the backcountry.

"Well, it's late and Red's probably ready to get home. I'll have more questions, but for the moment we thank you for your hospitality."

"Anytime," Cricket said.

"By the way, you seem to like art," Penelope said. "How do you feel about children's charities?"

"I was going to major in fine arts until I found you couldn't make a living. Is there a local art benefit for children? I'd love to help out."

"Good."

★ ★ ★

Once back in town, Penelope offered to drive Red home, but he insisted on taking a taxi. So she dropped him off, took Andy to his car, and led the way to the little twelve-acre ranchette she shared with Big Mike, Chardonnay — a spirited Arabian mare — Andy more often than not, Laney when she threw Wally out, and her sister on the rare occasions Dutch was out of commission for one reason or another — like murder.

"What have you two been doing?" Stormy asked. "Look at you."

Penelope did. Planting Guido, crawling around under police vehicles, and charging up hillsides had taken its toll. Her jeans and T-shirt were smudged with dirt. The windbreaker was ready for a trip to the cleaners, and she had broken a nail. "I'm a mess," she said cheerfully. "So are you, Andy."

Having spent the return trip bathing himself, Big Mike was his usual dapper self and ready to tuck into some lima beans.

"Does Dutch look like this? Is he all right?"

"Probably, but he's fine. It's a good thing you're staying here tonight though. He's not in a very good mood. Somebody blew up the hill over the crime scene and buried it."

"Blew it up? As in explosion?"

55

"Andy got pictures of the whole thing. He was very brave, but stupid. He shouldn't be taking chances with high explosives."

"You were there? You saw it? Are you sure Dutch is okay?"

"Tell her all about it, Andy. I'm taking a shower."

It was a very bedraggled prospector who approached the double-wide in the taxi, brushing his teeth. He rinsed his mouth from the canteen and spit out the window. At least, he could kiss Mattie without making her recoil. It seemed like several lifetimes since he had come out of the backcountry dreaming lurid fantasies about their reunion.

Mattie opened the door and stood in the square of light cast from the living room and watched her husband pay off the driver. She held a tumbler in her hand. "I heard you coming, you old fool. How was your day?"

" 'Bout usual. You?"

"The same. I take it we're not rich beyond my wildest dreams."

"Nope." He clumped up the steps and pecked her cheek.

"That ain't no way to kiss me, not after I've been missing you so badly."

"I smell."

"That is God's truth," Mattie agreed, "but we can fix that." She grabbed him by one ear and pulled his face down to her own. After a suitable interval, she released him and said, "That's the way to kiss."

"It surely is, darlin'," Red agreed. "It surely is."

"Here," she said, handing him the tumbler. "Have a little sipping whiskey. Where are Daisy and Lady?"

"That is a long story. I'll tell you after I'm clean."

Mattie smiled as she poured another drink. Red bellowed away in the shower. He had a terrible voice, and it didn't improve with whiskey.

She went into the bedroom with the drink, leaving a trail of clothes behind her. A little duet in the shower would improve the singing portion of the evening.

"Are you sure it was a dinosaur?"

"That's what Red said, sis. It looked like a bunch of big rocks to me. But the fact that Millicent DeForest had some excavating tools seems to support Red, even though they were gone when we got there."

"There's big money in dinosaurs," Stormy said. "Remember Sue? Four point eight million at Sotheby's, wasn't it?"

"How do you know that?"

"Morgan Fairchild told me. She's a science nut."

"I didn't know you knew Morgan Fairchild," Andy said.

"I met her once. We had coffee together. Great eyes."

"Great everything."

"Smart too."

"A terrific actress."

"Yeah, but can she cook?" Penelope asked.

"Who cares?"

After dinner Penelope arranged a set of Andy's photographs in order on the kitchen table. The first shots clearly showed what appeared to be big rock footstools.

Penelope examined the photographs carefully with the magnifying glass that came with the compact edition of the *Oxford English Dictionary*, but saw nothing that resembled a clue or an explanation for murder. Whoever he was, he sure knew how to contaminate a crime scene.

Andy had caught the moment of the explosion, and subsequent photographs showed its aftermath as the hillside tumbled down in a cloud of dust. "I'm proud of you, Andy, but that really was dumb. You could have been killed."

"Can't win a Pulitzer Prize under a Bronco. Besides, you were charging around like John Wayne."

"Jane Wayne, please."

The last two photographs were a little out of focus. "What's this?" Penelope asked.

"I think it's your backside. I was on automatic and still shooting when I dove under the Bronco."

"Oh, great. Just what Tweedledee and Tweedledum need. A shot of my butt."

"They'll probably have it framed by tomorrow," Andy said. "Give them something to look at until June gets here."

"Don't remind me."

The tale of Millicent DeForest's demise and a possible dinosaur find was the lead story on the late news. Lola LaPola, Empty Creek's very own contribution to television journalism, reported live from the scene, reciting the bare facts of the story (withholding the victim's name pending notification of the next of kin). It didn't look like the troops had made much progress in excavation as yet.

"There's my sweetie," Stormy exclaimed, blowing him a kiss.

"We're examining several leads," Dutch told Lola.

"Hah!" Penelope said.

"Can you be more specific, Chief?"

"Not at this time."

"Well, there you have it," Lola said, turning away from Dutch and looking directly into the camera. "The police have a big job ahead of them in the mysterious events at Lonesome Bend. This is Lola LaPola reporting. Now, back to you in the studio."

"A big job, indeed," Anchor Boy said, nodding sagely and preening for the camera.

"That Ralph Bando is an idiot," Penelope announced. She made the same proclamation at some point during every newscast. "I don't know how Lola puts up with him." Penelope hit the power button on the remote control and Anchor Boy disappeared. "I'm going to bed," she announced.

"Keep it down in there," Stormy said. "Remember, I've got only a teddy bear for company tonight."

"By the way, what happened to the wet T-shirt contest?"

"Postponed."

"Not for lack of interest, I trust."

"Nope," Stormy grinned. "We decided to charge admission. Might as well make a little money for needy rug rats."

"I wonder why Cricket changed her name?" Penelope tossed her blouse into the hamper. It was shortly followed by other articles of clothing.

Andy was propped up in bed, watching, waiting. Penelope could take the *longest* time to undress. "Would you want your mother to know you were a dominatrix?"

"That was Mistress Juliana."

"Even so. Besides, Cricket is a nice name."

"A little attracted to her, were we?"

"She's very pretty," Andy admitted reluctantly. "And she does have long hair."

"Well, I'd better not catch you groveling around her cowgirl boots. Any groveling is going to be done right here."

"Yes, dear."

"Beginning now."

"Yes, Mistress Penelope."

"And you can forget Morgan Fairchild too."

While considered a success in her many endeavors over the years, Penelope soon decided she had no future whatsoever in the dungeon field. Andy started at her toes and slowly nibbled and kissed his way to her face, quickly reducing Mistress Penelope to a whimpering shell with a voice stuck on

"Oh, wow, yes, ooh."

Much later, Penelope snuggled deep into Andy's arms and whispered, "How soon can you do that again?"

"Morgan who? And long hair is vastly overrated."

Penelope smiled. "I love you too, but I still wonder why she changed her name."

CHAPTER THREE

When Penelope and Mycroft finally straggled out of bed the next morning — neither was worth a damn without a solid twelve or so hours — the one stumbled her way into the kitchen and poured coffee before slumping at the kitchen table, the other hunkered over the liver crunchies and promptly fell asleep again with his head in the bowl until the life-giving aromas stirred him enough to take a tentative nibble or two.

Already at the kitchen table, Andy, Stormy, and Dutch ignored Penelope and the comatose cat. They were accustomed to their strange habits.

Until they were big enough to have their own rooms, Stormy had watched and listened many a school morning as Muffy and Biff played good parent–bad parent, taking turns, alternately cajoling or issuing horrendous threats if Penelope didn't get up right now. The promise of dire consequences had little impact. Frequent visits to the pediatrician shed little light on what Muffy and Biff considered an unnatural disorder. In the end, however, everyone agreed. Penelope just liked to sleep and she was very good at it. Even after graduating to separate rooms, Stormy was witness to mornings in the Warren household that were largely devoted to getting Penelope out of bed, dressed, and on the way to school in time. Stormy had once discovered that a tray of ice cubes dropped down the front of Penelope's pajamas had the desired effect, but the prospect of going to the prom with two black eyes dissuaded her from repeating the performance.

More recently, Andy had experimented after watching *The D.I.* starring Jack Webb as a Marine Corps drill instructor. It was Penelope's way of sharing the Corps with Andy. Webb seemed to have no trouble getting recruits out of bed. The next morning Andy rose very early and gathered the necessary props to re-create the mise-en-scene. An empty metal garbage can, the handle of a toilet brush, and a handy light switch completed the preparations. In the interest of accuracy, Andy waited until his watch reached the ungodly hour of 4:30 a.m. before flipping the light switch, flooding the bedroom with fierce blinding light.

"Reveille, dammit!" Andy shouted, banging the toilet brush in the garbage can in his best Jack Webb imitation. The din was horrendous. "You people are screwing up *my* Marine Corps," he screamed. "Get out of those racks! Reveille!"

Penelope leaped up and came to a naked attention at the foot of the bed. Big Mike went straight up three feet and landed ready for action, hissing and screeching hideously. The sight of Penelope's feminine charms quivering deliciously was definitely worth the subsequent tirade delivered in Penelope's best sergeant major imitation, demonstrating a rather colorful vocabulary that Andy didn't know she possessed, while insisting that he do several anatomically impossible feats.

Two bouquets of flowers, one box of candy, and several days later, Penelope admitted it was pretty funny, but Andy never did it again. If she wanted to sleep the day away, so be it.

Dutch knew all about his future sister-in-law's ill-tempered mornings, so he rather judiciously kept his mouth shut.

As Big Mike's favorite aunt, Stormy claimed privilege and opened a can of lima beans with the electric can opener. She knew how to get his attention.

"God, that's irritating," Penelope said. It was permissible to speak after her second cup of coffee.

"Mikey's hungry."

"What time did you get here?" she asked Dutch.

"About three. I got lonely."

"I didn't hear you come in."

"You wouldn't hear the Four Horsemen of the Apocalypse."

"That's true."

"Well, I heard them," Andy complained. "It sounded like a gymnastics meet in there. I couldn't get back to sleep."

"I was glad to see him," Stormy said.

Penelope leaned over and kissed Andy's cheek. "Good morning, sailor, thanks for last night."

"You ready to talk now?" Dutch asked.

"Crime fighters are always ready. Find anything?"

"They're still digging. Nothing yet. But we checked out the property. It's part of Lonesome Bend Ranch. It's a jagged little piece that juts out into nowhere, bounded on one side by Desert Development and the other side by BLM. Whoever surveyed it must have been drunk. Or crazy. Maybe both. Registered owner on the deed is NFN

— no first name — Cricket, a single woman. Weird."

"You don't know the half of it yet."

"An interesting woman," Andy said.

"Well, if there is a dinosaur under all that dirt, she can open a museum."

"What about Millicent DeForest?"

"Stoner's been checking her out. Assistant professor of geology at the college. Seems to have had a special interest in paleontology, kind of a sideline. Maybe just a hobby. Her apartment was decorated in early Jurassic."

"Tweedledum said that?"

"No, I did. According to Stoner, she had lots of little dinosaur models around, like kids play with. My T-rex has bigger teeth than your T-rex. Only child. Parents on a cruise off the coast of Africa. Last port of call was East London in South Africa. We're trying to reach them now."

"You've been busy."

"There's more. Stoner hit the programmed numbers on her telephone. He got the answering machine at the parents', naturally. But the second was her boyfriend, one Brian Abernathy, and he was home. Stoner brought him out here to identify the body."

"Any indication he did it?"

"Stoner said he was pretty broken up. He played her messages. All from the boyfriend. The last sounded pretty worried, like she should have been home much earlier."

Penelope shrugged. "He could have been setting up an alibi."

"Didn't have to. He was playing basketball. Plays every Saturday afternoon. Nine other guys will swear to it. Haven't had time to check it out yet, but he wouldn't make up something like that. Boyfriend would appear to be in the clear."

"One down and approximately four million to go, *if* population projections are correct. And that takes in only Arizona."

"Don't be such a pessimist. We can eliminate at least twenty or thirty more. Everyone who was at the Double B yesterday afternoon."

"We're *really* making progress now."

"What are you doing today?"

"I think I'll spend some time at the library. I find that my knowledge of dinosaurs is sadly lacking. They were rarely addressed in my doctoral program. How about you?"

"Watch people dig, I guess." Dutch paused. "You think the dinosaur is connected to the murder?"

"Don't you?"

★ ★ ★

The library opened at noon on Sundays, and Penelope managed to get there shortly after. She automatically stopped to look over the latest acquisitions. It was physically and psychologically impossible for her to pass the New Books section of a bookstore. Thank God, books weren't fattening.

The electronic card catalogue — Penelope still missed leafing through the old-style card catalogue — indicated a number of works on dinosaurs, only two of which were in the library, both in the children's section. The rest were noted as missing.

Penelope went to the reference desk and was surprised to find the head librarian herself behind the counter. "What are you doing here?"

"Filling in," Leigh replied. "Noogy is sick. The flu."

"Overdose of chocolate, more likely," Penelope said. "Or a woman."

Juan-Carlos Estavillo usually ruled his reference domain with ruthless abandon. No fact, however obscure, was safe when Noogy was in pursuit. But he could be easily distracted by any candy with a nougat-filled center, or a señorita. For a bald-headed man who stood five foot three and weighed two hundred and fifty pounds, Noogy had an uncanny ability to attract and seduce beautiful women who towered over him.

"Have you fallen into his web too?"

Penelope smiled. "I must admit I've been tempted."

"We all have. Our Noogy is a charmer. I can hardly wait to see him in the Men of Empty Creek Calendar."

"Dave could charge admission during that modeling session. I'd pay."

"Me too, but don't tell my honey. Has anyone asked Noogy to pose?"

"I haven't heard. Why don't you suggest it?"

"Oh, I couldn't. I'm his supervisor. It could be construed as sexual harassment."

"If political correctness is carried much further, the human race will be in danger of extinction — like dinosaurs. I see absolutely nothing wrong with a member of one sex approaching a member of the other sex with whoopee in mind. It should be done with grace, aplomb, and creativity, naturally."

"Of course."

"Andy's first words to me were 'Have you ever been to Africa?' When I said I had, he fled, tripping over the hitching rail, incidentally — I had to have it removed — and it took him several weeks to work up the nerve to return."

70

"Why, for God's sake?"

"His natural shyness, for one thing. He thought he had developed the perfect introductory line. I was supposed to reply, 'Why, no, I haven't.' He could then say, 'Neither have I. We have a lot in common. Would you like to have coffee?' "

Leigh laughed. "Even for Andy, that seems a bit much."

"I could have brained him. Imagine how long it would have taken had he feared PC as well. I'd be withering away, waiting for my dotage."

"Well, if you didn't come to see Noogy, how can I help you?"

"Your dinosaur books, like the creatures themselves, seem to be extinct."

"Blame Michael Crichton and Steven Spielberg. They've been gone ever since *Jurassic Park* came out."

"That was five years ago. Why haven't you replaced them?"

"We did, but they disappeared too, after *The Lost World*. Try the encyclopedia."

"I could have done that at home. I have a perfectly good 1967 edition of the *Britannica*."

"Try the Internet, then. You can use my computer."

"You're on the Internet now?"

71

"Don't tell the patrons yet. It's a secret until the library board decides how to handle it. They're afraid everyone will want to see *those* pages."

"Well, of course. That's what a library is for. Free access to information."

"They're worried about complaints, but the American Library Association is very clear on the issue. We have to protect freedom of information everywhere, not just with books."

"Your board members are chicken. Let me know if you need help. We'll inscribe the First Amendment on a baseball bat and beat them over the head with it."

"That might do it."

While Penelope entered cyberspace and Leigh pondered the vagaries of dealing with spineless library board members, Big Mike headed for Periodicals and his favorite chair. Call me if you find a saber-toothed tiger or one of my other relatives.

Penelope quickly discovered that Morgan Fairchild was right. Unscrupulous fossil rustlers trespassed on government land all over the western states with impunity, digging out whole chunks of earth, leaving gaping holes in the landscape. She also learned there were lawsuits and counter-suits over ownership of fossils discovered in the conventional manner by paleontologists seeking to advance knowledge of the earth and its creatures millions of years ago.

The Tyrannosaurus rex named Sue created a huge controversy with a South Dakota farmer claiming ownership because she was found on his land. The Cheyenne River Sioux wanted Sue because she was interred by nature within the boundaries of their reservation. The people who actually found Sue wanted her for a local museum. In its usual manner of conflict resolution, the federal government raided the place, sending the FBI and the National Guard to confiscate Sue and damned near everything else in sight. After a long and stultifying journey through the courts, poor Sue wound up at Sotheby's, awaiting auction with an initial bid list at one million dollars.

"Well, I'll be damned," Penelope said, reading through a bulletin describing five dinosaur skulls stolen from a Moscow museum. The bulletin made three requests. Report any knowledge of the missing skulls to the local police authorities. Penelope could just imagine the reaction of Tweedledee and Tweedledum to dinosaur skulls belonging to the Russians. The second was to pass the information on to interested persons. Finally, any suggestions on how to tackle the problem were welcomed. Penelope wondered if anyone had recommended better locks.

Having now absorbed as much paleontology as she cared to for one Sunday afternoon, Penelope decided to exercise her First Amendment rights and try for one of *those* pages. She typed in a keyword.

D-O-M-I-N-A-T-R-I-X.

There did seem to be quite a thriving cyberspace interest in the topic — and any number of related subjects. Penelope called up a Web page at random, one apparently authored by Mistress Domina, not the most imaginative of names.

Oh, my!

It was a good thing Mikey was lazing away in Periodicals. He wasn't old enough to see apparitions like Mistress Domina. A full-color photograph of a rather hefty, grim of visage but rosy-checked Mistress Domina slowly appeared on the computer screen.

A caption beneath the photograph read: CHAINS REQUIRED, WHIPS OPTIONAL.

Leigh gasped, but leaned over the screen for a closer look. "How do you suppose she got into that . . . thing?"

Mistress Domina wore a very tight black leather corset.

"With a great deal of difficulty, I should imagine."

"You certainly have varied interests this morning. Dinosaurs and dominatrixes. How can they possibly be related to the murder?"

"They're probably not. I was just curious."

Driving out to Lonesome Bend, Penelope noted with satisfaction that the crossing signs seemed to be working. There wasn't a single road kill to be seen. It was too bad that the No Shooting signs — which had been up for a number of years, peppered with bullet holes — hadn't helped Millicent DeForest.

Shooting.

Red had heard what appeared to be the ultimately fatal shot. He had fired a shot in return. But what, Penelope wondered, would have happened if Red had not fired a warning? Or better yet, what would have happened if Red had not come along just when he did? It was just possible that a fossil rustler had discovered Milly first, but was more than a little irritated when the DeForest woman arrived, dismounted, and showed tools of the trade.

"Are you paying attention, Mikey? We

may be on to something here." The pavement ended and the Jeep shimmied and bounced along the corrugated dirt road, dislodging Mycroft's front paws from the dashboard, and reminding Penelope once again that Empty Creek was, in many ways, much closer to the nineteenth century than the twenty-first. It was still a frontier community barely disguised by the trappings of progress. The amenities of civilization ended a mile or so out of town, and the primitive desert still ruled despite attempts to tame it with the bulldozer and housing developments. And the badlands of the backcountry could be dangerous, indeed.

Slowing only exacerbated the impact of the washboard road, so Penelope pressed the accelerator to the floor and the bouncing eased. Mycroft hopped into the backseat and watched the dust swirl in their wake. So much for paying attention.

"But if he had dynamite ready," Penelope said, "maybe he just wanted to bury the dinosaur. Then he could come back at his leisure and dig it out. Sell it and make the big score. Milly is probably worth as much as Sue if it's relatively intact. But the arrival of Millicent changed that. He shot her and planned to bury Milly *and* Millicent. He could take the horse someplace, turn him loose, and we'd just have a missing woman who got lost in the desert. That happens often enough."

Penelope slowed for a tour Jeep and then sped past.

"But Red came along and spoiled all that. So why didn't he just shoot Red too, and bury all three? Why wait until we arrived to blow the hillside up? Down? Whatever?"

There was the usual activity at Lonesome Bend Ranch. A group of Sunday horsemen and horsewomen rode in, returning from a trail ride. A young woman wearing chaps put her horse through the paces in a small riding ring. Penelope didn't see Cricket when she buzzed past, taking the left fork that led to the crime scene.

Penelope expected to see any number of police officers digging away diligently. She did not expect, however, to find three tour Jeeps, four television news crews — led by Empty Creek's own Lola LaPola — five city council members, six of her closest friends, seven dogs (with owners), eight horses (with riders), and an enterprising young man hawking soft drinks and sandwiches. Only the partridge in a pear tree was absent.

Because the narrow dirt road was blocked by the police Bronco, Penelope had to park behind a mishmash of other vehicles and hike in.

Sam Connors leaned against the fender of the Bronco. Except for the yellow windbreaker emblazoned front and back with the word POLICE in large block letters and the absence of a real steed, Sam might have been a cowpoke of old, clad as he was in cowboy boots, jeans, and western shirt. The ensemble was completed by a large sombrero tilted rakishly over his forehead, and, of course, his heavy gun belt and holster.

Penelope ducked under the sombrero and gave him an affectionate hug and kiss. After all, they had once been an item and might still be had Sam not awakened one night to find Big Mike using a rather sensitive portion of his anatomy as a scratching post.

"Dutch should put up bleachers, charge admission, and sell his own hot dogs," Penelope said. The crowd milled restlessly behind the yellow crime-scene tape that encircled what looked very much like an effort to unearth an ancient city. Diggers filled wheelbarrows with dirt. The wheelbarrows were, in turn, trundled to makeshift sieves and unloaded for the crime lab technicians to shake and rattle over the screens of the sieves in their search for clues. The leftover earth was then dumped at another site.

Penelope estimated they were still at late yesterday in their efforts to restore the scene to its Before condition.

Sam grinned. "He's not in a very good mood."

"I can imagine. Where did all these people come from?"

"The usual ghouls and sightseers."

There were more ghouls than diggers by Penelope's rough count. Hell, there were more dogs than diggers. Two of them — Alexander and Kelsey — greeted Big Mike effusively, bestowing a couple of wet terrier kisses. The other mutts, outraged at such treasonous behavior, set up a clamor. Clint Eastwood Cat looked at them disdainfully, raised his fur, and hissed, as if to say, Come on, you want some of this? Go ahead, make my day.

Now, a goodly number of Empty Creek canines had learned to their misfortune that no, they did not want a piece of this particular cat. But these dogs appeared to be tourists and none too bright either.

Laney knew the warning signs and cried, "Alexander, no! Kelsey, come!"

"Goddammit, Mycroft!" Dutch roared. "Leave those dogs alone!"

Too late.

79

Penelope stepped back out of harm's way.

Wally let out a rebel yell that would have brought tears to Robert E. Lee's eyes.

Led by a full-figured shihtzu named Ting, the dogs charged and Dutch's crime scene erupted into a flurry of scuffling animals and dog owners. Five against three — Alexander and Kelsey entered the fray on Mycroft's team — wasn't really fair odds. Big Mike could take that many by himself, but why deny his friends a little action? After all, things could get pretty boring at Laney's.

Big Mike reared up on his hind legs with a yowl that would curdle Count Dracula's blood. That took care of Ting. A cat was one thing, but a cat doing an excellent imitation of an angry grizzly bear was quite another. Ting changed sides and snapped at a speeding whippet. Alexander and Kelsey took out a cocker spaniel and a pug respectively, leaving a half-grown Doberman for Mikey.

Big Mike was bowled over by the sheer size of the Doberman, who skidded through the dust and turned for another attack when it would have been far wiser to head for the Arizona-California border. Big Mike came up swinging and clawed a stout woman, who was trying to rescue the whippet, with one paw and a puffing, red-faced man with the other before leaping to the Doberman's back and digging in.

The poor Doberman bucked and reared desperately in an effort to dislodge Big Mike, but Cowboy Cat was having none of it. It wasn't until the dog hit the dirt running — whining piteously — that Big Mike stepped off nimbly, ready to take care of the next dummy in line.

But there were no takers.

"Vicious beast," Whippet Woman said.

"He was minding his own business," Penelope said, "and you ought to keep your dog on a leash."

"I'm bleeding," Red-faced Man said.

"That'll teach you to interfere in a cat fight."

"Excuse me, prease."

"What do you want?" Penelope demanded, whirling to face a Japanese man wearing a blue suit. He held a camera in one hand.

"This cat. He berong to you?"

"He's my friend. He doesn't belong to anybody."

Japanese Man bowed politely.

Penelope returned the bow.

"I am Hiroshi Ishii."

"Penelope Warren."

"Ah, Penelope-san. I have pictures of the

encounter. I shall give them to you for brave cat. What is his name?"

"Mycroft."

"Ah, Mycloft-san." He bowed to Big Mike. "Samurai Cat," he said. At that moment Ishii-san's left little finger fell off.

Whippet Woman screamed and fainted. Some people had no manners whatsoever.

Penelope picked up the little finger as though this sort of thing occurred every day and returned it to its owner. "You dropped this."

"Ah, thank you, Penelope-san." Ishii-san replaced the finger and bowed once more in gratitude. "You have fossils?"

"Mysteries, but no fossils," Penelope said. "You must excuse me now. I have to see to Samurai Cat."

"Of course."

After two additional bows, Penelope checked Big Mike for wounds. He had come through the brief skirmish unscathed and looked up with an expression that said, You weren't worried, were you?

"I'm getting too old for this, Mikey."

"Some cat."

"Hi, Cricket. What are you doing out here?"

"Thought I'd better see what happened on my property."

"Hah!" Red-faced Man said.

"Who are you?" Penelope asked.

"McCory. Albert J. McCory. Vice president, Desert Development Company."

"So?"

If Vice President Albert J. McCory responded, it was drowned out by a shout from the dig. "Hey, boss," Burke shouted. "You better take a look at this."

Penelope ducked under the yellow crime-scene tape, followed by Big Mike and Cricket. Dutch and Burke were at one of the sieves.

A human skull stared up at them from the dirt, yellowed teeth grinning fiendishly.

" 'Let me see,' " Penelope recited. " 'Alas poor Yorick! I knew him, Horatio, a fellow of infinite jest, of most excellent fancy. . . .' "

"Got this too," Tweedledee said, waving a bone. "Looks like it might've been his shin. Broke pretty bad once, from the looks of it."

Cricket gasped and fled.

"Think a dinosaur got him, boss?"

"There were no men when there were dinosaurs."

"Sure there were. I seen them in the movies."

"Explain the bullet hole between his eyes, then."

"Oh, yeah. There is that."

Penelope turned to watch Cricket leap into the saddle and canter away. "I wonder what that's all about?" she said to no one in particular.

CHAPTER FOUR

Penelope envied Big Mike at times, especially when she suffered a severe case of information overload. Not that information was a bad thing, quite the contrary. But information at this stage of human civilization should make sense, contribute to the accumulated store of knowledge, be of value to the human condition — even in Empty Creek, a community noted for being so out of step that they didn't even have a drummer, much less a different beat. What other city in Arizona, or the world for that matter, persisted in having an Oktoberfest with an imported oompah band and a parade with about twelve people in it — six or eight bikers, three horsemen, and a bar stool race? No one in Empty Creek needed a reason to drink beer, imported from Germany or not. They preferred Coyote Dogs (hot dogs named for the local baseball team and not their source) to bratwurst. And Cackling Ed, who was only slightly younger than Milly the Dinosaur, was still fighting the Hessians, the Huns, and the Third Reich. One year he followed the band, shouting, "Remember the *Maine!*" between oompahs — he tended to get a little confused about threats to national security — although he still attempted to seduce any handy fraulein.

At least, Old Western Days and Cinco de Mayo were related to Empty Creek's rich heritage, and the big parades and celebrations were well attended, although there was a tendency to get very drunk and shoot up the place despite all official admonitions to the contrary.

Big Mike, on the other hand, responded to information as necessary. He was not a Big Picture cat. So long as the basic food groups — lima beans, liver crunchies, and frozen yogurt — were plentiful, vacuum cleaners stayed away from his tail, and there was the prospect of a nocturnal tryst with Murphy Brown, that sexy little calico who lived down the road, Mikey was content with life as it unfolded its wonders for him.

"Which reminds me," Penelope said, "how's your sex life?"

"How did we get from *your* information overload to *my* sex life?" Nora Pryor asked, blushing prettily to absolutely no one's surprise. She was a veritable blushing machine. David Macklin had revealed that Ms. July, when posing for her portrait, blushed from forehead to toes throughout the entire modeling session.

"A logical progression," Penelope said. "Well? Did you and Tony have a spat?"

"Of course not. What makes you think that?"

"You're wearing a new scent. Chanel?"

"Number Five."

"A present to make up for whatever distress Tony caused you?"

"He could just like to give me presents."

"Yes, he could."

"Oh, all right, he's still refusing to pose for the Men of Empty Creek. What about me? I asked. You certainly didn't mind when I took *my* clothes off. That was different, he said. How? I asked. Your body is a work of art, he said, and deserves to be shared with the world. Besides, I'm not a man of Empty Creek. We'll make you an honorary citizen, I said, so you can just plan to get your sorry English butt over to Dave's studio and take it off for art."

"A surprising attitude," Penelope said, "for a man whose idea of a party trick is to suddenly start stripping while bellowing 'Take it off, you Zulu warriors.' "

Nora reddened in absentia for Tony. She had fallen in love with him on the evening they met after just such a performance. "That's only after several glasses of port," Nora said.

"And the conclusion of your little heart-to-heart?"

Nora smiled. "He's not buying me off with Chanel. He'll do it. He just doesn't know it yet. How about Andy?"

"He suggested the Cats of Empty Creek. I find their stance disheartening at a time when the nonprofit sector needs all the help it can get."

"They'll come around."

"They'd better."

"This is all very interesting, but you were telling me about the information overload."

"Red the Rat is returning from one of his prospecting trips, hears a shot, and a few minutes later comes across a wounded Millicent DeForest. He rushes her to the hospital, where she dies. Her last words were, apparently, 'It's mine.' Before we can examine the crime scene, someone blows a mountain down on top of it, shouting a warning, by the bye, covering up any tracks he might have left and, incidentally, burying a dinosaur. The owner of the land financed her junior year abroad by writing pornographic novels. And then she disappears. If that's not enough, a former member of the Yakusa shows up, asking if I have any fossils. . . ." Penelope ran out of breath.

"Yakusa? In Empty Creek? How do you know he's Yakusa?"

"His little finger fell off."

"Ugh! Gangrene?"

"Repentance. I understand there's a big government crackdown on gangsters in Japan. As a result, there's a flourishing trade in prosthetic little fingers for Yakusa who want to reform and become respectable. They used to cut their little fingers off as a sign of loyalty."

"Double ugh!"

"They're also removing their tattoos. I wonder if Ishii-san still has his. Some tattoos would enliven the men's calendar."

"This isn't information," Nora said. "It's babble."

"Only until it's all put in its proper place."

"I can see why this would trouble a skilled detective like yourself, but I'm still not sure why we're here."

Here being the Empty Creek Museum and headquarters of the Empty Creek Historical Society. Serving her second term as president of the historical society and the preeminent local historian, Nora's *Empty*

Creek: A History and Guide was now in a fourth printing of the second edition.

"Yorick," Penelope said.

"Hamlet's Yorick?"

"Our Yorick, alas. While excavating the crime scene, a human skull with a bullet hole between the eyes was found. Dutch says there are no old missing persons cases open. I wondered if you, in all your research, had ever come across something that might shed light on Yorick's identity?"

"Something like that would have stuck in my mind. I don't remember anything, however. How long ago?"

"Before I moved here, presumably. Otherwise, I would have remembered a missing person. But no more than twenty-five or thirty years ago, perhaps 1970 to start."

"You think the murders are related?"

"It's all very strange," Penelope said. "First, a dinosaur, then a woman shot in the back, and now Yorick. I can't imagine what's next. A plague of locusts, probably."

"What happened to the woman who owns the land? Do I know her?"

"Her name is Cricket."

"What a pretty name. Unusual too. What's her last name?"

"Just Cricket. It's her only name. She had it legally changed. She was there when

Yorick was discovered. The next thing I knew, she was on her horse, galloping away. When I stopped at the ranch on the way home, her house was dark and locked up. I liked her. I hope she's all right. She's a definite candidate for the next calendar."

"First, the men."

"Absolutely. Well, if you can remember anything at all, call me. I'm off to the library to leave a message for Noogy. Maybe he can track something down."

"Has anyone invited Noogy to pose?"

"We don't know. Probably not. I don't know his Woman of the Month, but I'll leave an invitation while I'm there. I wonder how he does it?"

Nora's cheeks turned crimson. "He makes you feel like you're the only woman in the world. And those eyes . . ."

"You too?"

Nora nodded shyly. "A long time ago, after I was divorced, but before I met Tony."

"Well, aren't you the surprising little historian? You should write a tell-all monograph. It would be a best-seller in Empty Creek. You could give a talk at Mycroft & Company and autograph it for everyone. My Nights with Noogy."

"Penelope!" Nora wailed.

"Look on it as a public service."

"I'd rather cut off *my* little finger."

"That's a thought. We could all do it. A protest against the men who won't pose."

"Let's give *their* little fingers the chop-chop if they won't pose."

"An even better idea."

"Feeling better?" Penelope asked.

"Ah, the lovely Penelope." Juan-Carlos Estavilla rose, marched from behind the reference desk, took Penelope's hand, bowed gallantly, and kissed it. "A twenty-four-hour virus. Nothing serious, but thank you for asking."

Penelope giggled. "Your mustache tickles."

"A tickling mustache is but part of my charm."

"Well, you can display the rest of that charm for the Men of Empty Creek Calendar."

"I'd be honored."

"You would?"

"Of course. What cad would refuse such a request from a beautiful woman?"

"I know several."

"They should be horsewhipped. I, Juan-Carlos Estavilla, would crawl a thousand miles through the burning desert to be with the exquisite maiden who graces the month of June."

His eyes pierced her soul — again. Oh, to hell with it. Penelope jumped in and swam several laps in their black, limpid pools. When she surfaced after an eternity of seconds, her knees were weak and her stomach was doing backward somersaults. She took a deep breath and said, "That won't be necessary. A little research will suffice."

"Rebuffed again."

Penelope smiled. "I'm a one-man woman, Noogy, but if I were unattached, I might consider your application."

"I can provide references."

"I'm sure you can. For the moment, however, information is what I need." Penelope posed the same missing person question to the reference librarian.

"I'll call you with the answer."

"Thanks." Penelope paused. "And, Noogy, do something about those eyes. Register them as deadly weapons or something."

At the Tack Shack, Penelope took a Save Lonesome Bend T-shirt from the rack (her others were all in the wash) and changed in the dressing room while Big Mike went off to greet Leia, Lora Lou's big but shy white wolfhound.

"Don't you have enough of these?" Lora Lou asked at the counter.

"It's a good cause, and besides, I'm going out to the DDC. Might as well jerk their chain while I'm at it."

"In that case, it's on the house. I'll make the donation to the legal fund for you. Jerk their chain for me too." All proceeds from the T-shirts went to the Save Lonesome Bend effort.

"Well, thanks. I'll do that."

"Making any progress?"

"Not much," Penelope admitted glumly. She gave Lora Lou the brief update and then asked, "Do you know a woman named Cricket? She owns the ranch at Lonesome Bend."

"Sure. She has a standing order for feed. We deliver, but she occasionally comes in. She's pretty much a loner. She must have had a tragic love affair."

"Have you been reading Laney's novels again?"

Lora Lou grinned. "Yep. I just love all that swooning and stuff. I think she's a Hacker."

"Laney can barely turn her computer on."

"Not Laney and not that kind of Hacker."

"Lora Lou, what *are* you talking about?"

"Cricket. I think she might be a Hacker."

"Those Hackers? The Mahoney-and-Hacker Hackers?"

"The very same."

"I thought they were all in jail."

"Most of them are, but they get out, drink a little, fight a little, get caught doing something, and go back. The prison authorities probably keep their cells ready for them."

"I don't believe it. Cricket is too educated to be a Hacker. She's not trailer-park trash."

"You ever seen Ma Hacker? Cricket bears a definite resemblance."

Penelope rang the bell, pounded on the door, rang the bell some more, and tried the knob. Locked. Lonesome Bend Ranch was, indeed, lonesome. Penelope wandered around the stables and pens. The weekend cowboys and cowgirls were all off doing whatever they did during the workweek, but Cricket or someone else had been there, because the horses stared placidly at Penelope and Big Mike, showing no signs of having missed a meal or two, and their water barrels had been topped off recently.

"Where is she, Mikey?"

"Mewp," he replied.

"I don't think she's out dancing."

"Meorgh?" Mikey said, staring down a bird perched on a rail.

"I don't think she's transformed herself into a bird either."

Having established that neither of them had the foggiest notion of Cricket's present whereabouts, Penelope, Girl Detective, and Big Mike, Faithful Assistant, hopped in the Jeep and headed off to interrogate a certain vice president.

Penelope stopped the Jeep and let the dust settle before she got out and went to the gate in the heavy chain-link fence that surrounded the field headquarters of the Desert Development Company. The gate was locked with a heavy chain and padlock. The DDC was certainly poised to defile the desert. Bulldozers and other heavy grading equipment were parked next to a series of sheds. A single-wide mobile home provided offices.

Penelope rattled the chain in frustration, cupped her hands, and shouted, "Hello!"

"Go away!" A man wearing a uniform cap, blue shirt, and jeans slouched out from behind a shed and ambled toward the gate. His hair hung in gray, greasy coils to his collar. A gun belt and holster sagged around his hips. "Sign says keep out. Can't you read?"

96

"Actually, it says no trespassing. Where is everybody?"

"Gone home. Start early. Leave early."

"Who are you?"

"Watchman." He pointed to a tag sewn on the breast pocket of his shirt. "Says so right here. Can't you read?" He spit tobacco juice at Penelope's feet.

"It says security."

"What does?"

"Your tag. It says security, not watchman."

"Don't get smart. 'Course, if you was to be nice, we could maybe have a drink."

"I'd rather kiss a tarantula."

"Oh, yeah, I know all about you. Come out here with that shirt, trying to take away my job. You one of them liberals wants to destroy the country."

Penelope shrugged. "I'll come back tomorrow."

"You just do that."

"Make sure you take your surly pills."

"Huh?"

While not exactly lonesome, the crime scene was calm in comparison with the previous afternoon. There wasn't a tour Jeep or a news crew to be seen. Teams of police officers and crime analysts continued the tedious work of digging, sifting, and wheeling the dirt away. Two huge piles of dirt and rock rose beyond the wide perimeter established as the crime scene, which was actually beginning to resemble the Before rather than the After.

Harvey Curtis, an undercover cop until romance — and Penelope — had blown his cover, and now a card-carrying detective, seemed to be in charge of the current shift. Because Harvey was there, Penelope wasn't at all surprised to find Alyce Smith, Empty Creek's very own astrologer and psychic in residence. After all, Alyce might have been a dinosaur in another life, although she had never mentioned it. The lovely mistress of January was a serene figure in the midst of hubbub, standing, eyes closed, face raised to the breeze that ruffled her blond hair.

Harvey put a finger to his lips. "Shhh. Alyce is working," he whispered.

"I can see that," Penelope replied in a normal tone of voice. When Alyce went into one of her trances, little short of an elephant stampede was likely to disturb her.

"I thought Alyce might feel something," Harvey explained.

"I take that to mean the authorities are stymied."

Harvey nodded. "Dutch is not happy."

"Have you found anything else?"

"Some pretty rocks and a lot of junk. It's over here."

Penelope followed Harvey to a mound of miscellaneous items retrieved from the desert — an assortment of beer cans, some with bullet holes in them, a large tomato-juice can also riddled by gunfire, several spent cartridge cases of various calibers, but old and corroded, a rusted horseshoe, a lot of broken glass, a cardboard box that had once contained condoms, a tangled strip of cassette tape, an orange golf ball, the wooden handle of a paring knife, disintegrating boxer shorts, the clasp and tag of a brassiere (34C), and a shiny can without a label.

"Well," Penelope said. "It looks to me as if someone came out here for a picnic, played some music on their tape recorder, drank beer and Bloody Marys, got in some target practice, played a little pitch and putt, had sex, didn't bother to clean up after themselves, and forgot to put their under-wear on when they left."

"Pretty good," Harvey said, "but what about the horseshoe?"

Penelope smiled. "They either played a game of horseshoes in between banging away at cans and each other or they had to call their farrier."

"Could have brought it along for luck."

"This doesn't seem a very lucky place," Penelope said. "No more body parts? Human or dinosaur?"

"Not yet, but whoever belonged to the leg definitely broke it sometime."

"Presumably before he was shot."

"Oh, yeah, it had healed."

"Murder," Alyce said from her trance.

"Yes, we know," Penelope pointed out gently.

"Three so far, and more to come."

"How many? Who?"

"I don't know." Alyce blinked several times, tossed her hair, and returned from Fuzzy Wuzzy Teddy Bear Land, or wherever it was she went on these journeys of the mind. "Oh, hi, Penelope."

"You okay, honey?"

"He worries about me," Alyce said, brushing Harvey's hair back from his forehead. "I keep telling him it's just a form of meditation."

"What if you don't come back? I don't want you meditating right out of my life."

"We could always use her as a statue," Penelope said cheerfully. "Put her in front of city hall. Decorate her at Christmas. She could be the Statue of Liberty on the Fourth of July and other patriotic occasions. You could even have conjugal visits."

"With a statue?"

"She wouldn't really be a statue, Harvey. Just in a trance. You could make love in a trance, couldn't you, Alyce?"

"With the proper motivation. Like if my honey whispered, 'I'd love to pose for the calendar.' "

"Oh, no," Harvey said, backing away. "My mother would never speak to me again."

"I'll never speak to you if you don't," Alyce said.

"For someone who lives with an astrologer, Harvey, you could have come up with a better excuse. Mercury retrograde at the very least."

"He'd better not," Alyce said. "He knows very well that I'll choose the optimum day for posing."

"We may have a conundrum on our hands," Penelope said, "but it's nice to see the war between the sexes flourishing."

"I should have left you locked in the pillory," Harvey said with considerable disgust. He had once asked Penelope for a date while holding her prisoner in a pillory at the Empty Creek Elizabethan Springe Faire. The medieval device seemed to possess considerable aphrodisiacal qualities, having brought several couples together, and it now resided in the bedroom of one Lola LaPola, intrepid television reporter, and her husband.

"But then you would never have met me," Alyce said, "and rescued me from the stake." A madman had condemned Alyce as a sorceress and sentenced her to burn. It had been a most interesting Faire.

"That's true."

"This is all very interesting," Penelope said, "but we digress. You said there were three murders — Millicent DeForest and Yorick. Who was the third?"

"Milly, of course, the dinosaur."

"You went back a hundred million years?"

Alyce shook her head. "It's the aura. This has been a killing ground. Milly was stalked and killed by a predator. I can feel it."

"Wouldn't that be considered natural selection, survival of the fittest?"

"Murder by any other name . . ."

Penelope shuddered at a sudden chill. Someone had just stepped on her grave.

Pink clouds streaked the western sky as Penelope and Big Mike went down to feed Chardonnay and the rabbits. The Arabian mare snorted and tossed her head in greeting. Chardonnay took the peppermint candy delicately and munched happily while Penelope mixed the healthy concoction for her dinner. The rabbits emerged from the desert to sit in a semicircle around a small patch of grass, the only true cultivation on the twelve acres Penelope owned along the banks of Empty Creek. All the rest was desert in its natural state.

With Chardonnay eating and the rabbits munching on lettuce and carrots, Penelope sat back in the lawn chair, thinking yet again what a perfect time it was to enjoy a relaxing cigar and a double scotch. The only problem with that being she didn't smoke cigars or drink scotch as a general rule.

"Another day like today," she told Mycroft, "and I might just do it."

Big Mike, stretched out on the grass to watch the rabbits, turned lazily and looked up to place his order. Cuban, for me, please, and a nice single malt.

Alyce Smith was a most excellent astrologer and psychic, more often right than wrong, although she made no claims to prophecy. "Look on me as a guidance counselor," she often said. "I can indicate the best days to sign legal documents and the days better spent in bed with the covers pulled over your head." Her abilities, however, did not extend to herself. With a greater perspicacity on Alyce's part, for example, she might not have found herself tied to a stake with fagots piled to her shapely hips. Still, her musings were not to be ignored. When Alyce said trouble was coming, it was a wise cat who headed for the old hidey-hole.

Penelope was still pondering the wisdom of finding a good hidey-hole, when Andy came down the path and kissed her. She grabbed him and pulled him down, managing to collapse the lawn chair in the process.

Sprawled on top of her, not an altogether unpleasant experience, Andy cried, "What was that for?"

"Glad to see you," Penelope said before cutting off further conversation with a kiss of her own. Men were definitely good for making even the strongest and most independent of women feel secure on the occasions when someone trampled over their graves. Penelope was not about to confess to that fact though, and after a few intense minutes said, "I think you're all being rather childish about it."

"What happened to glad to see me?"

"That was then. This is now."

"It's the journalist's code of ethics."

"What about it?"

"Skinny reporters should never pose nude. It's a little-known subsection of the code."

"You're an editor."

"Still applies."

"Dan Rather would do it."

"He's a television journalist," Andy said. "They'll do anything."

"Noogy's agreed to pose."

"Oh."

Penelope smiled. That ought to get the I-can-pee-farther-than-you syndrome roiling among the males of Empty Creek.

After dinner Andy gingerly explored the possibility of continuing the glad-to-see-you routine without making a definite commitment to art and charity. When he put his arm around Penelope's shoulder, she purred, albeit silently, and snuggled close, turning her face up for his kiss. Emboldened, Andy unfastened the top button of her blouse, and the second, and the third. He tugged the blouse free of her jeans and kissed the soft swell of her breasts above the lacy brown bra she wore. By the state of her breathing, Andy judged that calendars had been forgotten for the moment and things

105

were really getting interesting, when the telephone rang.

"Oh, damn." Penelope removed his hand from her breast somewhat reluctantly, and said "Don't lose your place" before going into the kitchen to pick up the wall extension. As usual, Big Mike followed, leaping to the counter to see who was on the line. Penelope always wondered if he was expecting a call from Michael Eisner at Disney to ask him to star in *Cat Hunk*. It wouldn't surprise her.

"Hello," she said after untangling the cord from Mikey's paw.

"I was ten when he left."

CHAPTER FIVE

Had it been on a main highway, there might have been billboards advertising Eats, the Amazing Two-headed Rattlesnake, and Cactus Juice — Fifty Miles, Thirty Miles, Ten Miles, This Is It, but one out of four wasn't bad. Lacking the highway, the mutant reptile, and the juice, the Eats advertised at Betty's Coffee Shop looked as though they might be palatable if the little building freshly trimmed in blue and white with clean windows was any indication. The gas station was old; the convenience store new.

Bathsheba was one of those little places in the desert that existed solely for the truly reclusive, the hands on the vast ranches surrounding it, and the warring clans who lived on opposite sides of the highway some fifteen miles out of Empty Creek. No one remembered now what had started the feud, but it had continued down the generations. One group of interbred brats grew up and took over from their pappies and grand-pappies. Their junkyard dogs yapped and snarled and whined from behind the fence. The Mahoneys favored mongrels. The Hackers went in for mutts.

Trailers had been plopped down haphazardly behind chain-link fences on both sides of the highway. Shells of rusted cars and pickups, junk, railroad ties, old washing machines, were the prominent landscaping motif.

Cricket offered Penelope a choice. " 'A clean well-lighted place' or sleaze." Betty's was the clean well-lighted place. Having ended her Hemingway phase while in Africa, Penelope opted for sleaze. It was always far more interesting.

Maggie's Roadhouse was neutral ground. A huge white stripe, grimy with age now, had been painted down the center of the big room. A jukebox, also neutral ground, straddled the line. Hackers stayed to the left, Mahoneys to the right. Whoever happened to be out of jail at the time sat, drinking and staring sullenly across the room at their rivals.

Cricket was in a corner booth and waved when Penelope and Big Mike entered, blinking in the gloomy interior after the brightness of the day. Both Mahoneys present glared when Penelope went to the left.

"Hi," Cricket said. "Thanks for coming."

"My pleasure."

"The food's not bad and I can recommend the tequila."

"I'll have both."

Cricket smiled wanly. "Sometimes I miss San Francisco. Dressing up for the opera, theater, a new art exhibition."

"Why didn't you stay there?"

"He wouldn't know where to find me. I always thought he would come back for me someday."

"He still might. You don't know for sure that it was your father we found."

Cricket shook her head. "It's him. When that cop said the leg had been broken, I just knew. I painted pictures on his cast, and when they removed it, he wouldn't let them throw it away. It's probably still around here someplace. Ma doesn't throw much out."

"We'll know when we get back. I called Dutch and filled him in. He's going to have the dentist dig out your father's old charts."

"If he still has them."

"He does. Dutch called back to confirm."

"Ma always said Pop liked Dr. Dumont's whiskey. He wouldn't give me any though. I always got the novocaine instead. I suppose he might now if I asked. I'll have to get a cavity and see."

"You could just have your teeth cleaned. Rinse with whiskey."

"That would be more practical."

An old woman waddled out of the kitchen and headed for the booth. "Whatcha gonna have, Sally Anne?" she asked. "One of them tangerine martinis?"

"Maggie means Tanqueray martini. I was still the sophisticated woman when I came home. I forgot all the wine here comes with a screw top."

"Now, don't you be sassing an old lady none, Sally Anne. I can still spank your bottom if I needs to, just like that time I caught you smoking out back."

"I was fourteen and Maggie took me over her knee and whaled the tar out of me. Right in front of the Mahoney boys too. That was the worst part. I think it might have led to certain career choices later in life."

"Never smoked again, didcha?"

"No, ma'am, I surely didn't."

"So what you and your friend gonna have? I got a bottle of tangerine. Keep it just for you 'cept you never come visit no more. It's almost full."

Penelope watched the tears well up in Cricket's eyes. "Aw, Maggie, you're sweet.

How can I not have a tangerine martini?"

"Okay, then. 'Bout time. What's yours, hon?"

"The same, please, and a saucer of nonalcoholic beer for my friend."

Maggie and Big Mike surveyed each other.

"He's a big un." Maggie waddled off.

"Sophisticated ladies," Penelope said, raising her martini glass to Cricket.

"I don't feel very sophisticated when I come home. It's like I never left. I'm always afraid I'll get trapped into marrying some cousin three or four times removed and wind up living here, hating Mahoneys and myself."

"Why didn't your mother report your father missing?"

"It wasn't anyone's business. Hackers are supposed to take care of themselves."

"And so he just disappeared."

"September 8, 1973. Never found the truck or any other trace of him. He was just gone. I walked him to the truck, holding his hand. He had his lunch in a brown paper sack. Picked me up, kissed me, and drove away. He always called me Sunshine. I watched until I couldn't see him anymore."

"Where was he going?"

"Ironically, he was looking for fossils and gems. Ma's got the longest-running garage sale in history. Pop would find this stuff in the desert and bring it home for Ma to sell to the snowbirds."

"Hey, Sally Anne. Whyn't you and your friend meet us at white line? Teach you some new tricks."

"My name is Cricket."

"Cricket. Grasshopper. Whatever. You still Sally Anne to us. Sally Anne Cricket. Kinda purty. Ain't you gonna introduce us to your friend?"

"No."

"Aw, Sally Anne, don't be mean. You still the prettiest little thang around."

"That's Cully Mahoney," Cricket said to Penelope. "He's dumb. Sully is his brother. He's dumber yet. The smart one in the family's been locked up in the asylum since he was twenty-one. Poor Buxter. He was the nicest of the Mahoneys until he started hearing voices."

"Heard about this new thang. It's called the French kiss. Teach it to you."

"Good God. Can you believe it? It's enough to make me want to bring Juliana out of retirement."

"You boys leave Sally Anne alone," Maggie hollered, "or I'll get my vacuum

112

cleaner out. Give this place an early spring cleaning and start over."

Cricket laughed. "She'll do it too. Maggie's got a sawed-off shotgun under the bar."

The Mahoney boys evidently believed Maggie as well. "Gotta go," Cully said hastily. "You sure do look good, Sally Anne. Another time. You too, purty stranger."

"When 'Great Birnam wood to high Dunsinane hill shall come,' " Cricket said.

"Huh?"

"Would you care to translate?" Cricket asked.

"Delighted," Penelope replied. "When my cat flies," she said over her shoulder. "Sorry. It was the best I could do on short notice."

"Meow." *I could fly* if *I wanted to.*

"Of course you could, Mikey."

"You *did* have to reduce it to something they could understand."

"You'll let me know? I'll be at Lonesome Bend."

Penelope nodded. "As soon as I hear anything." Impulsively, Penelope hugged Cricket and was surprised to discover how frail and vulnerable she seemed.

Driving off, Penelope looked in the rearview mirror and saw Cricket standing, just like she must have when she was ten years old, watching her father leave for the last time. A chill seized her spine. "Dammit!" Penelope cried. "Whoever you are, stay off my grave."

Sitting at her desk in the back room of Mycroft & Company, Penelope was working herself up to a most excellent headache, wishing she could reduce the case of Millicent DeForest, and possibly Pop Hacker, to something comprehensible. It seemed inconceivable that the two murders, nearly thirty years apart, could be related. But irony piled upon irony. Pop Hacker, like Millicent DeForest, was out digging for fossils on the day he died. They both happened to find the same dinosaur on land now owned by the first victim's daughter. It was just too coincidental. It's enough to give anyone a headache, Penelope thought, when Kathy screamed.

Her worst fears realized at last, Penelope grabbed the claw hammer from its nail on the wall and raced into the store proper, prepared to repel an armed robbery in progress. Nothing less would induce such a terrified scream.

Kathy stood behind the counter as far

away as she could get from Hiroshi Ishii without actually leaving the premises, pointing in horror at a mug on the counter. "His finger fell into my coffee," Kathy shrieked.

"Solly," Hiroshi Ishii said. "So vely solly." He bowed to Kathy-san, Penelope-san, and Mycroft-san before dipping into the coffee cup to retrieve the offending member. "Do you have paper tower?"

"Ishii-san, you really must get some Krazy Glue for that finger."

"Klazy Grue?"

"Yes, Klazy Grue. Stick that sucker on once and for all." Penelope smiled. Conversations with Ishii-san were beginning to make her feel nostalgic for Africa, where the "L" and "R" sounds in Bantu languages were also interchangeable. Quite often the rions loared in East Africa. "Kathy, would you fetch a paper towel, please?"

"Will a tissue do?"

"Quite nicely."

With Ishii-san's finger more or less firmly in place once again, Penelope asked, "How may we help you?"

Ishii-san bowed.

Penelope bowed.

Kathy bowed.

Big Mike yawned. Except for Kathy's

scream, which had turned out to be no big deal, it had been a dull day. He was probably disappointed that Maggie hadn't blasted away at the Mahoney boys.

Ishii-san dipped into the inside pocket of his suit coat and withdrew a photograph. His little finger stayed behind.

It was an excellent shot of Mycroft on the back of the beleaguered Doberman. "Thank you," Penelope said, bowing automatically. "I shall have it framed and hang it in a place of honor."

"You are most kind," Ishii-san said. "In return, I must humbly beg a favor."

"If I can."

"I must have fossils."

"Are you a dealer?"

"I hope to be. It will erase the stain of Yakuza. I have dishonored honorable ancestors. I am, as you say, going direct."

"Straight. Going straight."

"Ah." Again he went into his pocket and brought out a small notebook and pen. The notation made, he bowed. "Thank you."

"You're welcome, but as you see, I deal in books, not fossils. I'm sorry."

"I am staying at the Razy Tlaverrel Moter."

"Naturally," Penelope said. The Lazy Traveller Motel, while not the only motel in

116

Empty Creek, was the finest, offering a restaurant, coffee shop, banquet rooms, Olympic-sized pool, and weekend getaways for consenting adults in one or another of the suites featuring water beds, some very interesting movies on cable television, and an assortment of erotic oils in the bathrooms. Penelope and Andy were partial to the Chrysanthemum Suite. "If I hear of any fossils for sale, I'll let you know."

Penelope returned to her office and opened the back door for a little air. All that bowing had a tendency to make her dizzy. She stood in the doorway, breathing deeply, and contemplating passion in its many forms. Her own hunger had always been for books and reading. When Andy was not staying over, it was physically and mentally impossible for her to doze off — as much as she liked to sleep — without reading, no matter how tired she might be. Red the Rat dreamed of finding one or another of his lost gold mines. Others lusted after money, power, stamps, diamonds, baseball cards, sex, classic cars. But fossils? Until the death of Millicent DeForest, Penelope would never have thought of bones, however old, inciting such deep fervor except among those in the academic community who studied them. "It's just one more example, Mikey, of the necessity for keeping an open mind."

"Psst!"

Penelope looked around for the source of the whispered hail. The alley was deserted. Seeing no one lurking to either right or left, she attributed the curious sound to a dust devil whisking through on its appointed rounds and turned, ready to address the business of selling books.

"Psst!"

Penelope stopped. "Who's there?" she called out.

"Knock, knock."

"It's supposed to be the other way around. I say, 'Knock, knock,' and you reply, 'Who's there?' "

"Who are you talking to?" Kathy asked.

"The spirit of the alley, apparently. Come out where I can see you, whoever you are, and stay off my grave."

A man, swarthy of complexion, peeked out from behind the Dumpster. He wore a brown fedora and a dark blue double-breasted Burberry trench coat with the collar turned up. "He's a crook, don't you know?" he said in an accent that was partially British, but mixed with a heavy dose of something vaguely Mediterranean.

"Have they updated the weather report?"

"Sorry?"

"You appear to know something we don't know. Is there a storm approaching? It wouldn't surprise me. It's the result of all the atomic fallout."

Fedora Man blinked.

"You're confusing him," Kathy said.

"Exactly. From the fifties?" Penelope elaborated, quite enjoying herself now. "In Nevada? Probably Bikini Atoll as well, although I'm not quite sure about the prevailing winds."

"You're confusing me too."

"Well, what do you expect? Someone skulks around behind *my* Dumpster, going 'psst' like he expects to interest me in his virgin sister, although I suppose in my case it would be his virgin brother, but Lord knows in this day and age, or I suppose the 'psst' could be preparatory to flashing me, and what a disgusting thought *that* is. Well, which is it to be?" Penelope demanded. "Virgins or flashing?"

"You are beautiful with your temper. Your nostrils flare."

"Of course I'm beautiful. What do you want?"

"Actually, I was hoping to interest you in a fragment from the Dead Sea Scrolls."

"Ah, you're working your way through college selling subscriptions to the Dead Sea Scrolls. Manufactured yesterday, I suppose."

"Madam, really. They've been aging for a month. I brought a supply from Israel. I also have several pieces of the true cross."

"And you call that nice little Japanese man a crook. What does that make you?"

"An entrepreneur." He removed his fedora, revealing a shaven head, and bowed.

"Oh, Lord, not another one. Why me?"

"You know about the dinosaur. I would like to buy it."

"It's not mine to sell."

"I will share the profits. No questions asked."

"Sorry, not interested."

"I am at the Lazy Traveller Motel if you should change mind."

"In the Lilac Suite, I suppose."

"How did you know?"

"Anyone who would shave his head would stay in the Lilac Suite. Or are you follically challenged?"

"Excuse me?"

"Bald."

Yitzhak Cohen replaced his fedora. "Please. It is the debonair touch." He marched down the alley, swinging his arms, looking like he was on parade at Buckingham Palace.

"And stay out of my alley," Penelope called after him.

"What is this all about?" Kathy asked. "Where are all these people coming from?"

"Japan and Israel apparently. They seem to think that Empty Creek is now the dinosaur capital of the world."

"What are you doing about all these foreigners in your fair hamlet? All that's missing is the zither music in the background."

"Who are you talking about?"

"Ishii-san, for one, although I rather like him. He's very polite. And Yitzhak Cohen, for another, whom I don't much care for. He just tried to sell me fragments from the Dead Sea Scrolls *and* the true cross. He's willing to trade for fossils. Doesn't that make you the slightest bit suspicious?"

"You're just mad because he thought you were gullible enough to fall for it."

"That's true," Penelope admitted.

"Wait until you meet Boris and Natasha."

"Good God! Now what?"

"Russian cops."

"You're kidding, right?"

Dutch laughed.

"You're *not* kidding."

"Nope. Better brush up on your Dostoyevsky. His name's Fyodor Popov and he likes quoting *The Brothers Karamazov.* She's Katerina Rakitin. Big gal."

" 'He may suddenly, after hoarding impressions for many years, abandon everything and go off to Jerusalem on a pilgrimage. Or he may suddenly set fire to his native village. Or he may do both.' "

"What?"

"*The Brothers K,*" Penelope said. "I'm quoting Dostoyevsky. I've always thought that would make a nifty epigraph for a novel."

" 'Well, Count.' "

"That's Tolstoy."

"I just wanted you to know I'm erudite too. Unfortunately, that's as far as I ever get in *War and Peace.* Nothing ever happens."

"Skip a bit. Napoleon does get around to invading Russia."

"There is that, I suppose."

"I guess he'll show up here next. Just what we need. A runt of an emperor invading Empty Creek." Penelope took a deep breath and shouted, *"Aux barricades!"*

"Dammit, Penelope, give me warning when you're going to scream."

122

"I *was* warning you. We have to tear up the cobblestones and barricade the town. We'll make our stand at the creek. The thin red line must hold firm."

"You're nuttier than your sister."

"I'm going to tell her you said that. She's any number of cashews short of a full can."

"Good thought. Bring some cashews when you come. I'm hungry."

"Come where?"

"Why, to meet Boris and Natasha, of course. Better bring two cans. Natasha looks a little famished herself."

Since Penelope's sense of curiosity rivaled Big Mike's, she packed up and pointed the Jeep in the direction of what had euphemistically been renamed the Public Safety Building. To Penelope's mind, Dutch's title should have been changed at the same time from Chief of Police to Chief of Public Safety, but Empty Creek bureaucracy was singularly lacking in such sensible judgment. She made one detour to pick up rations for Dutch and his new friends.

Penelope greeted the desk officer and veered off toward the august offices of the chief. Mycroft, as usual, headed for the jail, where he knew he would be warmly greeted and pampered by whatever officers were on duty there. It was a tradition started on the day Big Mike and Penelope had been arrested for obstruction of justice by Tweedledee in a fit of pique. If the object was to teach a surly cat and an equally surly book mistress a lesson, it had failed. Big Mike made enduring friendships with the jailers, Penelope was almost immediately released on her own recognizance, Dutch met Stormy, and Tweedledee narrowly escaped a long-term assignment to crossing-guard duty at the Empty Creek elementary school.

"Serendipity," Penelope said upon entering the office and tossing her purchase on Dutch's desk.

" 'The world stands on absurdities, and perhaps nothing would have come to pass without them,' " a man Penelope took to be Fyodor Popov said glumly. " 'We know what we know.' "

"What's this?" Dutch asked.

"Fat-free pretzels. Much better for you than peanuts."

"Pay my colleague no attention," Katerina Rakitin said, thrusting a massive hand at Penelope. "He carries the weight of Mother Russia on his back. It is a great burden. I am Katerina Rakitin."

Penelope was not a small woman — she

stood five nine in her stocking feet — but as she took the proffered hand she had to look up at the Russian detective. If women ever went into professional football, Katerina could play right tackle.

"I want cashews and you bring healthy pretzels?"

"I'm glad to meet you," Penelope said. Her hand disappeared in the clutch of Katerina, who pumped once, twice, thrice, before Penelope managed to extract it with her arm still attached to her shoulder. She turned to the man wearing jeans, a gaudy Hawaiian shirt, tennis shoes, and a cowboy hat decorated with feathers, and said, " 'They have their Hamlets, but we still have our Karamazovs!' "

Popov almost smiled. "You know the Master?"

"If you mean Dostoyevsky, I have a passing acquaintance. I try to read one Russian novel a year. They're so gloriously depressing."

Dutch ripped the bag of pretzels open.

"You should open them carefully," Penelope criticized. "Now you won't be able to reseal them for freshness."

"Cashew cans have little plastic tops for freshness."

"Why serendipity?" Katerina Rakitin

asked. She took a pretzel and chewed it delicately.

"I just read about missing Russian fossils on the Internet, and here you are."

"Yes, we are here. At the Lazy Traveller Motel. It's a wonderful motel."

"And doing a brisk international business, I understand."

Katerina took another pretzel. "What a wonderful country. Fat-free pretzels. Just imagine?"

"Forgive me, but do you lift weights?"

"When I was an athlete. I shot the put."

" 'Feed men, and then ask of them virtue!' " Fyodor said, grabbing a handful of pretzels.

"That's the Grand Inquisitor section," Penelope said to Fyodor, and directed her next comment to Katerina. "You mean put the shot."

"The greatest chapter in all of literature," Fyodor said, "but she means she shot the put in anger when we boycotted the Olympics. The bullets left scars on the shot. The big heavy ball?" he explained helpfully. "Katerina is a very passionate woman."

"Oh. 'Better to reign in hell than to serve in heaven.' Evil is always more interesting than good."

"Milton stole that line from the Master."

"Milton was there first. Two hundred years or so first."

"He should have left it for the Master. That line was destined for Dostoyevsky. The Master would have done a better job of *Paradise Lost* anyway."

"An interesting point," Penelope conceded, "but hardly pertinent to the matters at hand. What brings you to Empty Creek?"

"Mr. Yitzhak Cohen," Katerina Rakitin said. "He has our fossils and we want them back."

"I want cashews. My heart is set on cashews."

" 'I punish myself for my whole life,' " Popov cried, " 'my whole life I punish.' "

"Have some more pretzels," Penelope said.

"You are most kind."

CHAPTER SIX

After sending Boris and Nastasha off to the Lazy Traveller Motel, Dutch convened a meeting, hollering for Tweedledee and Tweedledum to haul it into his office.

"Who is Millicent DeForest?" Penelope asked by way of beginning, "or, more precisely, who was Millicent DeForest?" She had always admired the opening line of Ayn Rand's novel *Atlas Shrugged*. "Who is John Gait?" Rand had asked, and then spent about a million words answering the question. At the rate this investigation was proceeding, Penelope thought it might take an equal amount of words and time to discover DeForest's true identity and therein the motive for her murder.

"Loving daughter and girlfriend," Tweedledum said, finishing off the pretzels.

Penelope tapped the stack of papers in her lap, the results of the many interviews conducted by Tweedledee and Tweedledum since Millicent DeForest's death — her parents and Brian Abernathy, the devoted boy-friend. Penelope had listened to the taped interviews and studied the reports. Tweedledee and Tweedledum had done a good job, Penelope admitted. She couldn't find anything they had missed. "A young woman who never forgot a birthday or an anniversary and who probably always had sex in the missionary position. It borders on hagiography."

"Haggle what?"

"Hagiography. Writings dealing with saints." Penelope riffled through the interviews. "Everything here suggests Millicent DeForest was a saint."

"Saints don't have sex," Tweedledee said.

"Some do before they leave their worldly lusts behind."

"Well, they shouldn't. Jeez."

"A college teacher," Dutch interrupted. "Her colleagues liked her."

"Yes, an instructor at Empty Creek College, apparently well respected by students and other teachers, but that's strange too. There are always academic rivalries, jealousies, angling for position in any college department. 'It's my turn to teach the modern British novel.' 'I don't want freshman comp again.' That's what goes on in English departments. I suppose the same attitudes would exist in the local geology department. 'It's *my* dinosaur.' That sort of thing."

"You still think the dinosaur is connected?"

Penelope shrugged. "The sudden descent of fossil seekers would suggest the possibility."

"They're here for the big gem show in Tucson. They saw the story on television, so they popped up here to investigate."

"What do gems have to do with dinosaurs?"

"See, you're not so smart," Tweedledee chortled. "They always have fossils at gem shows."

Penelope ignored him. "But, then, we also have the death of Pop Hacker. I don't look forward to telling Cricket."

"It was a long time ago."

"Cricket is still grieving. It's like the families of MIAs in Vietnam. They want to know what happened to their husbands, fathers, brothers. Until I tell her, Cricket can still hope that one day he'll return."

"I'll tell her if you like," Dutch said.

Penelope shook her head. "Thanks, but I'll do it."

"Does she remember what day he disappeared?"

"September 8, 1973. It was a Saturday. She was ten years old."

"It pinpoints his death anyway."

"Possibly, but not necessarily. He could have been struck by amnesia and wandered around for several years before his death, or he could have been kidnapped, for instance, and held for a time, until they found out he wasn't worth anything, or he could have . . ."

"Why do you always have to complicate things? You read too many mystery novels. The murders can't be connected anyway."

"Probably not, but . . . For example, Pop Hacker might have found Milly and was killed because someone else wanted the dinosaur, or . . ."

"So how come the dinosaur is still there? Why didn't the killer take it in 1973?"

"A good point. I'm working on it."

"Better work on this year."

"Okay, play nicely, children. What else we got?"

"What about the guy who tried to blow us up?" Tweedledee asked. "We coulda been killed."

" 'It is a riddle wrapped in a mystery inside an enigma.' "

Dutch groaned. "No more Dostoyevsky, please. My head hurts."

"That's Sir Winston Churchill, actually," Penelope said. "It *was* a reference to Russia though."

" 'I am a Bear of Very Little Brain, and long words bother me,' " Tweedledee said.

Penelope clapped her hands delightedly. "I didn't know you read works of quality."

"*Winnie the Pooh*'s a kid's book."

"Hardly."

"Well, what's an enigma, then?"

"Inscrutable. Not a long word."

"Long enough."

"Antidisestablishmentarianism. That's long. And an excellent example of word building."

"Stop!" Dutch banged his palm against the desk. Big Mike, resting peacefully on the windowsill, jumped. "Is that short enough for both of you?"

"She started it, boss," Tweedledee whined. "She always does. Can we go home, or we gonna send out for pizza?"

"Go home. I'm not springing for your pizza again. As for you, sister-in-law-to-be, bring cashews next time."

Penelope loved college campuses, especially near the end of the academic day, when the sun was falling, the shadows were long and cool, and sounds muted. As an undergraduate, she had often lingered in the quadrangle, a stack of novels beside her on the bench, while other students hurried off to dorms, fraternity or sorority houses, the student union, a favorite bar. She had continued the practice as a graduate student, and again in Ethiopia, where the custom was altered to sitting on the veranda of her little house, watching the sun set over what the old British expatriates always referred to as miles and miles of bloody Africa. A novel was always close at hand, and she discovered that a gin and tonic was a most agreeable complement to a setting African sun. It was during one of those moments when a kitten, eyes barely open, tumbled out of the bougainvillea that climbed the wall and bordered the roof, raised his hair, hissed, and spit, before accepting Penelope's offer of a lap and looking up with an interested expression that said, Okay, what's next, babe?

Empty Creek College was built in the southwestern style, with the natural vegetation of the desert for landscaping. Most of the students had left for the day, but the door of the gym was open and the basketball team was practicing hard, working on a set play while the coaches yelled encouragement.

On her way to the science building,

Penelope stopped at a pay phone and called Andy.

"Editorial, Anderson," he growled. He thought H. L. Mencken must have answered the telephone that way. And if it was good enough for old H.L., it was damned well good enough for the crusading editor of the *Empty Creek News-Journal.*

"Detecting, Warren," Penelope growled back, hurting her throat a little.

"Hey, darlin', I was just thinking of you. Want to play caveman and cavewoman?"

"You've been talking to Laney again."

"She does have good ideas."

"Well, you're not bopping me with a club and dragging me around by the hair, even when it gets long enough."

"It's a rubber club."

"Good God, she provided the props?"

"I can hardly wait to see you in the leopard skin. There's not very much of it."

"Faux, I hope. Mycroft wouldn't approve of people murdering his relatives."

"Absolutely faux."

"Can it wait until tomorrow? That's the reason I called. I'm going out to see Cricket. It *was* her father. She may want some company. I don't know what time I'll get back."

"Of course. Damn, that's too bad. Give her my condolences."

"I will. Would you feed Chardonnay and the rabbits for me?"

"Sure."

"You're a sweetie. I'll call you later."

Climbing to the second floor of the science building where the faculty offices were located, Penelope's footsteps echoed in the stairwell. Entering the corridor, she heard an angry voice.

"But you've never found any fossils on our property!"

"Yes, but we have a new situation, and I answer to the city."

"Well, tell them it's a fluke."

"I report the facts."

Penelope stopped in front of a bulletin board filled with the usual clutter pertinent to a college — scholarship notices, books for sale, final exam schedules.

"The fact is, you'd better not find any fossils on DDC land. This development has been delayed enough."

Vice President Albert J. McCory stormed away without glancing in her direction. Good thing. Penelope didn't think he would like her knowing the edict he had just delivered, and while she might pass for a student engrossed in some posted announcement, he would have certainly recognized Big

Mike as his nemesis of the Great Lonesome Bend Fight.

When McCory was gone, Penelope went to the office he had left and found Dr. Hayden Chudnik, chairman of the geology department, sitting behind his desk with a smug expression on his pasty, moon-shaped face.

"Yes, may I help you?" he asked impatiently. "Are you one of my students?"

"I'm Dr. Penelope Warren," she said, offering her academic bona fides. Chudnik looked like the sort of man who would need them. "I teach here."

"Oh, really. What department?"

"English."

"Yes, well, how can the geology department help the English department?"

"What can you tell me about Millicent DeForest?"

"Poor Millicent, I told her, but she refused to follow my counsel."

"Told her what?"

"To give up her foolish quest and focus on her work here. But she was determined to make a major discovery. Poor thing. She might have been better off in a less-demanding discipline like the English department. Unfortunately, I could not recommend tenure for her."

Less demanding discipline indeed! Penelope resisted the urge to tweak Chudnik's prominent nose — hard — by watching Big Mike leap silently to a rock-littered credenza behind the desk. Presumably they were of some geological significance. "Why is that?" she asked finally.

"As you know, we are a teaching institution. Research is useful, but secondary. Millicent, unfortunately, hoped to make her mark here and move on to a major university. She often neglected her students as she sought the fossil that would establish her reputation. She hoped to have some great T-rex named after her."

"She does. I named her Milly."

"A sentimental gesture, although I very much doubt it is a T-rex. More likely, it will turn out to be Diplodocus. They were more common to the Southwest."

"There's no mention of the tenure issue in what you told the police."

"Personnel matters are none of their business, and how do you know what I told the police?"

Penelope went into her purse and pulled out the leather case that held the badge signifying she was an honorary member of the Empty Creek Police Department. She flipped it open expertly, masking the "honorary" with her finger.

"I thought you taught here."

"I do," Penelope said, "but I'm also Police Reserve." That was stretching it a little, but in a good cause.

"Well, I have nothing more to add. This affair has taken too much of my time as it is. I have work to do."

"Preparing for your classes, no doubt."

"I am an excellent teacher."

"With tenure?"

"Of course. And you?"

"Oh, I'm just a part-time instructor."

"You've misrepresented yourself. I shall report this incident to the president."

"Please do, and be sure to tell Clara that she should have pursued her degree in a less-demanding field than chemistry."

"You may leave now. This interview is terminated."

Penelope rummaged through her purse again and found a safety pin. She handed it to Chudnik.

"What's this for?"

"Use it to burst that pompous balloon on your shoulder, jerkface. Come, Mycroft, we're leaving."

"Mycroft? Who are you talking to?"

"My cat. You didn't see him come in? He's an honorary police officer."

"He's in my rock collection," Chudnik screeched.

"He is indeed," Penelope agreed cheerfully.

Big Mike peered at Chudnik with a friendly expression on his face.

Chudnik copped a major attitude. "Shoo, shoo, scat!" he cried, waving his hands wildly.

Well, if that's the way you're going to be.

Big Mike scatted. He could have done it gracefully, of course, but instead kicked out with his hind paws, sending rocks flying in half a dozen directions. So much for winning the hearts and minds of the people.

"Clumsy beast!"

"Very good, Mycroft," Penelope said. "See you around, Hayden. Give the prez my best."

Still fuming from her encounter with the geology department, Penelope persuaded a friendly custodian to let her into the late Millicent DeForest's office. Like the office she had just left, Millicent's faculty den was furnished with a desk, three chairs, a bookcase, and a filing cabinet. The bookcase held textbooks, scholarly journals, and a number of works dealing with what appeared to be never-ending hunts for dinosaurs. Barney, the purple dinosaur, served as a paperweight, although the desk was neat and uncluttered. A bottle of mineral water stood next to Barney.

Framed movie posters of *Jurassic Park* and *The Lost World* hung on one wall. Another wall held a series of photographs of Millicent on various digs. In each, she wore dusty jeans, boots, T-shirts or sweatshirts, and a scarf around her neck. She wore a cowgirl hat perched jauntily or held it in her hand as she smiled for the camera. In each photograph, she looked hot, tired, dirty — and happy.

There was a light tap on the door. "Excuse me, I'm looking for Dr. DeForest. She wanted this material."

Penelope turned to find a tall young man in the doorway. He held a sheaf of papers in his hand and looked puzzled at finding a stranger in the office.

"I'm sorry," Penelope said. "She's not here . . . she's . . . you haven't heard?"

"I was out of town for a long weekend. I just got back."

"I'm sorry," Penelope repeated, frowning. "Dr. DeForest is dead. She was killed on Saturday."

Disbelief, anguish, pain, denial, swept over his face. He dropped the papers on the desk and slumped in a chair, blinking helplessly, opening and closing his mouth, wheezing for breath.

"Were you one of her students?"

A nod.

Penelope glanced at the papers, allowing the young man a semblance of privacy to regain his composure. She saw the same missing fossil bulletin from Moscow she had found on the Internet, the same timeless treasures that had brought Boris and Natasha to Empty Creek.

"What happened?" the student croaked.

Penelope looked up. He stared at her with a fierce intensity through the tears clouding his eyes. Penelope opened the mineral water and passed it over. "Drink this."

He drank thirstily. "Tell me," he said.

"Dr. DeForest was shot. Murdered."

"Oh, God, no!" he wailed.

Penelope patted his shoulder helplessly. "Did you know her well?"

"We were in love."

Penelope stopped at the market for a bottle of tequila to take to Cricket. Then she put orange juice in her basket. Passing the cheeses, she decided that a few snacks would do no harm. By the time she was ready to check out, she no longer qualified for the express aisle, having added all of the ingredients for a Penelope Tuna Salad Special — two cans of tuna packed in water, two tomatoes, a bunch of radishes, a cucumber, a green pepper ($1.99 a pound!), a red wine vinegar fat-free dressing, and a can of lima beans for Big Mike.

Driving out to Lonesome Bend Ranch, Penelope speculated on the sudden dissolution of Millicent DeForest's sainthood, the blatant misogyny displayed by Chudnik, and the unfeigned suffering of Schyler Bennett at the news of her death.

Overwhelmed at the enormity of his loss, Schyler had refused offers of assistance. Penelope had briefly considered having him taken to the station for questioning, but his grief was so obvious, his pain so great, Penelope only elicited his address, telephone number, and a mumbled promise to meet the next day at Dutch's office.

The sudden appearance of Schyler Bennett dispelled the image of faithful girlfriend. And there was the question of why Millicent wanted the Moscow bulletins.

Chudnik was another matter entirely. Although Penelope firmly believed that political correctness had been carried to outlandish extremes, Chudnik showed no evidence of sensitivity whatsoever. It was strange behavior when justifiable sexual harassment suits were quickly filed.

"Millicent DeForest was being denied tenure, Mikey, but if we pursue that particular aspect of her life to its logical conclusion, she should be the murderer, not the murderee. There was a professor on my dissertation committee I would have cheerfully killed. But I don't understand this at all. Why did Chudnik have it in for her?"

When she pulled up in front of the ranch house, Penelope turned her thoughts from the dead to the living.

They found Cricket behind the house, cleaning horse pens. She stopped work and leaned on the applepicker. "It was Pop."

Penelope nodded. "I'm sorry."

"Thank you." Cricket left the pen. "I'll finish this tomorrow."

"If you'd like to be alone . . ."

"No, come on in the house."

"I brought some things."

"That was thoughtful. You're very kind."

Embarrassed, Penelope shrugged. "Do you have any Irish background?"

"Mostly German."

"That would explain Mistress Juliana. I'm one-quarter Irish so we qualify for a wake anyway."

"Pop would like that. I think. I don't

really know. It'll make me feel better, I guess."

Together, they unloaded the Jeep and went into the kitchen, putting bags on the counter. "I wasn't sure what you had, so I brought everything."

Cricket smiled wanly. "Thank you."

"I *am* sorry. It must be hard, even after so much time." Penelope embraced Cricket and was again struck by how tiny and frail she felt. "How tall are you anyway?"

"Almost five two."

"You seem bigger."

"It's my toughness," Cricket replied, wiping tears from the corners of her eyes.

"I'll fix the drinks," Penelope said.

"Here's to you, Pop. I've missed you so much."

"All I wanted that first Christmas was for Pop to come home. I prayed so hard. After that I knew God didn't care about me."

"If you look in the dictionary under dysfunctional families, you'll find the Hackers and the Mahoneys."

"Do you remember anyone who might have had a motive for killing your father?"

"I was too young, but I asked Ma about it. She said there was nothing."

"Is the Hacker-Mahoney feud violent enough to kill?"

"We just fight and argue mostly, and there's not much of that anymore. I don't think we'll ever know what happened to Pop. It's too long ago now."

"You're probably right, but I wonder what was going on in 1973. Watergate was big that year, I think. We pulled out of Vietnam. But I don't know what Empty Creek was doing."

"The same as always. Nothing much."

"I'll check it out anyway."

As impromptu wakes went, the celebration of Pop Hacker's life went very well indeed. They sat in the dark and Cricket cried and laughed and remembered her first time in the saddle with her father leading the horse around the ring, his praise for her report card in the third grade, a picnic at the edge of the Superstition Mountains, helping him change the oil in the old truck that was never seen again, a Fourth of July parade when he wangled a place on the fire engine for her, letting her camp out in the backyard in the warm desert night. . . .

Big Mike, always sensitive to unhappiness

in people he liked, spent much of the evening stretched out in Cricket's lap, communicating his sympathy by snuggling against her, rubbing his head along her arm, content to lavish rather than receive attention.

Penelope listened, cried a little, laughed, nibbled on cheese and crackers, poured drinks, looked at old photo albums. Cricket had been a gorgeous child, with wide eyes and an innocent face; she had been a beautiful hippie — "I couldn't stand having missed the sixties, so I brought them back just for me" — she was a beautiful woman, her face shrouded in the shadows cast by the one lamp they had lit in the living room, her hair in pigtails. "It keeps it out of my face when I'm working — and crying."

Cricket's father had been a lanky man, a workingman whose customary dress was jeans, cowboy boots, a western shirt, and a face shadowed by a wide-brimmed Stetson.

Penelope turned the page of the album. Cricket smiled for the camera, holding blazing sparklers in each hand. The photograph was labeled July 4, 1972. Next to it was a snapshot of a young man, grinning and mugging for the camera, about to light a Roman candle.

"Who's that?"

"I took that one," Cricket said. "It's

Buxter Mahoney before the voices started and he went away. He always did the fireworks for the younger kids. We had kind of a truce on holidays."

Penelope stared at a picture of Cricket, energetically hosing down the fenders and hood of the gleaming yellow truck, her dress wet and clinging to her legs. Penelope memorized the license plate number of what Cricket told her was a 1931 Ford Model A one-ton flatbed with dual wheels.

They blinked in the bright light of the kitchen. Penelope took the tuna fish cans from the refrigerator, where she had put them to chill. "I don't like lukewarm tuna," she explained. Big Mike disappeared somewhere when they went into the kitchen, but he raced in when his favorite tune was played on the electric can opener, and danced around her legs. Penelope dished out a little tuna for Mikey's hors d'oeuvres, which occupied him just long enough for her to prepare the tuna salad.

She quickly sliced the tomatoes and arranged them around the mounds of tuna on the plates, complemented the red with the white of the cucumber, diced radishes, and green pepper, splashed dressing over it, and said, *"Voilà,* my tuna mess."

They ate at a breakfast nook in the kitchen while Big Mike growled over his lima beans.

"You better stay here tonight," Cricket said.

Penelope giggled, faking a tipsiness she did not feel. "I should have taught Mycroft to drive."

The walls were thin enough for Penelope to hear Cricket sobbing softly. Big Mike, who couldn't stand a woman in distress, padded away to offer comfort to his new friend, leaving Penelope alone in a strange bed, her thoughts careening wildly, trying to make sense of "a riddle wrapped in a mystery inside an enigma."

CHAPTER SEVEN

The first light of dawn outlined distant mountain peaks, casting a pale yellow sheen that soon turned to pink. The air was cool, even brisk, but fresh, as though it had slept undisturbed through the long night and awakened like a girl in the throes of her first passion, the memories of ardor sharp and clear, eager to kiss her lover awake while birds fluttered and danced, singing joyously in greeting and celebration.

Leaning against the corral and drinking coffee, Penelope appreciated the beauty of the sunrise, but with regret and longing. She had slept fitfully in the strange bed, even after Cricket's soft sobs had quieted, missing the reassuring presence of Andy and Mikey, dreaming of great creatures wandering vast plains, and a dinosaur named Milly fighting fiercely for its life as it was overwhelmed by giant predators and slowly rolled over and settled in its deathbed to await the arrival of Pop Hacker and then Millicent DeForest.

Penelope sipped the coffee, unable, unwilling to speak and disturb the unfolding grandeur over the eastern horizon. Cricket and Big Mike were quiet too, watching the sky burst into flames, turning the high scattered clouds red with heavenly fires. A horse whinnied. Another snorted in reply.

With the silence broken, Cricket said, "Thank you."

"You're welcome. Will you be okay?"

"It's over now."

Penelope nodded agreement, but she knew it was a false gesture. It wasn't over. Not yet. Perhaps not ever. "What are you going to do about Milly?"

"Paleontologists have been calling. They all want to study it. I guess I'll let one excavate the site after the police are finished."

"I think you should. It could be worth a lot of money. Better hire a night watchman too."

"Not a bad idea."

"Did a Hayden Chudnik call?"

"He was one of them. I didn't care for him. He was a little too pushy. He seemed to think it was his right because he's at the local college."

"There's another thing, Cricket. I named the dinosaur after Millicent DeForest before I knew about your father. You should rename it in his honor. Apparently, he found it first."

"I don't know. Milly sounds kind of nice."

"What was your father's name anyway?"

"Cornelius." Cricket giggled. "Isn't that awful? He should have changed *his* name."

"We could call it Corny-Milly."

"That's too perfect. Let's do it."

"It'll drive museums crazy."

When they stopped laughing, Penelope said, "We'd better be going."

"Thanks again. And you too, Mikey." Cricket scooped up Mycroft and carried him to the Jeep. "He was wonderful last night. So comforting."

"I know. Whenever I'm sad, Mikey always cheers me up."

Yitzhak Cohen was the first to leave the Lazy Traveller Motel, trench coat tightly belted, collar turned up, fedora tilted over his forehead. He glanced around furtively before slinking away, keeping to the shadows.

Fyodor Popov and Katerina Rakitin followed him.

Hiroshi Ishii crept after them.

The eastern sky had not yet turned red

when Nora Pryor, out on her morning run, approached the man wearing a trench coat and fedora. He suddenly found an acute interest in the wares displayed in the windows of the Cookhouse Boutique.

"Good morning," Nora said cheerily.

His reply was a muttered "Shalom."

She looked back at the hunched figure scurrying away. How very strange, she thought, even for Empty Creek.

Resuming her run, Nora nearly barreled into an amazon of a woman and a much shorter man. Startled, she managed an apology and another cheery greeting. "Good morning," the amazon said. The man merely nodded.

Nora ran backward for a few steps, watching the couple duck into a doorway.

The Parade of Nations continued with a hurried bow from a slight man of Japanese origin peering out from behind a corner of a building. *"Konnichiwa,"* he said.

"Good morning," Nora said, "I think."

By now Nora, who exercised only out of guilt, had reason enough to terminate the torture, and found a doorway suitable for some serious lurking of her own.

The sky brightened.

The Israeli slipped from doorway to shadow to doorway.

The Russians maintained a one-block interval.

The Japanese man hurried to keep up.

In what she considered an inspired movement, Nora crossed the street and kept all four personages in sight. She was still two blocks away from the Israeli when he turned abruptly and entered Mom's Doughnut Shoppe and Coffeehouse. He was followed by the Russians, and then the Asian chap, as Tony Lyme-Regis would say. There seemed to be no point to skulking about the deserted parking lot of the bank, so Nora shrugged her shoulders, hitched her running bra, and crossed the street again.

As a place to hold a clandestine meeting, Mom's Doughnut Shoppe and Coffeehouse at six a.m. ranked just ahead of Happy Hour at the Double B, but it was better than gathering at the Snake Crossing sign, trying to look inconspicuous. In point of fact, there were no good places to lurk furtively in Empty Creek. While Penelope and Big Mike might sleep through the dawn in the normal course of events, the desert telegraph never rested, and Mom's was an important informational way station.

Mom's Doughnut Shoppe and Coffeehouse was once plain old Mom's Do-Nuts. Somewhat belatedly, however, Paul Bowers

— "Who wants to eat Dad's jelly do-nuts?" — discovered on one of his infrequent trips to Phoenix that the nation, unknown to him, had inexplicably taken specialty coffee shops to heart. He returned wearing a black beret, the first stubble of what was to become a magnificent handlebar mustache, and the makings of a sidewalk café in the bed of his pickup truck. Mom's now offered a variety of exotic coffees and a meeting place for Empty Creek's literati at the four tiny tables Paul had plunked down on the sidewalk.

"Dammit, Pop, whatcha do that for?" the regular customers grumbled. "Don't want coffee lat-te. Want regular coffee."

"Don't call me Pop."

"Well, hell, Pop, what we supposed to call you?"

"Monsieur Bowers will do."

"Sewer's where this stuff oughta go."

But the human mind being adaptable, even for cops and cowboys, the regulars soon adjusted, although they left the caffe lattes, espressos, and cappuccinos to the more adventurous, like Nora, who entered Mom's and said, *"Café noir, s'il vous plaît, Monsieur Paul."*

Nora was on her second tiny cup of

brackish coffee and memorizing the mise-en-scène for later reporting, when Penelope and Big Mike stumbled in. "Good God!" Nora exclaimed. "What are you doing up at this hour?"

"Not a word until I have more coffee." Penelope leaned against the counter while Monsieur Bowers filled a cup for her. She managed to make her way back to Nora's table without stumbling over anyone. "Now, what are you doing here?"

"I was running, when I came across this most curious procession. First, there was the guy in the hat and trenchcoat. He said, 'Shalom.' He must be an Israeli. . . ."

"Yitzhak Cohen. Don't buy any Dead Sea Scrolls from him."

"Then the couple came along. They were following the Israeli."

"Boris and Natasha. Russian cops. They think he has their dinosaur skulls."

"And then the Japanese fellow was following them. He's the former Yakusa?"

"The very same."

"Well, if you know all this, why am I here?"

"Because you're a good trouper and you might have picked up something interesting."

"I think this stuff is growing hair on my

chest." Nora pushed her coffee away.

"Tony wouldn't like that. At least, I don't think he would, but you can never tell with men. They are the strangest creatures. Still, you could run off and join a sideshow. The woman with the bearded bosom."

"You're babbling."

"The dawn does that to me. So, what have you learned?"

"Natasha drinks caffe latte. Boris went for this stuff. Ugh. Perhaps he needs hair on his chest. And he said, let me see if I can get it word for word. He said, 'You understand the first half. That half is a drama, and it was played out there. The second half is a tragedy, and it is being acted here.' What do you suppose that means?"

"Boris — his real name is Fyodor Popov — is fond of quoting Dostoyevsky. It's probably from *The Brothers Karamazov*. And what have Mr. Cohen and Mr. Ishii had to say for themselves?"

"Nothing. They just sit there staring at each other. I think they're trying to be invisible."

Penelope got Brian Abernathy's telephone number from information and placed the call, wanting to catch him before he left for work.

156

"I still can't get over it," Abernathy said after Penelope convinced him she represented the authorities in the case.

"Did Millicent seem any different to you?"

"No, we were very happy together."

More questions elicited the same response. Apparently, Millicent DeForest was very good at keeping Schyler Bennett a secret from Brian Abernathy.

"If we're going to spend so much time in the library," Penelope announced, "I should get my own desk and Mikey should have a nice soft chair or couch reserved for his use. And," she added, watching Mycroft dig his claws into the carpet, "a scratching post, although I doubt he would use it." At home, a perfectly good scratching post and cat condominium were ignored while Mycroft shredded *The Complete Works of William Shakespeare*.

"Noogy is distraught, and it's all your fault," Leigh accused.

"He's changed his mind about posing?"

"No, he remains enthusiastic about sharing his masculinity with the world, but he can't find your missing person. I've never seen him so upset and, frankly, he's driving me crazy."

"That's one of the reasons I dropped by.

The search is off. We identified Yorick yesterday."

"Thank God. He can dispense with the sackcloth and ashes now. I speak metaphorically, of course."

"Of course."

The reference librarian slumped in his chair, staring across the big room at the video section.

"Don't be upset, Noogy," Penelope said. " 'We'll always have Paris.' "

"I am a failure. I should resign from the American Library Association."

"We identified our missing person yesterday. You shouldn't blame failure on yourself. He was never reported missing. It was an impossible task."

"Nothing should be impossible for Juan-Carlos Estavillo. I shall transfer to acquisitions or cataloguing as penance."

"Before you do, I have another request," Penelope said, "1973."

Noogy brightened. "Constancia," he replied. "What a magnificent woman."

That was an interesting response, Penelope thought. "And 1974," she said.

"Isabella."

"How about 1975 and 1976."

"Ah, dearest Carolina and wonderful Phoebe."

"No one should be allowed to name their daughter Phoebe. Go back to Constancia."

"Sweet Constancia. I lost my virginity that year. I was sixteen. She was twenty-seven. She was my teacher. I died when she ran off to Las Vegas and married the assistant basketball coach."

"You recovered nicely, but I meant the year of 1973. What happened around Empty Creek in 1973?"

"Probably nothing."

"Quite likely, but I'd better take a look anyway. Saddle up! Call H. G. Wells. Cue the time machine. Hit the whizbang switch. Retreat, hell! We're making a one-hundred-and-eighty-degree turn and attacking on a new front."

"I just love crazy women," Noogy said, watching Penelope stride purposefully to the newspapers on microfilm.

The world suffered its annual allocation of calamities, both natural and man-made, but Empty Creek bumbled through the Year of Our Lord 1973 in its usual somnolent fashion, which is to say untouched and unimpressed by the outside world.

Watergate and Vietnam dominated national and international headlines. The vice president resigned. The end of the military

159

draft was announced. USC clobbered Ohio State pretty good in the Rose Bowl. The Miami Dolphins won the Super Bowl. Secretariat took the Kentucky Derby. Oakland won the World Series, beating the Mets in seven games.

The great Empty Creek crisis of 1973 was a prolonged debate over new stop signs. No less than seven city council meetings had the topic on the agenda. The *News-Journal* decried the proposition in a number of editorials, basing its opposition on an infringement of personal liberties and a betrayal of the public trust.

The Empty Creek High School Gila Monsters had an unenviable hat trick, managing to finish last in their league in football, baseball, and basketball.

Reporters for the *News-Journal* recorded births, deaths, marriages. The society page was filled each edition with photographs of Empty Creek's elite at work and play — matrons in white dresses and hats lawn-bowling, bake sales to benefit the Horsemen's Association or the library or any number of worthy charities, the debutante ball.

The photographs of the entire ECHS graduating class were published in a special section. There were no Hackers or

Mahoneys among them.

"I'll be right back, Mikey." Penelope quickly found the high school yearbook for 1973 and riffled through the pages. A bespectacled Miss Constancia Alvarez (her hair in a severe bun), B.A., general science, home economics, Spanish, looked into the camera with a most serious expression, perhaps hoping to disguise the fact that she had seduced a student. Penelope wondered if Constancia had found happiness with her assistant basketball coach.

A dreamily ecstatic Juan-Carlos Estavillo, junior class president, on the other hand, looked like he had left Miss Alvarez's bed just in time for the photo session.

Penelope checked the remainder of the class photos for Hackers and Mahoneys, but found their names only in a list headed "Not present for pictures."

Penelope went back to her time machine to find Mycroft pushing the fast-forward button, watching the days and weeks swirl past in a blur. "You've lost my place, Mikey. Go back to September."

Mikey removed his paw and the microfilm slowed and finally stopped at a crime report in the edition of Saturday, November 10 — the one hundred and ninety-eighth birthday of the United States Marine Corps.

161

November 8 — An Empty Creek man was reported missing from the state hospital. He is not believed to be dangerous, but he is armed with a paring knife and is reported fond of apples.

The crime reports, then and now, were always the most interesting part of the *News-Journal*. Advertisers clamored to have their placement on page five, where the reports always started. Penelope reversed time and went back to September.

Sunday, September 9 — A citizen reported aliens took barbecue tools and $2.27 from beneath her bed. This was the third set of barbecue tools taken by aliens, which is the reason she now kept them under her bed. The investigation continues.

Monday, September 10 — Officers broke up a fight at the Double B. The altercation began at half time of the Monday night football game. A television set was damaged.

Tuesday, September 11 — A naked man was reported walking down Empty Creek Highway. The naked man said it was too hot. Officers gave him a blanket and a ride to the psycho ward, where he registered a complaint that the blanket was cruel and unusual punishment.

Tuesday, September 11 — A shoplifter

was arrested, but he had already finished the pilfered beer.

Tuesday, September 11 — A washing machine was taken from a garage in the 1200 block of Diablo Drive. The door was open. Burglary is suspected.

Wednesday, September 12 — A citizen reported hearing shots. A man was shooting watermelons on a fence post.

Wednesday, September 12 — A woman was arrested for indecent exposure. She was sunbathing on a chaise longue at the Lazy Traveller Motel and refused to put on her top. She was kept under observation.

Wednesday, September 11 — An eight-track tape player was taken from a vehicle parked in the 900 block of Empty Creek Highway. Egress was gained by breaking a window. A brother-in-law is suspected.

Penelope looked back and forth in the weeks preceding and following September 10, 1973, and found no apparent references to Cricket's father, fossil discoveries, or another visitation by aliens. That was too bad, really, Penelope thought. Aliens, with their advanced intelligence, might be able to make some sense out of this mess.

Schyler Bennett was late.
Penelope paced nervously in Dutch's

office. "He said he'd meet me here at two o'clock."

"It's two-thirty."

"I know that."

"Why didn't you get him in here yesterday?"

"He seemed like a nice young man."

"So did Ted Bundy," Dutch said. "Even Charles Manson had a mother."

"He'll be here. Trust me."

"Ha! He's probably in Mexico by now."

Tweedledee and Tweedledum poked their heads into the office. "He ain't home, boss. Nobody's seen him since early yesterday. He's probably in Mexico by now."

"Go polish your handcuffs or something," Penelope said.

"That's where I'd be if I'd killed my girlfriend."

"He didn't know she was dead. I told you, he was very upset. He wasn't faking."

"Ha!"

Penelope grabbed the Empty Creek telephone directory from a shelf and wound up. Tweedledee and Tweedledum ran. They knew Penelope had a pretty good arm. "Dolts," she said, although she felt rather doltish herself right about then. Schyler Bennett had seemed truly devastated. Perhaps Boris was right. The tragedy was being acted out here, and she had been fooled by a consummate actor. But why had he shown up at Millicent's office? Why not just take off for Mexico and be done with it?

"He didn't do it," Penelope said. "I don't care where he is. He's innocent. And if you say 'ha' one more time, I'll scream."

"Ha!"

"Aieeeeee!"

"Feel better?"

"Not really."

"It's two forty-five."

"You have a really cruel streak in you, Dutch. I'm going to tell Stormy. It's my duty as a sister. I can't have her marrying someone who's going around saying 'ha' when he's upset."

The intercom crackled. "Chief, I've got a collect call for Penelope on line three. Should I accept charges?"

Dutch rolled his eyes. "Jeez, this isn't your personal office, you know."

"Who is it?" Penelope asked.

"Somebody named Schyler Bennett."

"Put it through," Dutch said.

Penelope smiled and stuck her tongue out. "Ha yourself."

Dutch hit the speaker.

"Schyler? Where are you?"

"At a McDonald's in Palm Springs."

"California?"

"I was too upset to sleep, so I just got in the car and drove. And then I fell asleep at a rest stop."

"Keep him talking," Dutch whispered, leaving the room.

"Do you know anyone there?"

"No. I didn't even notice where I was heading until I got to the Colorado River. I just kept going. I'm sorry I'm late."

"You should have stayed here. With friends."

"Dee was my only friend."

"Dee?"

"That was my pet name for her. You know, from DeForest? She liked it when I called her Dee."

"What did she call you?"

"Sky or Sky King. You know, from the old program? Oh, God, I miss her so much. I should have been there with her. None of this would have happened if I had been there."

Penelope listened to him sob for a moment. "I'm sorry, Schyler."

"She was so beautiful, and now she's gone. I feel like killing myself."

"Don't talk like that!" Penelope said sharply. "Dee wouldn't like it."

"We were going to do so much together."

"Schyler, listen to me. You've got to come home. Are you okay to drive?"

"I got here, didn't I?" he said bitterly.

Dutch returned and sat on a corner of the desk.

"I want to help you," Penelope said.

"No one can help me now. God, I want to die!"

"No, Schyler. You'll get through this."

"Chief Fowler? You there?"

"Who are you?" Penelope asked. "What happened to Schyler?"

"Officer Randover, Palm Springs P.D. We've got him. Just like you asked. You are Chief Fowler?"

"I'm Fowler," Dutch growled. "Good work. He's a material witness in a murder case. Hold him tonight and I'll get somebody down there tomorrow to bring him home."

"He's just a witness," Penelope said. "Make him comfortable, but keep an eye on him. He talked about suicide."

"Chief?"

"Do it."

"You got it."

"Pretty sneaky," Penelope said.

"How many McDonald's can there be in Palm Springs?"

"Thanks, Dutch."

"You never considered suicide, did you?"

"What shall we do while my hair grows out?" Penelope asked, watching the flames dance in the fireplace.

"I shall kiss it, caress it, brush it, stroke it, cherish it, and find a scarlet ribbon for your hair," Andy replied, taking her in his arms. "Together we will walk hand in hand, laughing, talking, crying, whispering, sharing, wondering at what has been and what will be. And, yes, we shall love each other, exploring multitudes of mysteries. We will dance and listen to songs of love."

Andy kissed her and the cares of the day fell away. "Mmm," Penelope murmured. "Mmm." Slowly, tenderly, they kissed, teasing and caressing. She shivered when his hand dipped beneath her hair and touched the nape of her neck. Imprisoned in his embrace, Penelope beat a gentle tattoo against his chest.

Mycroft, disgusted with being ignored, leaped from the couch and stretched out before the fire.

No one noticed his departure.

They held each other tightly and prolonged the kiss on the road to their very own entry in the *Guinness Book of World Records*.

"Mmm."

When they finally parted, they stared into each other's eyes, smiling and practicing their heavy breathing exercises. "God, I love necking with you," Penelope said. "It really should be an Olympic sport."

"Synchronized necking."

"Heavy petting."

"The necking decathlon."

"What's the scoring system?"

"Who cares?"

CHAPTER EIGHT

An hour after touchdown at the Palm Springs airport, they were heading home. Schyler Bennett was ready to go. His old Jeep Cherokee was gassed — a professional courtesy on the part of the P.S.P.D. — and there was only a brief argument over who got to ride shotgun. Penelope let Tweedledee win and took the backseat after Schyler pushed rubble aside. He did not keep a tidy car. The floor and the backseat were covered with textbooks, soft drink cans, an old copy of the *New York Times*, the odd *News-Journal*, some wrinkled sheets of geology department letterhead, a pair of tennis shoes, a gym bag, and an assortment of candy bar wrappers.

Despite the night in jail, Schyler looked refreshed and his despair of the day before had visibly dissipated. He even managed a smile when a female jailer shook his hand and said, "Come back and see us real soon, now, you hear? Our chipped beef on toast is the best around."

"I once knew a master gunnery sergeant who ate SOS for breakfast seventeen straight mornings," Penelope said.

The officer curled her lip. "Our SOS isn't *that* good."

Once on the interstate, Schyler hit seventy-five miles an hour, the posted speed limit, looked over at Tweedledee, who nodded. "Cool," Schyler said, and set the cruise control at eighty-one miles per hour.

Once through Indio and heading up the long grade toward Desert Center, traffic thinned and they passed a few cars, the odd RV, and the big trucks laboring through the gears in the right lane.

"Feel like talking, kid?" Tweedledee asked.

"Might as well get it over with."

"Where were you when Millicent De-Forest was killed?"

Penelope frowned at the question, but it had to be asked and there was no tactful way to do it. Tweedledee could be the bad cop.

"Flagstaff," Schyler replied, keeping his eyes on the road. "My mom's been sick and I went home to help out."

"What were you doing on Saturday between ten and three?"

"Helped my brother change the oil on his

171

car. Had lunch. My sister came over with her kids."

"Lots of witnesses."

"Ten or twelve altogether."

"Okay. Who might've had a reason to kill Millicent?"

Schyler shrugged. "Do you think I haven't been racking my brain? Everybody liked her."

"She had a boyfriend. She was cheating on him."

"He didn't know about us, but Dee was going to tell him. She just wanted to wait for the right moment."

"You always go out with older women? Your teachers?"

"It just happened. We didn't do anything wrong."

"Just curious."

"What was her relationship with Hayden Chudnik like?" Penelope asked.

"They didn't like each other."

"You said everyone liked her," Tweedledee interjected.

"Almost everyone. I don't know. I'm confused."

"That's good enough for me," Tweedledee said. "He's a suspect."

"Did you know that Chudnik was trying to deny her tenure?"

"Yes, but it was nonsense. She was going to fight him with a sexual harassment suit."

"I'm not surprised," Penelope said.

"You know him?"

"I've met him."

"He hates women."

"That's an understatement."

"Dee was a terrific teacher. She spent time with her students. We had seminars at her house. She did everything she could for her students. Chudnik was jealous of her. Dee should have been chairman of the department."

"Was he jealous enough to kill?" Tweedledee asked.

"Objection, counselor," Penelope said. "Asks for an opinion."

"That's what I want. An opinion."

"Witness is not qualified to speak to the suspect's state of mind."

"Gotcha!" Tweedledee crowed. "You agree he's a suspect now?"

"Of course, along with everyone at the DDC who has a job in jeopardy if construction is halted, assorted fossil entrepreneurs, and the butler."

"What butler?"

"Never mind."

"You guys don't know anything, do you?" Schyler said.

"Not enough yet," Penelope replied. "But we will. What were you delivering to Dee?"

"Just some things she wanted downloaded from the Internet. There's always a lot of dinosaur information. She wasn't on it yet."

"Descriptions of fossils stolen in Moscow?"

"How did you know that?"

Penelope smiled. "A lucky guess. Why did she want them?"

"She wanted anything I could find. She was interested in everything."

Big Mike was irritated at being left behind and spent the day on a variety of personal and household chores. Once awake — far earlier than normal — and after suffering the indignity of having the door shut firmly in his face, Mycroft leaped to the windowsill in the living room and assumed the mournful expression designed to make Penelope relent. But she only blew him a kiss and drove off.

"Damn," he said in cat, batting the curtains in frustration.

There was nothing to do but eat, so he went into the kitchen and hit the liver crunchie bowl for a bit and then jumped into the kitchen sink to coax a few drops of moisture from the tap (there was a perfectly good water bowl, freshly filled, on the floor, but he sometimes liked to fend for himself). Fortified by food and drink, he gave himself a good bath fore and aft (as a colleague in the naval service might say). After one final swipe of his paw over his face, he pronounced himself clean and looked around for something to shred. While contemplating the various possibilities, he dozed off in a convenient pool of light cast by Mr. Sun.

Upon awakening an hour later, greatly refreshed by his nap, Mycroft went into the living room to sharpen his claws. Ignoring the three-story cat condo and *The Complete Works of Shakespeare*, his normal whetstone, Mikey picked out a virgin piece of territory on the back of the couch and, in short order, was satisfied with the state of his weaponry and the new hole in the fabric. That would teach a certain person to leave a certain cat behind while she went off adventuring.

Such industriousness dictated the need for another nap. Adept at opening cupboard doors, he chose the hallway linen closet and settled in on top of the fluffy towels, kneading them to his satisfaction before relaxing at a job well done. He soon fell asleep to dream fondly of Murphy Brown, that sexy little calico — and the mother of his kittens — who lived down the road a piece.

The afternoon was spent in hidey-hole maintenance. Big Mike went from the linen closet to the top of the refrigerator to the hamper in the bedroom closet to the top of his favorite bookcase in the living room, stopping along the way to push at the door of Penelope's home office. No luck there. The door was firmly latched to protect the computer and its printer from a few more cat hairs shed into vulnerable spots. Oh, well. Mycroft was content to bide his time. One day, sooner or later, Penelope would screw up and presto — computer cat hammock.

He knew how to open the latch on the window in the guest bathroom and briefly considered breaking out of solitary confinement in the cat slammer. If Murphy Brown were in season, Mycroft would have been out of there in an Empty Creek minute, but she wasn't. It was too early to go and play with the rabbits, and, while he liked Chardonnay, the mare was no cat and rather dull company. No, it was definitely time for a midafternoon snack and nap.

★ ★ ★

When the president of the Empty Creek Historical Society made a duty visit to Lonesome Bend Ranch, hoping to convince Cricket to donate the dinosaur or, at least, the odd hoof bone or two — whatever they were called on dinosaurs — to the museum, she did so with her usual sense of optimism, forgetting to check her horoscope for the day. If she had, Nora Pryor might have stayed home, but she didn't.

Cricket, who had looked at Sagittarius but dismissed it since there was no eligible bachelor looming to discuss marriage plans with, went out to the crime site with Dr. Chester Handley, a museum curator and a specialist in fossils, blithely unaware of the ominous position of the stars and the fact that Mercury, the planet of communications, was perversely retrograde. For his part, Handley was much too excited about the potential scientific value of the Corny-Milly find to consider his day might be better spent looking for Etruscan coins.

Alyce Smith knew of Mercury's state, but went out to visit Harvey anyway because she was singularly unable to predict events in her own life with any degree of accuracy, a failure that had sometimes caused no end of trouble in the past. Besides, she missed

Harvey, who had been working long hours of late and wanted to make sure he had fresh hot coffee and a nice Danish. Alyce also planned to take him behind a convenient cactus and jump his bones.

However, poor little Cupid, going about his own business of amour, was destined to get trampled by two clodhoppers named Dr. Hayden Chudnik and Albert J. McCory — the former put no stock in the folderol of astrology and the latter never read beyond the sports pages, so they headed out to Lonesome Bend in equally surly moods.

Unaware of the mob trekking in his direction, Harvey Curtis was trying to decide between red and black for the new Corvette he planned to buy if the overtime pay kept piling up — a Z28 Camaro convertible would do if the extra money lapsed, as it appeared it might. The crime scene very nearly resembled the Before now. Although no additional human bones had been found, the debris had continued to pile up. The footstool-like things were uncovered and definitely appeared to be the remains of some great creature.

Cricket and the good Dr. Handley were the first to arrive. Introductions were made all around — Sam Connors and Sheila Tyler had also drawn the overtime duty —

and Cricket and Handley were allowed past the crime-scene tape to examine the remains of the dinosaur.

Following Harvey's admonition to tread carefully, Handley peered and poked, circled the footstools, squatted, rose for more circling, and said, "Hmmm."

"What is it?" Cricket asked.

"Biggest damned lizard I've ever seen," Handley said, removing his New York Mets baseball cap and scratching his shiny bald pate.

"Hmmm," Cricket said in response to the curious non-academic nature of Handley's declaration. Big lizards were good.

"Hmmm, indeed."

"You have to let me in there. I am Dr. Hayden Chudnik."

Cricket and Handley turned to find a geology department chairman wagging his finger at Harvey Curtis, a gesture that did not endear him to the police officer.

"This is my crime scene and you're not going in there."

"You let them in."

"They're authorized."

"Hi, Harvey."

"Hey, Nora, how you doing?"

"Fine. Can I go in and talk with Cricket?"

"Sure."

"What?" Chudnik screeched.

"She's authorized."

"It's mine!" Chudnik hollered, dancing back and forth behind the tape. "It's mine!"

"It's not yours," Handley shouted back. "It's mine!" He turned to Cricket. "It is mine, isn't it?"

"I was hoping for a donation to the Historical Society," Nora said.

"That might be arranged," Cricket said to Nora. "And, yes, it's yours for study."

"Hot damn!" Handley jumped in the air and clicked his heels. "It's mine. It's mine."

"What is it?" Albert J. McCory cried. "Tell me it's not a dinosaur."

Handley pumped his fist in the air. "Oh, yes, it is, and it's mine."

"Hi, sweetie, I brought coffee for everyone."

"We might have a situation here, honey. Can it wait?"

The lab team leaned on their shovels. Sam Connors and Sheila Tyler hitched their equipment belts and sidled closer to the increasingly apoplectic madman.

"Nope," Alyce replied cheerfully. "Fresh coffee will put a new perspective on things for everyone. We'll sit down and discuss the situation, whatever it is, sensibly, like adult human beings."

Along with misjudging the alignment of the planets as they pertained to her day, Alyce also overestimated the maturity of the little gathering at Lonesome Bend.

"What is it?" Chudnik shouted.

"Seismosaurus," Handley responded. He thought it extremely gracious on his part to tell Chudnik that much.

"That shows what you know. It's definitely Diplodocus."

"Seismosaurus, you fool." Handley turned his back on his rival. "You see, right there," he said, pointing. "The size alone definitely indicates . . ."

The baseball-sized rock struck Handley in the small of his back. He grunted and fell to the dirt, writhing in pain, gasping for breath.

"Dippy," Chudnik said, wincing at the pain in his throwing arm.

Handley struggled to his feet and staggered a few yards toward Chudnik. "Is that all the harder you can throw?" He charged Chudnik, yelling, "Seismo!"

"No!" McCory heaved a rock at the offending fossil that threatened to stop development on the DDC project. Unfortunately, his aim was wide.

Fortunately, Nora saw it coming and ducked, but the missile whizzing past her ear sent her little redheaded Irish temper into overdrive. She retaliated with a wicked sidearm, curving *her* rock neatly past McCory's ear.

At the threat to womanhood, Cricket and Alyce joined Nora in pummeling McCory with rocks.

The sight of two doctors of philosophy duking it out in recreations of the Thriller in Manila and the Rumble in the Jungle deterred Harvey not one whit. He waded in, ducking a roundhouse from Chudnik and a haymaker from Handley.

The crime lab team cheered in a welcome break from sifting dirt.

Sam Connors and Sheila Tyler saved McCory from serious harm.

"Everyone's under arrest," Harvey shouted with the dueling paleontologists subdued.

After handcuffing Alyce — not for the first time in their relationship — he did the same to Nora and Cricket. It was a lot more fun putting the handcuffs on pretty women than sweaty and battered educators fighting over some old bones.

"Honey," Alyce wailed. "What did I do?"

"Disturbing the peace."

"Harvey, you release us this instant," Nora demanded.

"Be quiet, or I'll send you home to Tony like this with a note pinned to your shirt saying you've been a bad girl."

"You wouldn't dare. It was self-defense."

"Try me."

Nora opened her mouth and then wisely decided to shut up. Harvey just might do it. Even though Tony was in Los Angeles, Regina, her sixteen-year-old daughter, wasn't, and Reggie was perfectly capable of grounding her mother for a month or two.

Being the cuffee rather than the cuffer was a new experience for the former Mistress Juliana. Cricket tugged experimentally at what she had always considered exotic bracelets and found herself truly under arrest.

"Thank you," Nora said.

"You're welcome," Cricket said.

"We couldn't let that jerk throw stones at you," Alyce said. "We have to stick together. Besides, it was fun."

Harvey read them their rights. "Do you understand these rights as I have explained them to you."

"Police brutality," Alyce said.

"Definitely," Nora said. "False arrest too."

"What do you have to say?" Harvey asked, turning to Cricket.

"Brutality, false arrest, *and* a violation of our civil rights."

"Good one," Alyce said.

"You're going to fit right in," Nora said.

They stopped in Blythe, where the Empty Creek Police Department paid for lunch to go at McDonald's. Fifteen minutes later they were back on the highway.

There were no saguaros on the California side of the Colorado River. But once over the bridge, they appeared almost immediately, dotting the rugged hillsides. Penelope always wondered how they knew to stay at home in Arizona, to show the eminently good sense not to go beyond the Colorado River. It was a sentiment she shared even though she was a native Californian and often hopped down to San Diego during football season to watch her beloved Aztecs of San Diego State University play at Jack Murphy Stadium — she refused to call it by its new name of Qualcomm Stadium.

"Got any Chicken McNuggets you don't want?" Tweedledee asked from the backseat. "Fair is fair," Penelope had pointed out during the brief stop. "And besides, if I don't get to ride up front, I'll pour coffee down your neck when you fall asleep, and you *will* fall asleep eventually." It was a persuasive argument.

"We just stopped. You can't have finished yours already."

"Well, I did."

"Gluttony is a sin."

"So is starvation."

"All right, but just one."

"Thanks, Penelope. You're a peach."

"And you're several bones short of a complete dinosaur."

"Aw, don't be mean."

"Let's take the back road."

"The speed limit's only sixty there."

"The interstate's boring. If we get stopped, you can flash your badge."

"There ain't no comfort stations."

Penelope rolled her eyes. "You just went to a comfort station. If you have to go again, we'll pretend we're in Africa."

"What do they do for comfort stations in Africa?"

"Go into the bush."

"Ain't that dangerous?"

"Only if you pee on a spitting cobra."

"Penelope! Don't talk like that. It ain't nice."

"All right, never relieve yourself on a spitting cobra. It makes them mad. Is that better?"

When they reached the turnoff, Schyler

left the interstate and took Highway 60 heading for Vicksburg, Salome, and Wickenburg. Past Wickenburg it was a straight shot into Empty Creek. He didn't think Penelope would pour coffee down *his* neck, but . . .

"Good lad," Penelope said.

"Dee liked the back roads too."

"Tell me about Dee."

"Like what?"

"The real Dee. What made her mad, for example?"

"She hated department meetings and committee meetings. She thought they were a waste of time. She always used to say, 'This is the problem. These are the potential solutions. Choose the best one and implement it. Don't talk about it for weeks. Don't write reports. Don't ask for further studies. Do it.' "

"Sensible."

"She was a very sensible woman. Organized. Efficient. Brilliant. That's the real reason Chudnik didn't like her. Dee was much smarter."

"It's tough being the brightest kid on the block."

CHAPTER NINE

When they pulled into the parking lot of the police department, Schyler Bennett turned the engine off and looked over at Penelope. "What happens now?"

"You'll make an official statement and that'll be it for now, I think." Penelope paused. "You're not going to do anything foolish, are you?"

Schyler shook his head. "I'll be all right. I did a lot of thinking while I was driving and last night. Dee would want me to carry on her work."

Penelope dug around in her purse, pulled out a card, and scribbled on the back before giving it to the young man. "These are my numbers, home and work. Call me. Anytime."

"Thanks."

"Wake up, Larry. We're back."

"Just a few more minutes, honeybunch," Tweedledee mumbled.

"I'm not your honeybunch and I'm going

to put Big Mike in your lap."

The homicide detective shot up and looked around wildly. "Jeez, Penelope, don't say things like that. Give me a heart attack."

When Tweedledee took Bennett away to make his official statement, Penelope went to Dutch's office and peeked in. "So what's been happening here?" Penelope asked.

"We need a paddy wagon," Dutch replied glumly.

"What on earth for? Are you expecting a riot?"

"Already had one."

"I go away for half a day and you have a riot?"

"A little one anyway. Kind of like a domestic squabble."

"Well, which is it? A little riot or a domestic squabble?"

"Big domestic squabble."

"Are you going to tell me what you're talking about?"

"Look for yourself."

Penelope looked out the window in time to see Cricket, Nora Pryor, and Alyce Smith being helped from the back of a police car. They were handcuffed.

Dr. Hayden Chudnik, red-faced and sputtering (also handcuffed) emerged from the backseat of a second car.

Albert J. McCory climbed out of a third car.

A stranger appeared from a fourth unit.

" 'Course, if we had a paddy wagon, they might have killed each other."

"What on earth?"

"Disturbing the peace, resisting arrest, and a whole bunch of things I haven't thought of yet. It's too bad we don't have chain gangs. We could put 'em all to work beautifying highways."

"It's too bad the Supreme Court ruled against the Inquisition. You could really have fun."

"They did? When?"

"And rubber hoses."

"Don't go all liberal on me, Penelope."

"I am a liberal. Sort of."

Cops made choices and dispensed street justice all the time. A motorcycle officer on traffic duty might let a speeder on the highway off with a stern warning. The same officer on duty near an elementary school with children present, however, might write up his grandmother for driving two miles over the posted speed limit.

Harvey Curtis had made the choice to teach his miscreants a lesson, including his own ladylove in the interests of impartiality.

Now Dutch also faced a choice. He could allow the misdemeanor charges against the riotous little group to go forward, or he could throw a monumental hissy fit.

He chose the latter, ranting and raving, making dire threats, promising swift and severe punishments if the two academic types and the vice president of development even jaywalked in his jurisdiction during the foreseeable future. "Another confrontation like this episode today . . . well, the consequences would be too hideous to consider," he concluded.

Dutch then stormed off to the women's section of the jail, where Cricket, Nora, and Alyce awaited his wrath.

"Do you know how many windows there are in my police station?" Dutch asked them.

They shook their heads collectively.

"A lot. Take my word for it. And there are floors to scrub and walls to wash and bars to polish. Get the drift?"

They nodded.

"Good, because if you pull a stunt like this again, I'll make sure that your community service includes cleaning every square inch of this place. Twice. You understand me?"

"Yes, Dutch," Nora squeaked.

Dutch smiled, but it was not a pleasant smile. "Penelope is your unofficial parole officer."

"Why me?" Penelope protested.

"They're *your* friends. Have a nice afternoon, ladies."

Penelope took her charges to the Double B and bought them a drink in exchange for the details of their harrowing experience.

"You're just mad," Nora said, "because you weren't there."

"It's not nice going around instigating mini-riots without me," Penelope agreed. "What was that all about anyway?"

"Professional jealousy," Nora said. "That would explain Chudnik and Handley, but I can't imagine why McCory would want to throw a rock at me."

"He wasn't," Cricket said. "He was trying to hit *me,* I think."

"What did you do?"

"He blames me for having a dinosaur on my land and causing the halt on the project while they look for dinosaurs on his land."

Penelope dismissed her parolees with stern warnings to avoid confrontations with all and sundry for the immediate future.

"Unless I'm present, of course." She then crossed the street to Mycroft & Company.

"Yes, may I help you?" Kathy asked.

"Sarcasm is unbecoming in one so young."

"I'm growing old in your absence."

"Nonsense. I saw you only yesterday."

"The day before."

"Really?" Penelope looked around her little domain.

"I'm pregnant."

"That's nice, dear. No, I'm sure I was here yesterday."

"See. Even when you're here, you're not. I said I was pregnant."

"You're what!"

"Just wanted to see if you were listening."

"Thank God. You're too young for motherhood."

"You have messages. I wish you'd get an answering machine at home."

"Anything important?"

"Two sales reps want to stop by. Stormy called. So did Laney. She said to ask you, Grrr. Whatever that means. She wants a complete report."

"Caveman and cavewoman. She's in her prehistoric mood."

"Oh."

"I'm not sure how Andy would look in a

faux leopard-skin loincloth. I might giggle."

"I'm sure I would."

"Anything else?"

"That nice Mr. Cohen stopped by."

"You didn't buy any scrolls, did you?"

"No, but they look quite authentic."

"I'll bet."

"Actually, he bought a copy of *The Maltese Falcon*. And when he left, Mr. Ishii came in and asked to buy the same thing Mr. Cohen had purchased. His finger stayed on this time, thank God. He was followed by a Russian gentleman who also wanted the same thing. But those were the last two copies. He was quite upset and wouldn't leave until I loaned him your copy."

"My God, that's a first edition."

"He promised to be very careful, and he's going to return it."

"He'd better."

"He sure mutters a lot."

"Boris is very intense."

"Where's Mikey?"

"I left him home. I had to go to Palm Springs today." Penelope switched to Humphrey Bogart. "Picked up a material witness, sweetheart."

"You sound like Sydney Greenstreet. Or Nero Wolfe. I've always thought Nero Wolf would sound like Sydney Greenstreet."

"I do a good Humphrey Bogart."

"Have it your way."

"I was going to suggest that you close early, gather up Timmy, and have dinner on me. But if you're going to disparage my . . ."

"Penelope, you do a wonderful Humphrey Bogart. The best ever. I tell everyone that."

"I thought so. Have a nice time."

"I miss having you around," Kathy said wistfully. "I wish you'd solve this case."

"Me too."

Big Mike heard the Jeep and raced to the door before remembering he was mad at Penelope. He retreated to the back of the couch and flopped, paws hanging down, doing his very best lion imitation.

"Honey, I'm home," Penelope called.

Big Mike ignored her.

"So you're going to sulk. All right. I'll fix you." She marched into the kitchen, hit the electric can opener, and waited, counting. "One thousand one, one thousand two, one thousand . . ."

Big Mike arrived in a rush, putting on the brakes and skidding across the floor. Obviously, Mikey had heard a lima bean calling his name.

"You're too easy," Penelope laughed. "Just like a man. Speaking of which, I wonder where Andy is. I thought he'd be here by now."

Andy, Shmandy. Open that can.

After dishing out the goodies, Penelope took a glass of wine into the living room and settled in to wait for Andy.

An occasional field trip might be a pleasant diversion for Tweedledee, but Penelope was disappointed in the Palm Springs excursion and sorry she had missed the Lonesome Bend melee. While she tried to live her life according to the classical Greek ideal of the Golden Mean — nothing to excess — Penelope admitted to a number of faults, impatience being foremost among them. It was a trait that sometimes led her to skip ahead and read the end of a novel.

It drove Andy nutso. "How can you do that?" he railed.

"I want to make sure the girl gets her guy." Penelope admitted to herself that it was a pretty lame explanation.

The lack of patience was also one of the reasons she did not join organizations. Membership meant appointments to various committees, which led to meetings and endless discussion of mundane matters. Like Millicent DeForest, Penelope preferred action. Get it done. Now! Move on to the next task.

So it was with detecting. Unlike Big Mike, Penelope did not have the personality to sift through one clue after another until the solution presented itself. Big Mike could stare at a particularly noisy bird, a bit of ribbon, or a piece of paper seemingly endlessly, examining all ramifications of his target, plotting his stalk, putting the coordinates into his gunnery system — or he could roll over and go to sleep. For Penelope, it was "Aha! Eureka! He did it. Put him away. Next case, please."

She was particularly impatient with the current situation. The known facts concerning Millicent DeForest's murder were that she was shot in the back by a person unknown using a 30.06-caliber rifle. Dynamite was then planted and exploded in such a way as to obliterate the crime scene and, incidentally, the fossilized remains of a dinosaur now named Corny-Milly. The compassionate dynamiter, however, issued a warning before setting off the big Lonesome Bend bang. Beyond this, however, there was a scarcity of hard information, only speculation.

Big Mike climbed into her lap and purred when Penelope stroked his fur softly. "I'm forgiven, huh?" He purred louder. "Thank you," she said, continuing to pet him.

Chudnik might be good for the murder of his colleague. Penelope was surprised that more murders were not committed in the academic world. Professional jealousy was a powerful motivation. Chudnik's reaction to Handley indicated he was far more interested in excavating dinosaurs than he admitted.

But why not McCory? He very easily might have come across Millicent DeForest and, understanding the threat to the DDC, eliminated her. As the project manager for Lonesome Bend Estates, his future livelihood was at stake and he, doubtless, had access to dynamite for construction purposes. But he couldn't be that dumb.

Could he?

Besides, Penelope found it difficult to envision either Chudnik or McCory on a snoop-and-poop mission through the desert, although it might be worthwhile checking out their military records. One or the other might have been in Special Forces or a paratrooper in younger, more adventurous days. Penelope didn't like to think of suspects being former Marines.

Both Chudnik and McCory had substantial motives for removing Millicent De-

Forest if Corny-Milly were a factor — professional jealousy and completion of the Lonesome Bend development project respectively. But what of opportunity? Each had alibis. So did the two men in Millicent's life. Her parents too, for that matter.

Murder for hire? Who, then? So far as Penelope knew, professional assassins did not advertise their services in the *News-Journal.* Still, she had read enough mysteries to know that there were any number of undesirable persons who would commit murder for the price of a drug fix or a six-pack of beer. But they would be unreliable and would likely sell out their employer for the next fix or drink. Mercenaries? The oddball militia member?

And what of the foreign contingent? Hiroshi Ishii seemed harmless, but the Yakusa were ruthless, even in decline. Look at what happened when Mafia leaders were imprisoned. Their women took over and the godmothers were often more relentless than the men. Of course, the parallel was a little shaky, but it was certainly interesting. And since Penelope always made it a point to beware of Israelis wearing fedoras and trench coats, bearing splinters of the true cross and fragments of the Dead Sea Scrolls, Mr. Yitzhak Cohen's presence in

Empty Creek was certainly questionable.

And there was always 1973 and Cornelius Hacker.

Surely, Mr. Sherlock Holmes had something to say on the subject, but Penelope couldn't remember it at the moment.

If all that wasn't enough, Andy was uncharacteristically late. Infinitely anal-retentive, he was the kind of person who arrived at parties a half hour early and then drove around for an hour so he could be fashionably late. Penelope had taken to packing a book and a bottle of wine to pass the time.

"Oh, bother, Mikey."

Big Mike twitched an ear. And then the other. He opened his eyes. He scampered into the kitchen and leaped to the windowsill. The day might not be lost after all.

As a trained observer of cat instincts, Penelope immediately followed. She was also curious to find out why Andy was in the backyard, shouting, "Can Penelope come out and play?" She arrived at the kitchen door just in time to see the basket attached to a huge red, white, and blue balloon settle gently on the ground.

Andy, wearing just about the most foolish grin Penelope had ever seen on his face, toasted her from the basket with a raised glass of champagne.

Mikey whimpered with excitement.

"What are you doing?" Penelope shouted.

"Romantic balloon rides," Andy shouted back. "Come on. I'm writing a feature."

Penelope shook her head slowly. "I don't believe this."

Big Mike suspended his disbelief long enough to leap into the basket, having no intention of being left behind again.

A young man with long hair and a blondish beard poured champagne and held out the glass. "Hi, I'm Ralph, I'll be your pilot and server tonight. Where would you like to go?"

"Lonesome Bend," Penelope said, accepting the glass.

"That's work," Andy said. "This is supposed to be romance."

"You're working."

"Not for long."

"We can neck over Lonesome Bend just as well as anyplace else."

"That's true."

They sailed off into the early evening. Once aloft, earthly noises hushed and they became a part of the air, floating effortlessly, riding the winds.

"Help yourselves to hors d'oeuvres," Ralph said, "and make yourselves comfortable. I'm very discreet."

Below, Empty Creek was a disembodied presence, silent and faraway. Tiny cars and trucks moved through the streets. Ralph provided binoculars and Penelope scanned the scene below. Floating serenely past the slopes of Crying Woman Mountain, Penelope picked out the house her sister shared with Dutch, and adjusted the focus. "Stormy has a new gardening outfit."

"I'll bet it's nice," Andy said. "Let me see."

Penelope handed over the binoculars and waited.

"My God, she's topless!"

"Why are you blushing? You've seen them before."

"Yes, but . . . but . . ."

"You're stammering, dearest."

"But that was in the movies, where nudity was an integral part of the story line. This is . . . different."

"Hah!"

"Really. Someone could see her."

"Give the binoculars back, then."

"In a minute, sweetie."

"See what Nora's up to."

Andy swung the binoculars around, a little too readily, Penelope thought. Stormy had probably gone into the house.

"She's got the curtains drawn. Tony must be in town."

"Imagine. Keeping secrets from the press. The selfish little ingrate."

Penelope was a sucker for strong arms embracing her from behind, soft lips nuzzling her hair and neck, and endearments whispered into her ear. Since Andy was now doing all three, she went all tingly and felt compelled to do her imitation of a helpless maiden. "What nice lips you have, Mr. Wolf," she murmured.

"All the better to kiss you with, my dear."

"What are you waiting for, then?"

Even with their endless hours of practice, Penelope and Andy still sought the elusive perfect kiss. On a number of memorable occasions they had come close, scoring nine point sevens, nine point eights, and, twice, nine point nine. One of the near-perfect kisses had come with Penelope imprisoned in the pillory one moonlit night at the Empty Creek Almost Authentic Elizabethan Springe Faire. She could only flutter her fingers — setting a world record for finger fluttering that still stood by her reckoning — while Andy did all the hard work. The second nine point nine had come when they were parked at the view area high atop Crying Woman Mountain. Penelope still believed that they would have reached ten that evening had Dutch not come racing down the road, disturbing the night with red lights and siren. But, of course, there was nothing for an inquisitive amateur detective and her equally inquisitive journalist companion to do but go ambulance chasing, as it were.

Now, however, soaring high above the desert floor with their lips and bodies melded and their souls intertwined, their respective hormones rapidly approached the red line on the tachometer of love.

"Oh, my God," Penelope whispered. "We did it. Ten point zero, even from the Bulgarian judge."

"Eleven," Andy said. "Definitely an eleven from my perspective. The Albanian judge agrees."

"So does your pilot."

"I thought you were discreet," Penelope said rather huskily.

"I am usually," Ralph said. "But when you're in the presence of greatness . . ."

"We'd better throw him overboard," Penelope said.

"We can't. We don't know how to make this thing work."

"Mikey can fly it. Mikey can do anything."

At the sound of his name, Big Mike glanced over. The expression on his face said, Damned straight!

"Hey, I've got a wife and three kids," Ralph said.

"Too bad. We'll have to be merciful. I guess we'll have to settle for necking."

"Not necessarily. You can be members of the thousand-foot club."

"Another time, perhaps," Penelope said, "although I can probably give you a referral or two." She turned her attention back to Andy. "Want to try for a twelve?"

Ralph was skilled at riding the winds, although Penelope and Andy were too busy to notice until their pilot announced, "Approaching Lonesome Bend."

"Damn," Penelope said. "Couldn't we go around Central Park one more time?"

"I don't think so."

Penelope disengaged herself from Andy's embrace. "I better take a look, but don't lose our place."

If Penelope had expected a different perspective and sudden revelations, she was disappointed. Lonesome Bend from above looked much the same as from ground level. There were no visible outlines of gigantic creatures from the beginning of time or missing trucks from 1973. "I could have climbed a tree and seen this much," Penelope said. She waved at Sam Connors, who apparently had the duty. Sam waved back.

"More champagne, my dear."

"Why, thank you, sir."

Lonesome Bend receded. Penelope and Andy held hands, sipped champagne, and watched the western skies as the sun descended.

"What a wonderful idea this was," Penelope said, squeezing his hand. "You show remarkable promise in the romance department."

They were about to renew their quest for a twelve on the kissing scale of one to ten, when a strange sound disturbed the tranquillity of the evening.

Penelope had heard that particular crack before. During qualification or the annual requalification with the Marine's best friend — the M-16 rifle — all shooters took their turns pulling and marking targets in the butts. Even with 150 Marines squeezing them off from the firing line, the personnel in the butts always knew when their target had been fired upon. It was a distinctive crack when the round passed overhead.

Penelope disengaged herself from Andy's embrace. "Get down," she said calmly, picking up the binoculars. "Someone's shooting at us."

"Who?"

"I don't know, but I suspect it's someone with a 30.06 and a grudge against fossil hunters — and romantic balloonists."

"Shouldn't you get down too?"

"In a moment, dearest, I'm looking for the flash if he fires again. It's too bad Dutch didn't order some hand grenades for me. We could drop bombs on him."

"How about the champagne bottle?"

"That would be littering. Besides, there's some left."

"Ralph, can you get us out of here?"

"Working on it, boss. Working on it."

"He's working on it," Andy told Penelope.

"I heard."

Frustrated by the hidden sniper and his refusal to fire again, revealing his position, Penelope said, "If I weren't a lady, I think I would make a rude gesture."

CHAPTER TEN

Big Mike was rather pleased about gliding through the air in a balloon. It put him on a level with those hawks that soared arrogantly through the desert skies, lording it over earthbound creatures. Still mewing happily, Big Mike seemed to be saying Get me one of these things, preferably with a couple of machine guns, and we'll have serious discussions with the hawks. Ralph, however, was angry at the sniper and worried that his reputation for providing gracious outings for the romantically challenged would be sullied. Andy, too, was worried because Penelope had yet again put herself in harm's way. For her part, Penelope was elated, basking in the adrenaline rush that came with a shot fired in anger.

"I'm sorry your evening was spoiled," Ralph said.

"Nonsense," Penelope replied. "I'm going to recommend you to all my friends.

Lora and Laney and Nora and Samantha and Alyce and Stormy and . . . well, everybody. You'll have more business than evenings."

"Thank you, but you still get a rain check. We guarantee satisfaction. It's company policy."

Penelope and Andy watched Ralph sail away in the darkening skies and waved good-bye.

"You know," Andy said, "it could have been just some maniac."

"Yes, but unlikely. Not with all those cops just down the road. It's far too coincidental for this simple little country girl to accept. Someone is out there protecting Corny-Milly. Or something. There's something he doesn't want us to see. Hmmm. I wonder?"

"What?"

"Oh, nothing. Just a thought."

"And since when have you been a simple little country girl?"

"Never. But I might like to be. Someday."

"Yeah, right."

"I think Ralph needs a marketing plan and some spicy slogans."

"What's wrong with Romantic Balloon Rides?"

"Too bland. Sexy Sailing in the Sunset. Now, that's catchy. Boudoir Balloon. I'll have to give it some thought."

"Give this some thought." Andy reached for her. "Let's set the Universe record."

Penelope ducked away. "First I have to call Dutch. Then we can get naked and discuss whether or not aliens neck."

"Aliens? Discuss?"

"Sure. They probably sit around in their little whatzits, looking out at earth, holding antennas, and saying things like 'I love the green warts on your forehead.' "

Andy shook his head. "Warts?" he mumbled, following Penelope into the house. "Antennas?"

Stormy answered the phone.

"Hi, sis. What were you doing topless in the garden?"

"How did you know?"

"Big sisters know everything."

"Well, I've found it's better than talking to the flowers. They have libidos too. Makes them grow better."

"Oh. I should have known that. Is Dutch there?"

"Hang on a sec."

"Now what?" Dutch grumped.

"Did you know your fiancée holds peep shows for flowers?"

"Sure. Makes them grow better. Everyone knows that."

"You might fit into this family yet, Dutch. You show definite promise."

"That only means I'm probably certifiable."

"Yes," Penelope agreed, "but you'll have such wonderful company with Stormy and me."

Dutch groaned.

"But before they arrive with the straitjacket, I have two things for you. First, I highly recommend taking Stormy on a romantic balloon ride over Lonesome Bend."

"Sounds okay, but I know you, Penelope Warren. There's a catch. What's the second thing?"

"You'd better wear flak jackets. Someone shot at us when we did it this evening. We were over Lonesome Bend at the time."

"You at home?"

"Yes."

"We'll be right over." Dutch hung up.

"No, wait," Penelope wailed. "I'll tell you over the phone. We've got some unfinished business here." The silence on the line stretched to infinity. "Damn."

"What's wrong?"

"The alien discussion is postponed. Go take a cold shower, sweetie, company's coming. Dutch and Stormy."

"I hope she wears her gardening outfit."
"You better stay in the shower."

Since both Penelope and Stormy had been brought up in a household where simple rules of civility demanded that all guests, wanted and unwanted, two-legged and four-legged alike, be fed and watered, a not-so-gracious-hostess-to-be quickly called Mr. Lee and placed a Chinese takeout order, opened a bottle of white wine, brought out four wineglasses — the good crystal, not the everyday cheapos — and set the table. As an afterthought, Penelope dimmed the lights and trotted out the candlesticks as well. Even a hardheaded Dutch might get the hint and make an early departure.

Fat chance.

Dutch and Stormy arrived before the dinner delivery. "Are you all right, sis? I was frantic when Dutch told me what happened."

"I'm fine."

"You've got to stop doing things like that."

"Doing what? We were minding our own business, weren't we, Andy?"

"She wouldn't even duck."

"You see," Stormy said. "It's stupid not

to duck when people are shooting at you."

"Fine talk from a kid who jumped off a three-story house using a sheet for a parachute. *That's* stupid."

"It worked. I didn't break anything."

"You limped for a month."

"A slight sprain."

"It could mean that someone with more bullets than brains is out there," Dutch interrupted.

"That's what Andy thinks. I'm voting early and often for the suspect of my choice as the shooter."

"And who might that be?"

"Oh, I don't know that yet."

"Just tell me what happened."

"Andy, will you pour the wine?"

"Of course, darling."

"And fill in if I forget something."

"Certainly."

"Penelope!"

"Relax, Dutch, I'm getting there."

"In my lifetime, please."

"Don't blame me. I could have told you over the phone and you'd know everything by now. How can you live with this guy, sis? He's such a curmudgeon."

Stormy smiled. "Yes, but he's my very own little Mudge."

"Sit! Talk! Now!"

"Yes, sir." Penelope sat at the kitchen table, took a sip of her wine and a deep breath. "Well, after you released the girls, I took them to the Double B for a drink to help them recover from their harrowing experience. . . ."

"Skip to the important parts."

"We'll never get done if you interrupt all the time."

"I swear I'm going to put in for early retirement and move to Montana."

"All right, all right. I was sitting here, pondering the imponderable, when Andy swooshed in with this hot air balloon. Champagne. Hors d'oeuvres. Very romantic."

Stormy clapped her hands. "Oh, what fun. Can we go, Dutch?"

"Only if Penelope ever tells me what happened."

"Hurry up, sis. It's not polite to keep Dutch waiting."

Mr. Lee's delivery person, with an impeccable sense of timing, rang the doorbell.

"Now what?"

"Dinner's here. Now we eat."

"Dammit, I don't want to eat. I want to know what happened."

"Don't whine, dear."

Eventually, over egg rolls, fried rice, and

shrimp with mixed vegetables, Penelope related the curious tale of the gunshot in the evening, leaving out only the perfect kiss. "I think . . ." Penelope paused in preparation for her dramatic conclusion.

Dutch, concentrating on Penelope's story, absentmindedly scooped mustard on the last egg roll and stuffed it in his mouth. Now, in the normal course of events, Dutch would not have done such a thing — no one but an unsuspecting tourist would. The reputation of Mr. Lee's lethal mustard was well known in Empty Creek. But Dutch, despite the occasional aggravation Penelope caused him, was really quite fond of his future sister-in-law, and when someone shot at her, he took it personally. "Go on," Dutch said.

"I think —"

"Arggh!"

Dutch leaped to his feet, knocking over the chair, and ran for the sink.

Mycroft, who had been sleeping next to the electric can opener, guarding it just in case someone decided to carry it off, jumped straight up and bumped his head on the cupboard. "Meorgh!" he cried, looking around for his assailant.

"Arggh!" Dutch hollered again, sticking his mouth under the faucet.

"Are you all right?" Stormy asked despite all apparent evidence to the contrary.

"Should he be drinking from the faucet?" Andy asked. "That's where the cat drinks."

Fortunately for Andy, the cat was too busy hissing to hear the insult.

"Doesn't anyone want to know what I think?" Penelope asked.

"Damn, that's good mustard," Dutch croaked after emerging from the sink. "Where were we?"

"Before you started destroying the furniture, began shrieking like a banshee, scared poor Mycroft out of several lives, and sent my water bill soaring, I was about to tell you what I think."

"So what do you think?" Dutch wheezed. Mr. Lee's mustard had that effect on vocal cords.

"Well, I think we should find the bullet," Penelope said. She was quite willing to jerk Dutch's chain a little in retaliation for frightening Mycroft. Partners had to stick together.

"Just like that?"

"It shouldn't be that hard. Just send a couple of guys out looking. If Sir Isaac Newton was right, it had to come down somewhere. Compare my bullet with the one that killed Millicent DeForest and I'll bet it's from the same rifle."

"Look for a bullet in about a hundred square miles?"

"Surely not. Probably only one or two."

"Forget it."

"You could use a metal detector."

"No way."

"Well, if you're going to be recalcitrant." Penelope paused. "You could, at least, call out there and find out if anyone heard the shot."

"I already did."

"Oh."

"They didn't hear anything and they didn't find anyone."

"Hmmm. That *is* a good idea. *Do* you have a metal detector?"

"We can get one. Why?"

"Just a hunch. I think you should sweep the crime scene."

"We don't have enough beer cans yet?"

"I want you to look for a 1931 Model A Ford flatbed truck."

Andy had lap duty and Big Mike did not want to be disturbed again, even for his favorite aunt, and he hadn't forgiven Dutch yet, so Penelope walked Dutch and Stormy to the car.

"Thanks for dinner, sis."

"You're quite welcome."

"You watch your six," Dutch said.

"I will."

Penelope watched them drive away and then stood in the darkness looking up at the stars, breathing deeply of the chilly night air. Despite the shot, it really had been a wonderful gesture on Andy's part, and Penelope was quite ready to take up some unfinished business. "Twelve," she whispered. "Here we come."

Penelope went in and shut and locked the door firmly behind her. "Finally, we're alone."

Andy humphed by way of reply. He was joined by Big Mike, snoring a lusty backup.

"Fine," Penelope said, "just fine. The perfect end to a perplexing day."

Penelope carried Mikey with one arm and poked and prodded Andy to the bedroom with the other. After brushing her teeth and dabbing a little perfume behind her ear and between her breasts, Penelope climbed into bed, hoping that Coco Chanel's concoction would waft a little desire in her sleepy man. There was a moment of lucidity when Andy took her in his arms and said, "Melons. We should plant melons this year."

"Yes, dear," Penelope agreed, putting her

lips to his, knowing full well that the comment was probably inspired by Stormy's gardening attire. Either that or he had been rereading *Candide* and was misquoting Voltaire.

Andy fell asleep in mid-kiss and the snoring contest resumed. What a waste of good perfume.

Penelope stared at the ceiling. How can anyone sleep after floating over the desert, she wondered, drinking champagne, achieving the perfect kiss, *and* getting shot at? Well, who needed men anyway? A little conjuring seemed in order. Penelope quickly reviewed the possibilities among the old favorites — Dance Hall Girl and the Gunfighter, Mysterious Female, Captured by Gypsy Prince, Ravished Redhead (Laney's favorite), Imprisoned in the Tower of London (Penelope's own preferred choice), Getting Shot at by Strangers. . . .

Penelope sat up in bed, disturbing the serenade briefly.

Dammit! Who was running around the backcountry, shooting at people, and, incidentally, blowing up the occasional hillside? Penelope blamed the local water supply for any number of things, up to and including the raging hormones demonstrated by the citizenry, but murder? More likely, the desert sun had baked some brain. It was time to consult an expert on the desert.

"And stop that damned snoring," Penelope said.

To her amazement, Andy fell silent and Mikey switched to a purr. Of course, Mikey's purr was as thunderous as his snore, but it was rhythmic, at least. Penelope settled back and closed her eyes.

Do your worst, the beautiful Princess Penelope told the evil Chancellor of the Exchequer, I will never give you my lands.

To the dungeon with her, the evil chancellor sneered.

The black-hooded executioner grasped her arm.

Princess Penelope rattled the heavy manacles on her wrists and shook off his clutch. She went to meet her fate bravely, knowing that her dashing young prince rode furiously through the night on his mission of rescue — if he hadn't fallen asleep at the side of the road somewhere. He'd better be on his way or a certain dashing young prince was in deep doo-doo.

Among her friends in Empty Creek, Penelope admired Red the Rat and Mattie for several reasons. Penelope thought that Red's perseverance in searching for one or another of the legendary lost gold mines for some thirty years now was commendable and deserving of success. Mattie was a fiercely independent woman who had worn out or discarded several husbands along the way. And, although not a raving feminist, Penelope was proud of her own accomplishments as a woman in the still-cowboy-macho world of Empty Creek and found Mattie praiseworthy in that regard as well. Too, although they had been married for some time now, Red and Mattie were still all atwitter about each other, like teenagers playing doctor for the first time in earnest, holding hands, necking in public, and otherwise demonstrating that hormones could still rage in senior citizens — Mattie was a well-preserved temptress of fifty-five and Red was a constantly horny sixty-one.

So Penelope was not at all surprised to find them outside on the patio with Mattie sitting in Red's lap when she pulled up to the double-wide they now shared.

"Howdy-do," Red and Mattie said almost in unison. "How's my favorite cat?" Mattie added.

Big Mike was just fine, which he demonstrated by leaping nimbly into Mattie's lap, where he received a good chin scratch. Penelope briefly considered making it a foursome — she still felt a little romantically deprived after everyone fell asleep on her the night before — but decided the patio chair was a little too frail for another body.

"Hey, Mattie, Red. Have I got a deal for you."

"Let me get you something cool to drink," Mattie said.

"Stay there. I'll get it. I know where everything is." Penelope popped into the mobile home and took a diet soft drink from the refrigerator. By the time she returned, Mattie had put Mikey into a state of helpless ecstasy. If she had the same effect on her man — and Penelope was sure she did — Red had better be taking his vitamins.

"Lemme guess," Mattie said. "You come out for a bit of exercise."

Penelope laughed. Mattie had once tied Penelope, Nora Pryor, and Samantha Dale to the hot walker, a machine that automatically walked horses tethered to its four arms, and sent them to traipsing around in a tedious circle. It was the same confusing night Red proposed to Mattie, but then, most nights — and days — in Empty Creek were confusing to one extent or another. "No, but sometimes I think that's the only way to get me to exercise."

"That might be a good retirement business," Mattie said. "Tie a bunch of ladies to the hot walker, let 'em have a good trot, work up a sweat, and then give 'em mud baths and massages. Be a regular salon. Whatcha think, Red?"

"Can I hose the mud off?"

"Maybe it ain't such a good idea."

"I don't know, Mattie, you may be on to something here." Actually, Penelope thought it a rather good idea, especially in a town that boasted of such bizarre enterprises as the Desert Surf and Flower Shop (surfboards and bouquets), the Tack Shack and Art Gallery (bridles and nudes), and the Cookhouse Boutique (the latest designer fashions for the happening roundup), to say nothing of the Dynamite Lounge (topless coeds dancing to Andrew Lloyd Webber and New Age music), a mystery bookstore named for a cat (not Sherlock Holmes's elder and smarter brother, as devotees thought), and a video store that featured the complete filmography of a B-movie actress named Storm Williams (including every SuperBra commercial she had ever done).

"You reckon?"

"Most of the women in Empty Creek are strange enough to patronize the Ranch Gym and Spa."

"Turn the walker to trot and they'd get a good workout, better than the machines in a gym."

"But they can watch television in the gym," Penelope pointed out. "Or read. That might be a problem."

"Red could read to 'em, I reckon."

"That might work. I could provide a reading list. Something elevating. The romantic poets, perhaps. Yes, I like it. Exercise mind and body. Mud bath, massage, facial. Mattie, I think you're on to something here."

"Why can't I hose 'em off?" Red asked. "I already seen most of them in the calendar."

"Now that you mention it, Red, when are you posing for the men's calendar?"

"I ain't. I got bunions."

"I'm posing for the next one," Mattie said.

"You are?"

"And you're posing for this one."

"I am?"

"Good," Penelope said. "Now that that's settled . . ."

"It is?"

"You should take a romantic balloon ride. Andy and I did it last night and it was fun right up to the point where someone took a shot at us."

223

"Romantic balloon rides and shooting gallery sure gets me excited," Red said.

"Just don't go over Lonesome Bend. I think that's where we made our mistake. Someone's out there trying to intimidate people, which brings me to the real reason for my visit. You've spent more time in the desert than anyone I know. Have you ever met any weirdos out there?"

"Besides me, you mean?"

Penelope smiled. "You're perfectly normal to my mind, Red, but I *do* have a rather wide definition of normal."

"Met some witches once, dancing around a fire under a full moon, but that was way back in the sixties. They was more hippies than witches. Made me an honorary warlock."

"And just what are the duties of an honorary warlock?" Mattie asked.

"Aw, honeybunch, that was way before I met you. And I *was* the only man around."

"How nice for you."

Red smiled dreamily. "Yep, there was this one old gal wearing nothing but some straggly beads — ooofff!" Red whooshed. "Whatcha do that for?"

"Sorry, hon, my elbow slipped."

"How about 1973?" Penelope asked. "Do you remember anything about that year?"

"Cain't say as I do. I've seen flying saucers though. Lots of them."

"Were any of them barbecuing?"

"Honest, I've seen 'em."

"I don't doubt you, Red, but there was a crime report back in 1973. A woman claimed that aliens had stolen her barbecue tools. Twice."

"Seems a long way to come just for a long-handled fork."

"That's what I thought."

"What you're really asking is if I've seen anybody the last couple of trips or so?"

Penelope nodded.

"You know as well as I do, Penelope, that if a man wants to live out there in the backcountry and not be found . . . well, he probably ain't gonna be."

Penelope had taken day rides into the Superstition Mountains, that vast wilderness area of the storied Lost Dutchman Mine and unexplained mysteries. Some said that wild Apache warriors still lived there, guarding the home of their gods as of old. You could ride for days in that beautiful barren wasteland and not see another person. Even if the desert and hills around Empty Creek were not as splendid as the Superstitions, the same was true. A man could live in the desert and never be seen —

unless he wanted to.

"Want me to ride out there and take a look?"

"Thanks, Red, but it would be wasting your time. I'll just have to go to Plan B."

"What's that?"

"I'll let you know as soon as I think of it."

CHAPTER ELEVEN

Big Mike had to be pried out of Mattie's lap. That woman sure knew how to scratch a chin. When it was Mattie's turn to get up, she did so a little reluctantly. That old desert rat sure was cuddly. But, at least, she didn't dig in her claws and growl in loud protest.

Walking to the Jeep, Penelope said, "You haven't been to town lately. Big Mike hasn't had anybody to drink with at the Double B."

"Tell you the truth, Penelope, this thing shook me up pretty good. Haven't felt much like leaving home. Maybe it is time to retire. Help the little lady give mud baths." He squeezed Mattie's butt affectionately.

"I ain't your little lady, Red, so get that idea right out of your head."

Penelope noticed that little lady or not, Mattie didn't shake off his hand.

"He's had nightmares about it." Mattie took Red's hand and squeezed. "I keep telling the old fool he did everything he could."

"Mattie's right, Red. I'm sorry, but you couldn't have saved her. According to the autopsy report, she was already dead when you got there. She just didn't know it yet."

"Seemed like a fine figger of a woman," Red said sadly. In his bachelor days, nearly every female of his acquaintance was a fine figger of a woman to him. "Ain't right. You catch the SOB who done it, Penelope."

"We'll get him, Red," Penelope said with a confidence she didn't feel. "Count on it."

Penelope was beginning to think of the crime scene at Lonesome Bend as CSLB. It was also beginning to take on the appearance of a meeting of the Empty Creek Police Benevolent Association. Tweedledee and Tweedledum stood at the fender of the police Bronco, polishing off a couple of foot-long subs. Harvey was manning a metal detector (good old Dutch!). Good old Dutch was standing apart from the activity, wearing a thousand-yard stare on his face. It would be a good day for a crime spree in town, Penelope thought, and immediately pointed that out to Dutch.

"It's your fault," Dutch said, bringing his

eyes back to the immediate vicinity.

"*Moi?*"

"Flying around, getting shot at, wild ideas about an old truck being buried. God knows what you'll come up with next."

"Now that you mention it, I think we need to go back through the crime records for 1973. We might find something."

"The one murder is not connected to the other. I think we'd better concentrate on catching the current murderer. Then you can play time detective."

"That's the trouble with you, Dutch. No imagination."

"I've got lots of imagination."

"We have a dinosaur that hasn't been anywhere for millions and millions of years, two murders are committed at the same spot, and I think there just might be a connection."

"Come on, Penelope, that's stretching it, even for you."

"Well, it's obvious to me," Penelope said firmly. "We need a whiz bang."

Dutch shook his head slowly. "I'll bite. What's a whiz bang?"

"It's a top secret magic machine, one that takes you away when you're a child and haven't done your homework. Didn't you have a whiz bang when you were a kid?"

"I had a paper route, and I always did my homework."

"How awful for you. I'll bet if you asked nicely and said pretty please with blueberries on it, Stormy would let you play with her whiz bang."

"You had matching whiz bangs?"

"Of course not. Hers was blue. Mine was red."

"Black," Dutch said.

"Black, as in your mood?"

"Black, as in the color of my whiz bang. I'd like a black whiz bang."

"For a Mudge, you're not such a bad sort. If this keeps up, Dutch, I might even let you take D.P. out for a test drive."

"You named your whiz bang Displaced Persons?"

"Diana Prince, silly. Wonder Woman in disguise."

"My first love," Dutch said. The thousand-yard stare returned.

"Diana?"

"Wonder Woman. Diana was too mousy. God, I was in love with Wonder Woman. What brains."

"What a skimpy little suit."

"Yeah," Dutch grinned. "That too."

"I begin to see your attraction to Stormy."

"Yeah, but remember, even Wonder Woman had weaknesses. Don't lose your golden rope."

"What's out there?" Penelope asked.

"Where?"

"Out there, where you've been staring," Penelope said, pointing. "About a thousand yards out. Three thousand feet. Thirty-six thousand inches."

"All the sadness of the world," Dutch said.

"Get a whiz bang, Dutch." Penelope made a mental note to call Ralph and make balloon reservations for Stormy and Dutch.

"Why'd the dinosaur cross the road?" Tweedledee asked.

"I don't know," Penelope said with a patient sigh.

" 'Cause they didn't have no chickens yet," Tweedledum chortled.

Penelope groaned. "Is this the famous cop humor I hear about?"

"Here's another one. What do you do if you find a dinosaur in your bed?"

"Find someplace else to sleep," Penelope said.

"Aw, you heard that one."

"When I was about six," Penelope said.

"It was an elephant joke then. My father probably heard it when he was six. What are you doing out here anyway? Shouldn't you be in town, tracking down leads?"

"Don't got none," Tweedledee said. "Besides, Dutch didn't like someone shooting at you. He was agoraphobic about it."

"Apoplectic?"

"That too."

"So, we been up there all morning, waitin' for the helicopter to flush somebody." Tweedledee motioned at the backcountry.

"Dutch sent a helicopter out?"

"Sure, he doesn't want to lose you to some crackpot. Don't understand why, of course, but there it is."

"I think he's sweet on you. Weren't for Stormy . . ."

"I'm touched. He didn't say a word to me." She looked back fondly at Dutch. What a good old Mudge.

"Doesn't want you to get a fat head."

"Did you find anyone?"

"Couple of tour Jeeps."

"Did they see anyone?"

"Nope."

"That's an idea," Penelope said. "You should interview all the tour Jeep drivers. Maybe they've seen something."

"Already have," Tweedledee said proudly.

"Well?"

"Nothing unusual."

"It was a good idea anyway. Big Mike's proud of you."

Harvey leaned the metal detector against the Bronco.

"Find anything?"

"More beer cans and a fifty-cent piece. Ain't seen one of those in years."

"Try upstream."

"Aw, Penelope, I've been upstream, downstream, all around the stream. There ain't no truck out here."

"Call Alyce and ask her to come out. I'll bet she can find it."

"Well, I'll get her out here, but she can't find something that isn't here."

"Humor me."

"Only because I like you. And it wouldn't hurt to see Alyce. This overtime is killing our sex life."

"What's that hairball on four feet doing now?" Tweedledee asked.

"Excavating a dinosaur, apparently."

Big Mike was, indeed, energetically scratching away at the fossilized bones of Corny-Milly. Apparently, he had overcome the catatonic state induced by Mattie's ministrations and was ready for a little action, sharpening his claws in preparation.

"Should he be doing that?" Tweedledee asked. "Those are valuable bones."

"Go read him his rights," Penelope suggested.

"I ain't getting near that coyote bait."

"Coyote wouldn't stand a chance."

"That's true."

"Mikey," Penelope called. "Stop that."

Yeah, right.

Mikey looked at her over the top of the footstool things with that quizzical expression that said Who me?

Penelope stepped gingerly through the crime scene even though everything that could be extracted was already in the rubble heap. Still . . .

She circled behind Mikey and was suddenly blinded by a flash of sunlight reflecting off a mirror. Shielding her eyes, Penelope crouched next to Mycroft.

"Bingo!" Penelope cried.

What looked suspiciously like part of a side-view mirror was embedded in the dirt between the bones of an ancient creature.

"Whatcha got?" Tweedledee asked. He walked over but kept a healthy distance and some fossils between him and Mycroft.

"Unless dinosaurs were equipped with

side-view mirrors," Penelope said, "or this particular dinosaur owned an auto parts store, we might have something."

"Harvey, what the hell good are you?" Dutch asked.

"Hey, I didn't look under the damned dinosaur."

Alyce took the cracked mirror and held it to her bosom. She closed her eyes, raised her face to the sun, and went away to wherever it was good psychics traipsed during a self-induced trance.

"Five bucks says she can't," Tweedledee said. "Particularly since there's nothing to find."

"You're on," Tweedledum replied.

"Shhh, Alyce is working," Harvey said, putting a finger to his lips. "I'll take that action too," he added loyally.

"I'm in for five," Dutch said.

"Mikey too," Penelope said.

"What about you?"

"I don't gamble."

"I'll get rich anyway," Tweedledee said, rubbing his hands gleefully.

"Rattlesnake gumbo," Alyce said.

"What's that mean?" Tweedledum asked with visions of a crisp five-dollar bill winding up in his partner's wallet.

"Probably some sort of incantation," Penelope said, "invoking the mysteries of the universe to aid her in the quest. Like the three witches in *Macbeth*. You know, 'Fillet of a fenny snake, In the cauldron boil and bake; Eye of newt, and toe of frog . . .' I don't think we have any fenny snakes in Arizona."

"Oh, right," Tweedledum said.

Eyes still closed, Alyce walked confidently toward the remains of the dinosaur. Her entourage groaned, all except Tweedledee, who, despite the advice of Kenny Rogers, was already counting his money.

"What is she doing?" Harvey asked. "I swept that area."

"We know," Dutch said. Losing a bet to Tweedledee was worse than traffic school.

"Quiet!" Penelope ordered. "Let Alyce work."

At the face of the bluff where Corny-Milly protruded, Alyce abruptly turned right and headed up the canyon for ten feet or so before executing a precise about-face and stepping off twenty paces in the opposite direction.

Alyce turned her face to the right, to the left, to the sun.

"I hope she's wearing sunscreen," Penelope said.

"There's a moth in the blender," Alyce said.

"What moth? What blender?"

Left, face. Forward, march.

The little group of gamblers followed in her trail. Psychic Cat dashed ahead.

"This is nuts," Dutch said.

"It's different," Penelope said. "No one likes to have their belief system upset. That's what got Socrates and Galileo in trouble."

"No, I mean it's nuts that I'm betting there is a truck buried out here someplace. No one buries perfectly good trucks. Sell it for parts, drive it to Mexico, that's what you do with trucks."

"We'll see."

Alyce stood quietly, breathing evenly, holding the mirror at arm's length now, like a divining rod. Big Mike sat at her feet, looking up at her and twitching his whiskers, either in anticipation of a great revelation or keeping an eye on *his* side-view mirror. He could be quite possessive about certain things, although Penelope couldn't imagine why he would want a mirror. He was always clean and well groomed, but he wasn't vain enough to spend time admiring himself. Wash the old bod down and get on to the next amusement of the day — herd a mouse into the house, play with a lizard, maul a fossil, find a lap for a quick snooze.

"Red sails in the moonlight," Alyce said.

"Meow," Big Mike replied.

"I'm glad someone understands her."

"Cats are psychic too," Penelope said. "Mikey always knows when I'm upset or sick and provides comfort. He's very sensitive that way."

The side-view mirror was now at a ninety-degree angle to the ground, swiveling back and forth like the gun of a tank seeking its target.

Unlike a tank on the move, however — whose tracks always sounded to Penelope like a family of noisy mice squeaking along as they moved hearth and home — Alyce moved quietly, following the mirror. It seemed to be pulling her with Big Mike beside her, following the red sails in the moonlight.

Mrs. Elaine Burnham, Empty Creek's very own unofficial town crier, climbed the steps to the second-floor offices of the *News-Journal*, presented herself to Harriet MacLemore, a former longshorewoman turned receptionist/classified advertising saleswoman/society editor/theater critic, and said, "Please, Mac, tell Mr. Anderson I have a scoop for him." In her brown tweed suit and sensible brown shoes, Mrs. Burnham looked quite pleased with herself.

"Not the aliens again?" Mac said.

"They've not returned since I threatened them with the vacuum cleaner. They seem to have an aversion to swooshy sucky things."

"I'm not surprised."

"Probably a genetic defect. They don't look very healthy."

"So you said. Well, if it's not aliens, what is it?"

"I can reveal that only to Mr. Anderson. I don't want to start a panic."

Mac sighed. "Hang on, I'll see if I can find him."

"Thank you very much, indeed, Mac."

Mrs. Burnham looked out the window and saw that very nice man from Israel get into a car and pull out. He was followed by that very polite Japanese gentleman, who, in turn, was followed by that grumpy man with the thick foreign accent and the giant woman with the pleasant smile and a caffe latte in her hand. Mrs. Burnham watched them depart, nodding with satisfaction.

Although it had issued from Mrs. Burnham's mouth, Andy could not resist the word — scoop! In the newspaper biz, you took your scoops when they came, however addled they might be in the telling. So Andy immediately ushered Mrs. Burnham into his editorial lair.

"They've found gold at Lonesome Bend," Mrs. Burnham said without preamble.

"Gold?"

"Yes, gold."

"How do you know?"

"Well, I'd just had a very nice cup of iced coffee at Mom's, and I was going to the bank and then the post office before doing my marketing — they have some lovely grapes on sale, the first of the season, they're usually so dear, but grapes are very good for you. They have no fat content whatsoever. Did you know that?"

"Yes, I did. You were saying . . ."

"And I do like a nice glass of red wine before bedtime." Mrs. Burnham giggled. "I'm not a drinker, of course, but if grapes are good for you, they should be healthy however they come."

"Would you care to sit down?"

"Goodness gracious, no, I have errands to run. I just came by to tell you about the gold, or was it black gold? Oh, dear."

"You were going to tell me how you found out about the gold."

"Of course I am, but you keep interrupting."

"Sorry."

"I had just finished my iced coffee . . ."

"You told me that part."

"You're doing it again."

Andy nodded apologetically. Woodward and Bernstein, he thought, never had to put up with this.

". . . when I ran into Alyce Smith. She was just leaving the Tack Shack and, of course, I stopped to chat, even if she is a sorceress, a very nice sorceress, but still. . . . Anyway, I asked where she was going on such a nice afternoon, and she said she was going out to Lonesome Bend to help the police make a find. So there you have it. A scoop. The police have struck gold at Lonesome Bend. Isn't it exciting?"

"Are you sure the aliens haven't returned?"

"Absolutely not. I gave them a good what-for, if you please. As I was telling Mac . . ."

"Yes, well, you give all the details to Mac. I have to get out there. Thank you for the tip."

"Anytime, dear boy. Please give my best to Penelope. Oh, bother, I nearly forgot," Mrs. Burnham said. "I must be having a senior moment."

Andy, who thought Mrs. Burnham an excellent candidate for poster girl of the Find a Cure for Alzheimer's campaign, smiled and waited patiently. "Yes?" he prompted.

Mrs. Burnham delved into her purse and brought out what looked to be a small and weathered leather patch. "I should think you'd want your photographer to take a picture of this."

"Why?" Andy blurted out. He was edging into a senior moment of his own, and he was only thirty-nine.

"It's a fragment from the Dead Sea Scrolls."

The side-view mirror now pointed directly at the slope assaulted by the head and horns of the buffalo. Alyce opened her eyes and said, "There."

Harvey scrambled up the slope with the metal detector. "There's something down there all right," he hollered, "and it sure isn't just another beer can. Get ready to pay up."

"Well, I'll be damned," Dutch said.

"Ye of little faith." Alyce smiled.

"Oh, hell," Tweedledee said.

"Pay Mikey," Penelope said. "Tweedledee bet against you," she explained to Alyce.

"He didn't think I could do it?"

"He didn't think it was here."

"I should put a curse on him."

"Come on, Alyce," Tweedledee whined. "I didn't mean anything by it."

"What do you think, Penelope?"

"Something really gruesome and horrible. Can you make him grow warts on his nose?"

"Too easy."

"Alyce, I'm sorry, you're the best psychic I know."

"I'm the only psychic you know."

"I can't help that. I don't get out much."

"I know," Penelope said. "Take away jelly doughnuts and make him eat broccoli."

"I hate broccoli."

"Good."

"Unless," Alyce said. "Unless . . ."

"I'll do anything," Tweedledee said.

"You, Mr. Policeman, are going to pose for the Men of Empty Creek Calendar."

"Aw, no, Alyce. My wife will kill me."

Alyce turned to Penelope. "I don't think broccoli is quite enough penance."

"No, wait. Jeez. I'll do it."

Dutch issued his own curse. "Dig," he said. "After you pay up."

"Aw, boss, why's everybody picking on me?"

243

★ ★ ★

A contingent of gold seekers arrived, hopped out of their respective vehicles, and rushed to the scene.

"This area is off limits," Dutch roared.

"But we are colleagues," Boris said.

"They're not," Dutch said, pointing to the Asian and Middle Eastern visitors to Empty Creek. "What are they doing here?"

"We don't know. We followed Cohen. Ishii followed him."

"Why?"

"A nice lady said you had found gold. I have never seen a gold mine."

"Well, you won't see one here either."

Andy parked and jogged the last few yards. "What are you doing here, Penelope?"

"I'm happy to see you too, honeybunch."

"You didn't call me."

"I was going to."

"You find gold and don't tell your favorite newspaper editor?"

"You too? Has everyone lost their senses. There's no gold out here. What *are* you talking about?"

"Mrs. Burnham . . ."

"That would explain it. Alyce, did you talk to Mrs. Burnham?"

"For a moment. She asked where I was

244

going and I told her about coming out to help you find something."

"That translated into a gold mine."

"I never said anything about a gold mine."

"No gord mine?"

"Sorry, Ishii-san," Penelope said. "No gold mine. Just an old truck." She looked up at the slope and whispered, "I hope."

CHAPTER TWELVE

Madam Mayor Nicole Pagliero had gone butch and Penelope wasn't sure she liked it, but the mayor was an adult and quite capable of making her own decisions regarding lifestyle. Penelope also wondered what Dr. Victorio Pagliero thought of his wife's new look. Probably, Penelope thought, he hasn't noticed yet. Psychiatrists were like that, particularly one who commuted every day to his office in downtown Phoenix when there were any number of potential candidates for his skills in Empty Creek. Still, his practice was lucrative, enough so that Nicole, also a psychiatrist, had given up her own practice in order to concentrate on saving animals scheduled for execution at the pound, the environment, and Lonesome Bend, to say nothing of playing a mean game of tennis and enlivening city council meetings with her pragmatic approach to local politics.

"So, what do you think?" Madam Mayor asked.

"I'm not sure," Penelope answered truthfully. "What does Vic think?"

"Oh, he quite approves. Encouraged me to do it, in fact. He thought I should experience life to the fullest."

"He suggested you go butch? That doesn't sound like any man I know, even a shrink."

"Oh, yes, Vic's a darling that way. So openminded and flexible, not at all dogmatic like so many Freudians."

"Well, it will give your colleagues on the council something to talk about, not that they've ever been at a loss for gossip. They'll wonder why you've taken it up at this particular point in your life."

"Oh, foo, I don't care what they say," the mayor said. "What do you think, Kathy?"

"I think it's very erotic. And I'll bet Dr. Pagliero finds it sexy. I would if I were a man."

"Hmmm," Penelope mused, looking at the mayor with renewed interest. "I wouldn't have thought of it in quite that way."

"Oh, yes," Kathy exclaimed. "Sometimes Timmy pretends I am."

"Andy is just the opposite, as you know,

but the important thing, Nicole, is whether you like it or not."

"It's new and different and I think it's rather fun for a change. Kind of exciting."

"Then, I'm happy for you," Penelope said. "We should be open to new experiences, and exciting is always good. I just hope Vic doesn't change his mind. It'll take forever to get back to the old you."

"Oh, not that long. It's just a matter of adjustment."

"I don't know about that. I've been trying for ever so long to make my change, but it just seems to creep along."

"Nonsense," Nicole said. "You're making wonderful progress, but perhaps there are some vitamins or something that will help the process."

"I wish there were. Andy won't be happy until I have hair dragging on the floor."

Madam Mayor turned to the mirror over the mantel in Mycroft & Company and brushed her newly shorn hair. "I think I like it. Butch is definitely in for me."

"Good for you, then," Penelope said.

"Now that we have that settled, let me tell you why I'm here."

"You mean, it's not just for fashion approval?"

"Of course not. I've added fossil preservation to the agenda for the next council meeting. I hope you'll be there."

"It's a '31 Ford dually, all right," Dutch said.

Yes! Penelope pumped her fist in the air. "Ow!"

"Ow? What did you do?"

"I think I dislocated my shoulder again. I haven't been so happy since the Aztecs beat Air Force on Thanksgiving Day. Stupid flyboys." A dedicated San Diego State football fan, Penelope had been angry at the Falcon coach ever since he said an alternate date to play the game was unacceptable because they didn't have an airplane to fly the team in. "What do you mean, the Air Force doesn't have an airplane!" Penelope had cried. "The defense cuts haven't been *that* bad." After a tailgate party of turkey dogs, Penelope had marched into the stadium ready for a bloodletting. Celebrating the ultimate victory, she had thrown her shoulder out of whack after a particularly enthusiastic high-five. She was also still mad at the San Diego Padres for preempting the original date for their stupid baseball game.

"Sometimes, I think we should keep you in a straitjacket so you don't hurt yourself."

"I'll be fine."

"How soon can you get here?"

"I'm on the way," Penelope replied. "Have you found anything yet?"

"It was your hunch. We'll wait for you to get here."

"Thanks, Dutch."

Penelope replaced the phone, wiggled her shoulder gingerly, pronounced herself fit for duty, and headed for the front of Mycroft & Company to round up Big Mike. "Important development, Kathy, I don't know when I'll be back."

"That's okay. Timmy's coming by later to help me with the new display."

"Just don't do anything in the window unless you draw the curtain first."

"Penelope! I'm a professional. We don't do things like that."

"What about that time in the back room?"

"The store was closed, and how were we supposed to know you were coming back? You should have knocked or called ahead or something."

"Fiddlesticks. That boy is oversexed, just like everyone else in this town, including you, while I, of course, am the epitome of virtue and purity." Knowing a good exit line just as well as Stormy, Penelope fled before a few of her own more interesting peccadillos could be mentioned.

On the way out of town, Penelope waved cheerfully at Guido, who stood implacable and unswerving in his duty to preserve the lives of wayward rattlesnakes, even though it was too early in the year for them to poke their little forked tongues out of hibernation. She also honked and waved at Schyler Bennett, who had just emerged from the coffee shop at the Lazy Traveller Motel, but his head was down and, if he heard the beep, didn't recognize it as intended for him.

She briefly considered stopping at Lonesome Bend Ranch to tell Cricket of the discovery, but decided against it. It would be emotionally disturbing for Cricket to watch the police go through the vehicle looking for clues, and God knows what they might find. The rest of Cornelius Hacker's skeleton might even be in the truck. "No, Mikey, we'll stop on the way back. We'll know more then anyway."

"Mewp," Mikey replied, although he was distracted by the dust swirling in their wake.

Penelope thought it sound like Mycroft had said, "Maybe."

To the best of her memory, Penelope had never before seen a 1931 Ford Model A one-ton flatbed truck with a marble knob atop the gearshift and a brodie knob fastened to the steering wheel decorated with the famed nude photo of Marilyn Monroe. In point of fact, she now saw only the front half of the truck, which was all that had been excavated so far.

The contingent of men — all cops save for a single newspaper editor with a camera in his hand — stood in a half-circle around the hood and fenders, speaking in hushed voices. They might have been in church waiting for the hellfire sermon they knew was coming.

"Man," Tweedledee said. "I'd like to have seen this when it was cherry."

"They sure don't make them like this anymore," Andy said.

"I had an old '46 Ford coupe," Dutch said. "Boy, I was dumb to give that up. I could probably retire by selling it now."

"Best car I ever had was a '57 Chevy," Tweedledum said.

"I had an Edsel," Tweedledee said.

"That figures."

"Aw, come on, boss. Edsels a collector car now. They even have clubs for them."

"Coolest car ever made was the '51 Merc," Dutch said. "The one James Dean drove in *Rebel Without a Cause*."

"Cute bug-eyes," Penelope said. The headlights were mounted between the fenders and the hood and did, indeed, look like eyes protruding from an astonished insect awakened after a twenty-five-year nap.

"Come on, Penelope, show a little respect. This here's a classic."

"This here's a crime scene," Penelope said, "not a classic car show."

"Wonder if this could be fixed up?" Tweedledee kicked at the shredded rubber that had disintegrated around the front wheel.

"I don't know," Andy said. "I doubt it after all this time."

Cornelius Hacker's truck was a mess. The flat windshield had been cracked. The windshield wipers were askew. Once a bright yellow, the truck was rusted and corroded now. The door windows were rolled up and dirt still clung to the glass.

"All right," Dutch said. "How did it get buried?"

"An explosion," Penelope answered promptly, "just like the one that buried the crime scene."

"You still think the murders are connected?"

"We have a modus operandi."

"Twenty-five years apart?"

"You have a better explanation?"

"God, I hate it when you might be right," Dutch said, "but why was Cornelius Hacker apparently buried over there and his truck on this side of the canyon?"

"No key," Penelope said, brushing dirt aside and peering through the window. "Whoever did it couldn't move the truck."

"Why not drag the body over here and bury them together?"

"Now, *that* is an interesting question," Penelope said. "Which comes first, the chicken or the egg?"

"Aw, boss, there she goes again," Tweedledee complained. "Don't let her get philosophical on us again."

"Think about it. What if the truck were buried first? Pa Hacker might have parked here and gone off looking for fossils. He hears an explosion, comes running back to find his truck buried, and encounters the person who did it. It would be reasonable to assume that there might have been a fight and Cricket's father was killed. He might even have been shot from ambush like Millicent DeForest. Now that I think about it, that's probably what happened."

"God, I hate it when you might be right."

Penelope smiled. "Well, if you gentlemen will excuse me, I'm going to take a look inside." She stepped forward and grabbed the door handle. It wouldn't budge. "As soon as some gentleman pries the door open for me. It's either locked or rusted shut."

"Slim Jim ain't gonna work, boss. Better get a crowbar."

"Do it."

"Try not to scratch what's left of the paint," Penelope said.

When both doors had been pried open and photos taken of the interior, Penelope climbed into the driver's seat, but the cab was still dank and wet. It was like descending deep into a cave. Penelope looked around with interest and found that Cricket's description of the truck had been accurate.

"Whatcha see?" Tweedledee asked.

"A lunch pail — you can examine that — a shovel, a moldy doll with all the hair gone, an empty Coke bottle, a butcher knife, and what appears to be one of those wrist bands from a hospital." Penelope squirmed behind the steering wheel and leaned over to pick it up.

"Well?" Dutch demanded. "Can you read it?"

"Surprisingly well, considering how long it's been buried."

"Dammit, Penelope, what does it say?"

"Buxter Mahoney. Now will you go

255

through the crime records for 1973?"

"Burke, Stoner. Get on it."

"Aw, boss, now?"

"As soon as you're finished here. You want to wait another twenty-five years?"

"I've got to get back to the paper. I can just make the deadline with these photos."

"Drive carefully, sweetie."

"Doing anything special tonight?"

"Brooding seems good right now."

"I don't care if we are on deadline. How about if I deliver the photos and then take the rest of the day off? We can resume our quest for the perfect twelve."

"I suppose I can always brood later. But give me a couple of hours. I want to stop by and tell Cricket about her father's truck."

"I'll be waiting."

"Get naked if you're there before me."

"I'll do better than that."

"I'm not sure what's better than naked, but surprise me."

Penelope and Big Mike found Cricket in the barn.

"Well, this is a nice surprise," Cricket said. "What brings you guys to Lonesome Bend?"

"I don't like always being the messenger," Penelope said.

"More bad news?"

"We found your dad's truck."

"Where?"

"Buried on the opposite side of the canyon. Almost directly across from where Millicent DeForest was killed. It's in surprisingly good condition for being buried all these years."

"He taught me to drive in that truck," Cricket said wistfully. "It was the year before . . . he went away. It took several pillows and I could still barely reach that button on the floor with my big toe. It's where the accelerator would be today."

"I wondered what that was for," Penelope said. "And what about that rawhide cord sticking out of the dashboard?"

"Pa installed a battery so he didn't have to crank the engine. Pull on the cord and it started." She shook her head sadly. "Come on in. I'll take a quick shower and then fix us a drink. Better yet, let's reverse that."

"Go ahead and take your shower. I'll play bartender."

Cricket picked up Big Mike. "Come on, Mikey, I'll bet we can find a nice saucer of milk for you." Although he was never averse to cuddling with a pretty lady, Mikey's expression looked like he'd had his heart set on a vodka martini garnished with a handful of lima beans on a toothpick, but he started purring anyway.

While Cricket jumped into the shower, Penelope mixed drinks and poured a bit of milk. If Big Mike was disappointed in the choice of libation, he didn't show it.

Penelope tasted her tequila and orange juice, reflected for a moment, and reached for the bottle to add more liquor. A double seemed appropriate under the circumstances. Satisfied, she handed one drink into the steamy bathroom to a towel-encased Cricket. "Thanks. I'll be right out."

At the bookcase, Penelope took a Juliana Masters classic and sat down to read. By the time Cricket emerged from the bathroom dressed in clean jeans and a fresh T-shirt, Penelope had worked herself up to a most satisfactory blush. Closing the book somewhat regretfully, Penelope said, "You were ahead of your time, way before presidential advisers and sports announcers took up the collar, so to speak."

"At least they couldn't cause any trouble while they were in the hands of Mistress Juliana."

"That's true," Penelope said, laughing. "Perhaps we should make an hour or two of domination each day a condition for White House employment. They couldn't raise our taxes if they were otherwise tied up. In fact, we might create a new position. Special Domination Adviser to the president. With someone going up and down the corridors of power cracking the whip, they might even get some work done for a change. Probably cut down on the need for so many special prosecutors too."

"We could turn the Lincoln Bedroom into a dungeon as a part of campaign finance reform. I'll bet *that* would cut down on illegal campaign contributions. You could still buy influence but . . ."

"Thanks for the $50,000 contribution. Now, get over my knee. You've been a baaad boy."

"Have you ever considered a career in politics?"

"Not seriously. I'm always reminded of what William Faulkner said when he was fired from the post office in Oxford, Mississippi. 'Good,' he said, 'now I won't be at the beck and call of every son of a bitch who happens to have two cents.' Or something to that effect. I'm afraid I'd very quickly adopt the same attitude toward my constituents."

"I don't know. I've always thought I'd like

to be in Congress for one term. That way I could have all the books I wanted delivered to me from the Library of Congress."

"There's something to be said for that."

Cricket took a sip of her drink and looked at Penelope over the rim of the glass. "Did you find anything in the truck?"

"They're still digging out the bed, but I was in the cab. Did you leave a doll in the truck, by any chance?"

Cricket shook her head. "Did you find one?"

"All its hair was gone and the cloth was in tatters."

"Pa stopped and bought it for me. He always brought me a little present. Something I could fix up my own way." Cricket bit her lip. "I'm not going to cry this time. It's just a damned truck and a doll. Do you think Dutch will give it to me? I mean, when the investigation is over."

"If he doesn't, the wedding is off. I won't have my sister marrying a cop who keeps dolls that belong to someone else." Penelope paused. "I found something else too, a hospital wristband that belonged to Buxter Mahoney."

"Oh, no!" Cricket cried. "You don't think he did it? Buxter's too kind and sweet to kill anyone."

"It doesn't look good. How else would it get there?"

"I don't know, but I can't believe Bux would hurt Daddy."

"Dutch has people checking with the hospital. Maybe something will turn up." Penelope glanced at her watch. "I'd better get going. I'm meeting Andy later. Will you be all right?"

"I'll be fine. This *really* isn't as bad as finally learning he was dead."

Cricket walked them out to the Jeep.

"I'm going to run out and talk to your mother tomorrow. Perhaps she'll be able to help."

"I'll go with you. I could pick you up anytime after I feed the horses in the morning. I'll be done by six-thirty or so."

Penelope laughed. "I've seen one dawn too many already this year. How about eleven? It's still too early, but it would get us there in time for lunch and a tangerine martini."

"Eleven is fine."

Penelope started the Jeep and leaned out the window. "What are you going to do with the truck?"

"Bury it again with my pop's remains if they find any more bones while they're digging out Corny-Milly. He loved that old truck. Be nice if he was buried with it."

Penelope giggled.

"What's that for?"

"You look ridiculous in that thing. I can't imagine what Laney was thinking, unless Wally looks better than you in it, which I doubt. You're the skinniest caveman I've ever seen, and it's not exactly what I meant by getting naked."

Andy wore the leopard-skin caveman outfit. A strap over one shoulder held it up, and he carried the rubber club over his other shoulder. With his lanky, Ichabod Crane-like body, he was all pointed elbows and knobby knees.

"Sure, you think it's so easy. Go out and bring home a woolly mammoth for dinner, dear. That's all you ever say. Well, I'd like to see you do it just once. I'll stay home and sit around the fire all day. You won't think it's so easy then. Here, take the damned club. You go chase woolly mammoths hither and yon. See how you like it."

"Never mind, dear. I'm sure cavemen had their geeks too. You probably invented fire or the wheel or something, and we're all grateful for it. Where's my costume?"

"In the bedroom."

The loincloth was skimpy and the halter was a trifle snug, but looking in the mirror,

Penelope decided she was just the thing to take a caveman's mind off woolly mammoths. She ran her fingers through her hair and shook her head to get the appropriate wild look. Perfect, she thought, haute couture for the prehistoric crowd.

"Ugh, big boy."

"Wow," Andy said.

"Cavemen don't say wow."

"What do they say?"

"Ugh, beautiful woman mine."

"You mine," Andy said. "Ugh," he remembered to add.

"You forgot the beautiful part."

"You beautiful," Andy said, advancing. "Still mine."

"Later, you brute. First we have to feed Chardonnay and the bunny rabbits. You can drag me off by the hair later. You *do* have a handy lair?"

Caveman and cavewoman ventured into the primeval wastelands of the Casa Penelope accompanied by their domesticated saber-toothed tiger. Chardonnay snickered when the duo approached — Penelope was positive of it — but the mare wisely did not refuse the peppermint candy. And if the bunnies thought the outfit of their meal ticket bordered on the absurd, they kept their opinions to themselves. As for the tiger, well, Big Mike had seen any number of things while rooming with Penelope, and very little surprised or shocked him anymore.

With the animals fed, caveman and cavewoman invented the kiss and then, as it turned out, prehistoric man had as much trouble with bra straps as his modern counterpart, but eventually accomplished the task. Penelope sighed. "That's much better."

After the second and third kiss, Penelope said, "Climb into the tree."

"We're going to make love in the tree?"

"No, silly, you're going to lurk in the tree, waiting for beautiful cavewoman — that's me — to come along. I'll be coming down to the river to do my laundry or something. We can improvise from there."

The lone scrub oak behind the barn did have a low branch suitable for lurking and pouncing. Andy dutifully climbed up and squatted, club at the ready. Big Mike joined him on the low branch with considerably less effort.

"My," Penelope said, "what a big club you have."

"All the better to . . ."

"Oh, dear, I seem to be interrupting something," Juan-Carlos Estavillo said.

Penelope shrieked and grabbed for the

faux leopard-skin halter. Andy fell off the branch on which he had been precariously perched. It wasn't one of history's more memorable pounces. Big Mike looked down at Andy with considerable disdain. How could anybody fall out of a tree?

"I rather like your outfit," Noogy said. "Very becoming."

"The least you could do is fasten the damn thing for me."

"Dee-lighted," Noogy said, baring his teeth in quite a good Teddy Roosevelt imitation. "Absolutely dee-lighted."

Penelope turned and looked down on her fallen caveman while Noogy fastened the halter. "Are you all right, Andy?"

"Not a word of this to anyone," Andy said. "Promise me, Noogy."

"My word as a gentleman."

"Whew."

"Only for you, Penelope," Noogy said. "I read the *Empty Creek News-Journal* for all of 1973." He turned to Andy. "I must say, you've improved the quality of the newspaper considerably."

"Thank you," caveman said.

"What did you find?"

"Nothing."

"Damn. Well, thanks for trying, Noogy. I appreciate it."

"There was this," Noogy said, smiling broadly and pulling a folded sheet of paper from his pocket. "I made a copy for you."

CHAPTER THIRTEEN

The lair was a mess.

Leopard-skin garments were flung about (the halter hung from a blade of the ceiling fan). The club leaned against the dresser. It had been largely unnecessary as it turned out, although the cavewoman had insisted upon being symbolically dragged through the prehistoric countryside by her hair. The bedding was rumpled and mussed. The saber-toothed tiger was sprawled across the foot of the bed. He had clawed at the door, demanding entrance and was mollifed only after the caveman invented pizza delivery — "See if they have woolly mammoth as a topping," Penelope had requested — and graciously shared the pepperoni and sausage pizza with the tiger. It was a wise decision on the part of the caveman. The pizza box now rested on the floor, and two empty wineglasses on the bedside table attested to the discovery of the vineyard.

An exhausted caveman — he had picked

the hottest babe in the primeval forest as it turned out — groaned at the insistent beep beep beep of the alarm and hit the snooze button, ensuring another four minutes of uninterrupted bliss.

Penelope snuggled in his arms and looked up at the ceiling fan. How did that get up there? she wondered. Don't care, she decided, and turned over to plant a big smackeroo on Andy's lips.

"Tomorrow, dear," he mumbled. "I'll mow the lawn tomorrow."

"We don't have a lawn."

"Whatever."

Well, this is a switch. I'm awake and he's out. There must be something to this caveman stuff. She turned the alarm off and swung her legs out of bed, planting them firmly on the floor. I'm getting up now. Yes, right now. Go ahead, brain, give the command to rise. Why aren't you getting up? Think caffeine.

That got the brain to kick in.

With Big Mike hitting the liver crunchies, and a cup of coffee at hand, Penelope realized that just seven days before she had also climbed out of bed early to save some local wildlife. If Red hadn't happened along when he did — if he had been an hour earlier or an hour later — Millicent DeForest might have been buried for another twenty-five years and Penelope would now be lying blissfully abed with nothing more urgent on her mind than an afternoon at Mycroft & Company and perhaps a video to watch with Andy and Mikey after dinner. But Red hadn't been an hour earlier or an hour later. . . .

Penelope looked at the ad in the personals section again. It had appeared a week after Cornelius Hacker disappeared. It was boxed and read simply: "If two cases of dynamite are returned, no questions will be asked."

Penelope called a familiar number.

"Good God, this can't be my sister. It's only nine o'clock in the morning. Who are you and why are you imitating Penelope's voice? What have you done with her? If you want ransom money, she's not worth it. In fact, you can keep her, and I'll get all her toys."

"You can't have my bondage starter kit."

"Who needs it? Cops come equipped with everything."

"That's true."

"What are you doing up? You're not sick, are you? Should I rush you to the hospital?"

"You're usually funnier."

"That's because we're still in bed and I'm not really awake. Dutch was out late. Again. I think it's all your fault. If you'd just stop discovering things."

"Well, nudge the Mudge. I need to talk with him."

"What?"

"Good morning to you too, Dutch. I hope you had a good night's sleep and that you're looking forward to another day of crime fighting."

"Stormy, no. Stop that."

"What's she doing?"

"None of your business."

"Well, try to concentrate. I have information. Better have your minions check the '73 records for stolen dynamite." Penelope read him the ad Noogy had found. "What do you think?"

"Ahhh," Dutch said.

"Ahhh as in that's interesting, or ahhh as in Stormy, I'll give you an hour to stop that?"

"Just ahhh."

"Focus, Dutch. It'll be good for your endurance."

Andy stumbled into the kitchen, draped himself over Penelope's neck, and started doing little things that set her to tingling. Not bad for a semicomatose caveman.

"Just pay attention," Dutch said. "Buxter Mahoney was schizophrenic. Still is, I suppose."

"If he's alive."

"He was two years ago when he wandered away from the state funny farm."

"Wandered away?" Penelope closed her eyes. "Mmm." For a brutish caveman, Andy had gentle, magical fingers.

"They went on a field trip, and he just disappeared. They didn't make much of an effort to find him, I guess. Overcrowded and underfunded. Just one more lost soul wandering the streets."

"Or the desert."

"It looks like you've solved one murder," Dutch said. "Now maybe you can concentrate on the DeForest case."

"Cricket doesn't think Buxter would kill."

"How'd his hospital band get in the truck, then?"

"That is a stumper."

"What'd you stop for?" Dutch asked.

"Stop what?" Penelope replied.

"I'm not ignoring you, honey. Penelope said it was good for endurance."

That what.

"I've got to go, Dutch," Penelope croaked into the phone. "Have a nice whatever."

"You too."

271

The line was abruptly disconnected.

By the time Penelope's pulse and heart-beat had returned to normal, the lair had been returned to a bedroom, she was show-ered and dressed, and, with a fresh cup of coffee at hand, ready to face the outside world in the new guise of General Penelope Warren. Stuff was happening and her sub-ordinates were on various missions. Andy was on the quest for a twenty-five-year-old classified ad. "My God, you want the im-possible," he complained.

"Don't you keep records at the *News*?"

"Of course we keep records. Mac never throws anything out."

"Then you should be able to find a simple little old insertion order. Shouldn't you?"

"I suppose."

After sending Andy on his way with a nine point two buss (there was a limit to anyone's stamina), General Warren decided to con-vene a staff meeting at her house at 1800 hours. Without an aide to get Dutch on the phone, Penelope pressed redial and waited. The answering machine picked up on the first ring. "I know you're there, but don't let me interrupt. We're meeting at my house at 1800 hours — that's six o'clock for the civil-ians in the group — to report in. The

Tweedles and Harvey are invited too. Warren out," she concluded in proper military radio procedure.

Cricket arrived promptly and accepted the invitation for coffee. Big Mike just as promptly confiscated Cricket's lap for a quick snooze.

"I'd like to make a quick stop at the market," Penelope said after filling a mug for Cricket. "I want to talk to the mayor."

"She hangs out at the supermarket?"

"One Saturday every month. She rescues animals from the pound and then gets people to adopt them."

"What a nice thing to do."

"She's also a psychiatrist. I want to ask her about schizophrenia. That's what Buxter Mahoney was being treated for. Before he wandered away from the hospital two years ago."

"Poor Buxter. He was always the best of the Mahoneys."

"Tell me everything you can remember about him."

"I think I've told you everything."

"Let's go through it again. With all that's happened since yesterday, I can make better evaluations now."

"He was nice, a gentle creature. On the Fourth of July he always shot off the fireworks for the younger kids. He liked things that made loud noises. He told me once that it scared the voices away."

"Dynamite makes a loud bang."

"But he couldn't have done it. He went into the hospital before Pop disappeared."

"He left the hospital once. He could have back then. We'll know soon. Records are being checked. Did he work?"

"In construction, I think. He had a red hard hat that he used to let me wear."

"Construction workers might have access to dynamite."

"It doesn't look good, does it? But where has he been for the last two years? No one's seen him that I know of."

"That's something we'll ask when we get out to Bathsheba. But he could be living in the backcountry with a rifle and a supply of dynamite."

"I still can't believe it."

"We better get going. Lots to do today. By the way, you're invited for dinner tonight."

Nicole Pagliero and her friend and partner in animal rescue, Lissa Jacobson, were sitting in beach chairs outside the market. The mayor had three cuddly kittens scrambling to get out of a cardboard box and a German shepherd puppy on a plastic rope happily lapping at every shoe that passed. Xanadu, Lissa's sleek black cat, was curled up in her lap.

Penelope greeted the black cat in her usual manner by solemnly reciting the opening lines of Coleridge's poem. " 'In Xanadu did Kubla Khan/A stately pleasure-dome decree. . . .' " She then made the introductions.

Big Mike growled at the kittens just to let them know who was in charge, and then turned to the puppy, who immediately sat on his haunches, looking over his new playmate, although he wisely refrained from dog kisses. With authority firmly established, Big Mike rubbed against the mayor's leg, purring, as if to say, This is a good thing you're doing. That done, he hopped into Lissa's lap to say howdy to Xanadu. They were old friends.

"How many kittens would you like, Penelope?"

"Oh, no. Big Mike is an only cat and he intends to keep it that way."

"What an adorable puppy," Cricket said. She knelt and gave him a friendly pat. He put his feet on her chest and licked her face.

"It looks like you've found a friend."

"I knew I should have waited in the car. How much is he?"

"He's yours for the price of the shots and neutering. Would you like some kittens too? Stanley seems to get along with them very well."

"Stanley? Who names a dog Stanley?" Penelope asked.

"It's my brother-in-law's name," Nicole replied.

"Oops, sorry."

"Don't be. He's a jerk. My brother-in-law," she added hastily, "not the puppy." Nicole turned the rope over to Cricket.

"Tell me about schizophrenia, Nicole."

"Does this have something to do with the murder at Lonesome Bend?"

"Murder at Lonesome Bend," Penelope repeated. "It would make a good title for a mystery novel. And yes, we may have had a break." Penelope quickly brought the mayor up-to-date, including what she knew of Buxter Mahoney.

"I wish city staff could make such succinct reports," Nicole said. "I'll try to do as well. Schizophrenia used to be known as dementia praecox, which meant early insanity. Schizophrenia means a splitting of the mind. There are several types, but from what you've told me, your Buxter Mahoney is suffering from the paranoid type. Its characteristics are unrealistic and illogical thinking, delusions of persecution, or, sometimes, grandeur, and frequently hallucinations. Quite often the victim hears voices and believes they are real. Visual hallucinations are also fairly common."

"What causes it?"

"Like so much in modern medicine, we still don't know that much. There are theories that range from the biological to the psychological and the social. A poor relationship between parents and child, some traumatic event, an inability to cope with reality . . ."

"A defense mechanism," Penelope said.

"In the simplest of terms, yes."

"And what's the best treatment?"

"A protective environment where the patient can work through periods of confusion away from the disturbing influences of his own home. Antipsychotic drugs are also used."

"Could someone like Buxter live alone in the desert?"

"I can't judge, of course, without knowing Buxter, but, yes, I suppose it is hypothetically possible. There are people who find the desert soothing and protective. Like us."

Bathsheba was crowded on a Saturday

morning. A number of cars were parked haphazardly at Ma Hacker's garage sale, and the treasure hunters swarmed over the tables, grabbing and discarding one bargain for another. Penelope immediately gravitated to a table laden with books and, while passing by on her way to be introduced to the matriarch, managed to pick out five novels — a Nero Wolfe omnibus, two Raymond Chandlers, Michael Connolly's *The Poet*, and a copy of Gary Amo's Edgar-nominated but out of print *Come Nightfall*.

"Ma, this is Penelope Warren."

Ma Hacker sat on a high kitchen stool behind an old cash register, presiding over the turmoil.

Mycroft leaped to the table.

"That's Mycroft, Ma."

Stanley barked. "And this is Stanley. He's moving in with me."

"Quite a crowd," Ma Hacker remarked.

"Bert, you take over for me and don't be giving the store away while I'm gone."

"Bert's my older brother," Cricket said. "He runs the gas station when he's not helping Ma."

"Making me old, more likely," she said, but she softened the words with a smile.

"Thank you for taking the time to see me, Mrs. Hacker."

"Might as well call me Ma like everyone else."

"Meah," Mycroft said.

"Smart cat."

"Yes, he is," Penelope agreed.

"Well, let's get on over to the Roadhouse. Could use a little pick-me-up."

The menagerie of women and animals navigated the route to Maggie's Roadhouse with only one mishap, when Stanley managed to wind his leash around Ma Hacker's leg. She was still getting untangled when she pushed through the door and stopped abruptly to glare at a woman sitting with Cully and Sully Mahoney on their side of the dividing line. Penelope took her to be Mother Mahoney.

The matriarchs glowered at each other, bristling like two hungry cats hovering over one bowl of cream. "And him," Ma Hacker said after staring down the Mahoney woman. "I wouldn't have sold him anything if I'd known he was one of them."

Penelope, eyes adjusted to the dim light now, saw Schyler Bennett sitting at another table. He was definitely on the wrong side to her mind. "Excuse me a moment, please," she said.

"What are you doing here, Schyler?"

"Penelope?"

"Indeed. Do you know where you are?"

Schyler looked more than a little guilty. "I suppose it is a little early in the day, but I was thirsty after wandering through the garage sale. Look." He held up a rock with the skeletal imprint of a small fish embedded in it.

"What is it?" Penelope asked.

"I'm not sure. I'll have to look it up when I get home. Dee would have known right off. Oh, damn, I miss her."

"I know." Penelope patted his hand gently.

"I just came out here for something to do. I guess I'll be going home now. See you later?"

"I'll stop by when I have some information," Penelope said.

"Okay."

Penelope watched him leave and then turned to the Mahoney table.

"I'm Penelope Warren, Mrs. Mahoney. I'd like to talk about your son, Buxter."

"Already told the cop all I'm gonna say. Don't have to talk to you."

"Ma, tell her to get on the other side of the line. She's one of Sally Anne's friends. She don't belong over here."

"No wonder Buxter hears voices," Penelope said. "I would too, if I came from this family."

280

"Hired a detective to find out what happened to my husband, but he never found nothing."

"You never told me that, Ma."

"Didn't want to get your hopes up, honey. I still think it was old Pa Mahoney. He was gone that whole weekend. Didn't come back till Monday afternoon. He was looking just too pleased with himself. But we could never prove anything. Then the old SOB dropped dead six months later. Heart attack, they said. I call it divine retribution. We'll never know now, I suppose."

"Oh, I think we will, Ma," Penelope said.

"Cricket said you were good. Guess you are if you can find Corny's truck after all this time."

The door opened and Penelope looked up to see a familiar figure framed in the light. "*Konnichiwa,* Warren-san." Hiroshi Ishii bowed and nearly lost the huge sombrero he had added to his ensemble.

Penelope stood and bowed. "Good day to you too, Ishii-san. These are my friends." After more bowing and some barking from Stanley, the Japanese gentleman bellied up to the bar and planted one foot jauntily on the rail — on the good side of the white line.

Penelope turned back to the door. "Ten,

nine, eight, seven, six . . . right on time," she said.

Yitzhak Cohen entered, said "Shalom," and took a table — on the wrong side.

"Can Boris and Natasha be far behind?" Penelope wondered.

Nope.

Gloomy Boris and voluptuous Natasha were right on cue — and on the proper side.

Now, isn't this interesting? Penelope thought.

After lunch, the Hacker menagerie left the foreign contingent to themselves and walked Ma Hacker back to her post at the cash register. Bert relinquished the stool and said, "Ma, wait'll you see what I just bought."

Ma groaned. "It happens every time I leave the boy to himself."

"No, this is great, really. You'll be proud of me this time. Look here. It's a fragment from the Dead Sea Scrolls."

"This meeting of the Baker Street Irregulars is now in session," General Warren said, mixing her metaphorical organizations. "First Sergeant, call the roll."

"Everyone present or accounted for," Stormy said, "except for the two people you really need."

"And who is that?"

"Sherlock Holmes and Dr. Watson, of course," Stormy said. "Nancy Drew wouldn't hurt either."

"Doubters will be assigned to mess duty."

"On the other hand, I've always thought them vastly overrated."

"I thought so. Detective Curtis, would you make your report, please?"

"The Mahoneys claim they haven't see Buxter since he went missing from the hospital. I went at them every which way but couldn't budge them. Those two kids of hers are creepy."

The reports continued.

Andy had found the insertion order for the classified ad. It had been placed by one Creighton Riley, who had listed himself as the owner of Red Rock Construction Company.

Bingo!

"How much do you want to bet that Buxter Mahoney worked for the Red Rock Construction Company before he started listening to the voices?"

"Thought you didn't bet?" Tweedle Number One said.

"Mycroft does, and this is a sure thing."

Tweedledee and Tweedledum had sifted through crime reports and found, after much sneezing and wheezing — "Those records are dusty, dammit, Penelope" — that it was Buxter Mahoney who had been walking down Empty Creek Highway in "a naked condition" on September 11, 1973. It was also Buxter who was reported missing from the hospital with a paring knife in his possession on November 8, 1973.

And, finally, Dutch provided the pièce de résistance. "Buxter Mahoney was checked out of the hospital the week before Cornelius Hacker disappeared. He was re-leased into the custody of his father."

"And Mahoney the Elder conveniently dropped dead six months later. Well, I guess we'll just have to find Buxter Mahoney."

"If he's out there, he could hide forever. Got any bright ideas?"

"Do you think you could borrow the First Marine Division? We could form a skirmish line and move north from Lonesome Bend."

"That'd be one big skirmish line."

"Yeah," General Warren said with a dreamy smile on her face. "Sergeant Major, get the commandant of the Marine Corps on the phone."

CHAPTER FOURTEEN

Going to Sunday brunch at the Double B was an exploit somewhat on the order of Sir Richard Burton — the explorer, not the actor — setting off into the interior of Africa in search of the source of the Nile. The expedition began with Laney and Wally riding their horses over to Penelope's with Alexander (the *good* Yorkshire terrier) happily ensconced in a saddlebag and Kelsey (his *evil* female companion) nervously clinging to the saddle horn — she refused to ride in the more comfortable rumble seat. By the time they arrived, Penelope was mounted on Chardonnay with Big Mike in *his* saddlebag and waving good-bye to Andy, who, although he could ride after a fashion, preferred Bloody Marys to horses and went on ahead to claim their table.

The people said howdy. Alexander barked and yipped until he got Laney to transfer him to Penelope's saddlebag so he could ride with his old buddy, Big Mike.

Penelope always thought he wanted a better view if Kelsey fell off.

Signs of civilization vanished as the little party rode off into a primitive and pristine paradise. It was peaceful riding through the desert. The late morning was bright and clear. The cloudless sky was a deep crystalline blue. A slight breeze ruffled the scrub. Birds chirped and warbled. Enveloped by the mysterious beauty of the desert, even Kelsey and Alex fell silent, communing with the grandeur of nature. Big Mike, always a Zenlike creature, had no problem in becoming one with the moment and the environment. It was a trait that Penelope, surely a cat in another life, usually shared.

But someone was trampling all over Penelope's grave again. A chill trotted up and down her spine, and she wondered if Buxter Mahoney was lurking in this paradise, sighting in on her with a 30.06, listening to voices, waiting for the command to kill.

"Did you bring a gun, Wally?"

"Sure."

"Good." Next time, Penelope thought, I'm not leaving home without one.

"Why?" Laney asked.

"Balloons."

"You want to shoot balloons?"

"Someone shot at my balloon."

"I see." Laney examined Penelope carefully. "You don't look feverish or chilly. Are you hallucinating? Are you sure you didn't catch malaria in Africa?"

"Andy took me on a balloon ride and someone shot at us. I recommend it though. Wally, you should take Laney. It's very romantic. You can join the thousand-foot club."

"And get shot at," Laney said. "I can hardly wait. It sounds like ever so much fun."

To Penelope's surprise, Wally paled. "Don't want to," he said.

"He's afraid of heights," Laney said.

"I didn't know that."

"I didn't either until he was supposed to storm the castle battlements to save me from another ghastly fate. I was rewriting the King Arthur legend. I played Guinevere, of course. But in the end I had to save myself because he couldn't climb the stepladder. And they weren't even pouring hot oil on him. I had to redo the whole thing so he could tunnel in under the moat."

"I'm sure your version of the legend was much better."

"Oh, it was. If you've never been ravished on the Round Table, I recommend it."

"My tables are all rectangular."

"Pretend." Laney swung in her saddle. "Wally dear, take me on the balloon ride."

"You'll be safe from antiaircraft fire so long as you stay away from Lonesome Bend," Penelope said. "I think."

"Can't," Wally said. He was never loquacious at the best of times.

"Please, honey. You don't have to look down. In fact, I'd prefer you spent all your time looking at me, adoring my splendid beauty."

"Aw, honey, not that."

"You think I'm ugly?"

"That's not what I meant," Wally said hastily. "I'll do anything but ride in a balloon." He was heading for the black hole of life — and knew it.

"Anything?" Laney smiled at Penelope. "Name it."

"Well, sweet darling honeybunch of mine, you *could* pose for the Men of Empty Creek Calendar. . . ."

Gotcha!

Penelope's uneasiness left her once they emerged from the desert and took the trail leading into town. Still, she didn't like the sense of suffocation in the desert she loved so much and where she usually felt so comfortable. It was one more reason to end this mess — and soon. Until the killer was put away, the disturbing ripples of his crime destroyed serenity in a tranquil community. Penelope resented the intrusion in her life almost as much as she deplored the senseless taking of life. She urged Chardonnay into a trot. Big Mike mewed with excitement. Alexander barked and stuck his face into the breeze. It was almost like hanging out a car window.

Penelope envied him.

Andy waved to them, which was hardly necessary, since he was at the same table they had shared for any number of Sunday brunches. Red and Mattie sat at the bar. They had saved Big Mike's stool for him. Alex would have preferred to be at the bar with the big kids, but he was relegated to sharing Laney's lap with his nemesis.

Nora Pryor and her Tony were snuggled in a corner booth, sitting close to each other on the same side, sipping their Bloody Marys and sneaking kisses when they thought no one was looking, which was hardly ever. Everyone in the Double B glanced at the couple occasionally just in case they might pick up a new technique or two.

The cowboy crowd, led by one Riley Stockard, sat at the corner of the bar, watching the tractor pull on television and downing tequila shooters, killing the few brain cells that remained. Real cowboys didn't cotton to sissy drinks like Bloody Marys, even though most people in Empty Creek believed that the Double B's Bloody Marys ought to come with warning labels.

The foreign contingent seemed to have come to a momentary truce, occupying a round table in the center of the room. Boris nodded morosely at Penelope, Natasha beamed and chugged her Bloody Mary, Ishii-san bowed, of course, and Cohen tipped his fedora. Penelope returned their greetings with a nod and a smile, wondering if she might borrow the round table for an evening.

Lora Lou Longstreet and David Macklin were with Samantha Dale and Big Jake Peterson. Had it not been for the calendars prominently displayed around the Double B, the life-size nude portrait of Lora Lou behind the bar, and the bank president's predilection for playing strip poker, the two couples might have passed for regular old ordinary churchgoin' folks.

Wally sat and took a healthy belt from a waiting Bloody Mary. "Gotta pose," he said.

"You too, huh?" Andy clinked Wally's glass in sympathy.

"Hi, darling," Penelope said. "Miss me?"

"I saw you just an hour ago."

"Well, you could still miss me. See if I give you a round table for Christmas."

"I've only had one drink," Andy said. "Honest. And I still don't know what she's talking about."

Albert J. McCory came in and took a seat at the bar. Penelope saw him and said, "Excuse me. I have to do a little business here."

She took her Bloody Mary and slid on to the stool next to McCory.

"You," he said.

"Me," Penelope agreed.

"What do you want? Haven't you caused enough trouble?"

"I'm not to blame for the delays in your project. In fact, a little cooperation on your part might speed things along. The sooner this case is resolved, the sooner we can get back to normal."

McCory shrugged. "Still haven't told me what you want."

"Do you have dynamite out at the construction site?"

"Sure. Couple of cases, I reckon."

"Are you missing any?"

"Of course not. We keep it locked up. I've already been through this with the cops."

"Have you looked at it lately?"

"What for? Got nothing to blow up. Nothing to build. Still think it's your fault."

"Would you check it with me tomorrow?"

"I guess."

"Thank you."

Penelope returned to the table.

"I missed you," Andy said.

Boris weaved his way over to Penelope. " 'My friends, pray to God for gladness. Be glad as children, as the birds of heaven. And let not the sin of men confound you in your doings.' "

" 'Hurrah for Karamazov,' " Penelope said. "Amen."

"Will you take your luncheon with me and Katerina tomorrow?"

"On one condition."

"What is that?"

"Cool it with the Dostoyevsky. I can't keep up."

Boris almost smiled. "I doubt that very much," he said.

Stormy entered the Double B with her usual regal magnetism, causing male heads to turn and watch her work the tables on her way over to where Penelope held court. She *was* statuesque, Princess Leogfrith ·in civilian clothes (a good thing since her entire wardrobe budget in the *Sword of Doom* trilogy hardly matched the crew's coffee allotment for the first day's shooting). Watching her sister, Penelope was again proud of the actress in the family. There was no doubt in her mind that Stormy would one day graduate from the B roles and become a major star. She wasn't about to tell her that, of course. Who needed a sister with a fat head?

"Where's Dutch?" Penelope asked when Stormy finally ended her triumphant entrance.

"On the phone. If he doesn't get off soon, I suppose I'll have to play carhop and take a Bloody Mary out to him."

"That's what this town needs," Andy said. "A drive-in with carhops on roller skates."

"What this town really needs is more hitching rails," Penelope said. "It's getting so you can't find a place to park a horse anymore."

Debbie sashayed up to the table, cocked a hip, and said, "This is too weird. One guy's sitting there mumbling something about an idiot —"

"That would be Boris," Penelope said,

"probably quoting *The Idiot*."

"The big gal was telling me how she wanted to be a ballerina, the Japanese guy, he's kind of cute, asked me for some Klazy grue, and the hat wants to trade a piece of the true cross for eggs Benedict. Thank God, you guys are normal."

What an insult.

"Who were you talking to for so long?" Penelope asked.

"Don't be so nosy," Dutch replied, reaching for the pitcher of Bloody Marys.

"You learn by asking questions. How did you learn where babies came from, for example?"

"In the tree house," Dutch said, "like any regular kid."

"Your father took you into a tree house to explain the birds and bees?"

"Nope. Billy Hayes swiped his old man's collection of girlie magazines. We didn't need to ask questions after that."

"Oh."

"He was talking to the guys out at Lonesome Bend," Stormy said.

"Traitor."

"Sisters have to stick together."

"Give, Dutch."

"Besides, I was talking to the lab. They

found some cassette tape in the truck's toolbox last night. Just a fragment, but it was long enough to get some words off it. After they did their mumbo-jumbo in the lab."

Dutch leaned back and took a sip of his drink. "Good," he said. "I hope you all have designated drivers or riders."

Penelope motioned to Debbie. "Would you bring me a pool cue, please?"

"Sure. Why?"

"I'm going to give Dutch ten seconds to start talking, and if he doesn't, I'm going to brain him."

"Aarooo," Dutch moaned.

"You think I'm kidding?"

"Aarooo," Dutch repeated. "You asked what was on the tape. I'm telling you."

"Aarooo?"

"Real spookylike. Like kids trying to scare each other at Halloween."

"That's it?"

"Of course not, but you keep interrupting."

"Sorry."

"After the creepy beginning, the same voice said, 'Protect the great creature at all costs. That is your mission. You must protect it. . . .' That's all they could get."

"Buxter Mahoney's voices came to him

from a cassette tape?"

Dutch shrugged. "Maybe he recorded them. If it was Mahoney."

"How can you record voices that come from your head?"

"High-tech schizophrenia?"

"Someone's controlling Buxter Mahoney."

"You're stretching again."

"Maybe, maybe not."

"I wish you'd concentrate on the De-Forest murder."

"I am," Penelope said. "There was some tape in all the junk your guys dug up. Have them work their magic on it."

"Come on, Penelope. You think that tape's the same that was in the truck?"

"Humor me."

"The hell I won't," Riley Stockard roared and promptly stripped down until he was wearing nothing but his cowboy hat and blue Jockey shorts. No one much cared about the Double B's No Shirt, No Service rule anyway. Riley downed another shot of tequila and put his boots back on before marching over to Natasha, where he doffed his hat, bowed, and said, "Would you care to dance, ma'am?"

To her great credit and immediate adoption as an honorary citizen of Empty-by-

God-Creek-Arizona, Natasha rose and said, "Why, thank you, sir." She practically carried Riley to the dance floor.

"Are you going to enforce the No Shirt, No Service rule, Dutch?"

"Doesn't say anything about dancing."

"Chicken?"

"Nope. I'm off duty."

"Start a pool?" Andy asked. "The time is one-fifteen."

Five-dollar bills promptly appeared on the table and times were chosen.

"One-twenty," Penelope said. Football and fight pools did not constitute gambling.

"It'll take longer than that," Laney said. "One-thirty."

"One twenty-one," Andy said.

"Sucker."

"Come on, Andy, let's dance. I want a good view."

Penelope settled into Andy's arms, rested her head on his shoulder, and kept one eye on her watch. Andy wasn't much of a dancer. He shuffled his feet awkwardly and moved his hips like they were set in concrete. To his credit, however, he was one helluva snuggler on the dance floor and almost made Penelope close her eyes and drift into dreamy dancing land.

Almost.

One-seventeen p.m.

One-eighteen p.m.

One-nineteen p.m.

And thirty seconds.

Oh, damn.

"The hell I won't," Vern Jeffords shouted, just in time according to Penelope's viewpoint. He hitched his jeans and clomped his way to the dance floor, tapping on Riley's shoulder with ten seconds to spare. "Cutting in," he said.

"Pay me," Penelope whispered, taking the lead and twirling her honey out of harm's way.

"Butt out," Riley said.

Vern persisted, clobbering Riley's shoulder with a clenched fist. "Cutting in, dammit!"

Now, in the normal course of action for such events at the Double B, Riley would have released Natasha, turned and hit Vern Jeffords with a powerful haymaker, knocking the shorter cowboy off his feet away from the jukebox (anyone who broke it was banned for a month), thereby setting off a wild melee where it didn't much matter who hit who — the fight was the thing.

In this case, however, Riley had taken step one by releasing Natasha and was winding up for step two, when the Russian woman stepped between them, saying, "Excuse me, please." She took Vern by the arms and slowly raised him to her eye level. Since she was a good six inches taller than her erstwhile dance partner, Vern's feet were dangling well short of the floor. "How is it you say, darlink, butt out?"

"Yes, ma'am," a stunned Riley replied, feeling the viselike grip of Cupid on his heart. This was one mighty fine woman.

"Good." She smiled at Vern. "You will butt out, please, yes?"

"Yes, ma'am."

Natasha carried Vern effortlessly to the bar and deposited him on a stool among the remaining cowboys — no fools they — now fully engrossed in the tractor pull. She patted Vern on the head, downed a shot of tequila, and returned to Riley.

"We dance more, no?"

"Yes, ma'am."

"Good God. What now?"

A sudden cackle with an English accent pierced the babble that passed for conversation at the Double B's Sunday brunch. "Stop, I say, stop it." Tony Lyme-Regis was under attack by Nora, who had her hands under his proper tweed jacket and was apparently intent on tickling him to death.

The Double B's Bloody Marys often induced erratic behavior, but this from the nearly always sedate and proper Nora Pryor — and she wasn't even blushing.

In his desperate efforts to escape Nora's fingers, Lyme-Regis had a brief argument with gravity but lost and fell out of the booth. Nora leaped on him, tickling his ribs relentlessly. Tears streamed down his cheeks, and he wiggled and giggled helplessly.

"Say it," Nora cried.

"I'd better investigate," Penelope said.

"Oh, God," Lyme-Regis spluttered between giggles, "will no one rid me of this meddlesome woman?"

"Henry II regarding Thomas à Becket," Penelope said, standing over the disheveled couple. "What *are* you doing, Nora?" Penelope had to shout to be heard over the Englishman's laughter and ragged wheezes.

"I'm going to tickle him until he agrees to pose for the calendar."

"Oh, is that all? Better give in, Tony. She's a very determined woman."

"I surrender," he cried.

"You do?"

"Yes, a thousand times, yes!"

Penelope nodded with satisfaction. Two gotchas in one day was pretty good work.

Nora got up, smoothed her blouse,

pumped her fist in the air, and leaped to the top of a vacated table, where she did a very credible bump and grind until she nearly threw a shapely hip out of joint, belatedly realizing everyone in the joint was watching with rather astonished expressions. The blush motor kicked to life and flushed with victory and perhaps one tiny sip of Bloody Mary too many, Nora shouted, "And I'm entering the wet–T-shirt contest too. So there!"

Poor Tony, who had regained his feet, said, "Of course you are, dearest." He grabbed a handy pitcher of ice water and poured it down the front of Nora's blouse.

"Eek! That's cold!"

The resulting dance to dislodge chunks of ice from within intimate apparel brought the crowd to its feet with thunderous applause.

"What is theese wet–T-shirt contest?" Natasha asked Riley. They were now in their own booth.

"Well, ma'am, I believe you'd win."

"There are prizes?"

Things were finally getting to be fairly normal for an Empty Creek Sunday afternoon.

Having determined that no one needed a designated driver or rider, the party broke up and everyone dispersed.

Riding back, claustrophobia enveloped Penelope as they left the trail and headed into the desert again. Her shoulders twitched and she shuddered at the chill along her spine. This is foolish, she told herself, nudging Chardonnay between Wally and Laney. "Hi, guys," she said with a cheer she didn't feel. "I didn't want to miss the next installment of Guinevere and the Cowboy Dude with Vertigo."

After tucking Chardonnay and the bunny rabbits into bed for the night, Penelope, Big Mike, and Andy went back into the house. Penelope left her guys on the couch watching the evening news and went into the bedroom closet. She fumbled behind the dresses, slacks, jeans, and blouses crammed on hangers and pulled out a long canvas container. Unzipping it, she removed the rifle and automatically worked the action to ensure it was unloaded. She brought it to her shoulder in a swift, practiced movement, sighted on the wall switch, and slowly squeezed the trigger.

Click.

"Get off my grave," she said. "Whoever you are."

CHAPTER FIFTEEN

After reassuring Andy that she was not sick when she got up with him at his usual ungodly hour of six a.m., Penelope kissed him good-bye and slipped away from the house herself, leaving Big Mike in bed to sleep for both of them.

She felt a little guilty for deserting Big Mike, but she didn't want a hearing-impaired cat, so he never went to the shooting range with her. He refused to wear earplugs — she'd tried — and she doubted he would wear earmuffs either, even if she had them custom made.

The sky had clouded up overnight and the grim overcast promised rain soon. With the threat of weather and the early hour on a Monday morning, Penelope had the rifle range to herself, although there were several handgun shooters on the pistol range.

By the time she had arranged her equipment — shooting stool, spotting scope, U.S. Marine Corps Competitive Rifleman's

Scorebook — the rangemaster called a cease-fire, a twenty-minute interval allowing the shooters to go down range and change targets. Penelope walked out to the two-hundred-yard line and placed the target for the first course of fire, two sighting rounds and twenty shots for record in competition.

Back on the firing line, Penelope donned her leather shooting jacket and cinched it tight. The Marine Corps utility cap was next. Shooting glasses. Earmuffs to protect *her* hearing. She took her position on the line and lifted an imaginary rifle to her shoulder — no one touched a weapon during a ceasefire — and visualized firing the first round right into the center of the X-ring, the smaller bull's-eye of the black circle that encompassed the nine and ten rings and was invisible at two hundred yards. The best shooters under the right conditions shot possibles, two hundred out of two hundred points and shots in the X-ring were used as tiebreakers. When a very good shooter, man or woman, was asked "How did you do offhand?" the response was usually something along the order of "Fifteen." That meant fifteen Xs. The two hundred was taken for granted.

The rangemaster recited all the safety instructions over the loudspeaker and then said, "The range is hot."

In her mind, Penelope went through the standard Marine Corps litany.

Ready on the right.

Penelope took her Colt Sporter, the latest civilian version of the military's M-16 service rifle, from the rack and set the sights from memory.

Ready on the left.

All ready on the firing line.

You may commence firing when your targets appear.

She inserted the magazine and loaded one round, letting the bolt slam forward. She twisted the rifle stock into the shoulder pad, seating it firmly, and slowly brought the rifle down on the target.

She thought of nothing now, focusing solely on the front sight, holding on the black bull's-eye at six o'clock. She took a deep breath, let out half, took up the trigger slack, and squeezed.

She called the shot and marked her scorebook — a ten at nine o'clock — before looking downrange through the spotting scope. The shot was in the black but in the nine-ring at ten o'clock. She adjusted for elevation and windage, loaded her second sighter, and repeated the entire process.

Again she called a ten at nine o'clock, marked it, and looked through the scope, smiling at the tiny gleam of light in the X-ring.

Thoughts of murder, old and new, and strange voices disappeared. Penelope fired for her own personal record, at ease with the rifle and the target and the familiar repetition of breathing in, the exhale, the slight pressure on the trigger, interrupting the squeeze if the sight drifted off the six o'clock hold, continuing when the sight picture was perfect again. Penelope sent her last round downrange and glanced at her stopwatch. Eighteen minutes. That was good, slow, methodical shooting, and she was rewarded with a score of one ninety-one and nine Xs.

Penelope nodded with satisfaction. It was something only shooters understood, that it soothed the soul to make loud noises with a finely tuned instrument and punch holes in a distant piece of paper.

It didn't hurt any to know that the next time somebody started blasting away with a high-powered rifle, this particular soul was prepared to blast right back.

By the time Penelope had returned home, cleaned and oiled the rifle, and cleaned and oiled herself, a light, cold rain was falling, which meant that one big baby had to be carried to the Jeep under the protection of a seldom-used umbrella. While Penelope enjoyed walking in the rain, the big baby didn't. It was one of the few things they disagreed about, but Mycroft was content to leave water to the fishes and worms. Good riddance too.

Once deposited safely — and dry — in the comfortable environs of Mycroft & Company, the big baby scooted for the fireplace and curled up before the fire laid by Kathy.

"It looks like you have a companion for the day," Penelope said, defying superstition by leaving the umbrella open indoors to dry.

"I take that to mean you're off again."

"I'm running out to the DDC to count dynamite, and then I'm having lunch with Boris and Natasha."

Penelope had to admit that the Desert Development Company kept their dynamite under tight security. McCory opened the locked warehouse. It was a temporary structure, but sturdy enough to withstand the casual thief. Inside, McCory pointed to a heavy screen from floor to ceiling. Behind it, two boxes sat on a shelf.

"There it is," McCory said. "All secure,

just like I told you."

"Did you open it when the police were here?"

"No."

"Why don't we just take a look?" Penelope suggested. "Just to be sure."

McCory sighed. "If it'll make you happy." He unlocked the door set in the heavy mesh and pried open the lid on the first box. He shrugged. "Dynamite."

"It's all there?"

"Yep."

"What about the second box?"

"You're persistent. I'll give you that." He carefully lifted the box off the stack and set it aside. When the second box was open, McCory said, "I'll be damned."

"What did you find?" Penelope asked.

"Bricks."

"Do you want to call the police, or shall I?"

By the time Tweedledee and Tweedledum arrived, Penelope had ascertained that several people had keys to the warehouse in addition to McCory — a foreman, several crew chiefs, security guards. But McCory had the only key to the area where the dynamite was stored. "I keep it with me all the time," he said.

"Anyone could take a cast of the padlock and get a key made," Penelope said. "Better start checking all the locksmiths in town."

Tweedledee nodded glumly. "It won't do any good. If he's smart, he just drove into Phoenix and had the key made there."

"Probably," Penelope agreed cheerfully. "But what the hell."

"Yeah, what the hell. What are you going to be doing while we're out in the rain?"

"Having lunch."

Penelope Warren, girl detective and astute observer, deduced immediately that Cricket was a libertarian when she opened the door holding a copy of *Reason* magazine. "I prefer Jimmy Buffet and the Parrot Head Party myself," Penelope said. "So does Mycroft."

"I enjoy reading about the folly of government."

" 'The less government we have, the better — the fewer laws, and the less confided power,' " Penelope said. "Ralph Waldo Emerson. I'm getting as bad as Boris. Always quoting someone. Is it still illegal to shoot jackrabbits from cable cars in San Francisco?"

"Probably. Come on in. Coffee?"

"Thanks, but I don't have time. Too much to do."

"You are out and about early for someone who doesn't like to get up."

"Busy day. Been shooting. Out to the DDC. Lunch with visiting Russians. Contemplation planned for later."

"One at a time. Shooting?"

"Just keeping my hand in. I can still hit a target. One of these days, I think I'll go back to competitive shooting."

"Are you afraid?"

"Not really. But the next time someone shoots at me, I think I'll shoot back."

"It's still hard for me to believe Buxter killed my father."

"If he listened to the wrong voices . . ." Penelope told her about the mysterious voice on the tape and the missing dynamite. "I think you should come into town and listen to the tape. Perhaps you'll recognize the voice."

"I'll follow you in."

Dutch played and replayed the snippet of tape. Cricket frowned in concentration, shaking her head. "It's too distorted," she said finally.

"See," Dutch said. "Now will you get your head out of 1973 and into the present?"

"What about the Mahoney clan?" Penelope asked.

"They all have alibis for the time of the DeForest killing."

"Not if they provide taped messages to their long-lost brother. You need to learn to suspend disbelief, Dutch."

"I need to teach my people to open boxes of dynamite."

"An honest mistake, but don't change the subject."

"All right, just suppose someone told Buxter Mahoney to protect the dinosaur twenty-five years ago, and Cricket's father, may he rest in peace, came along and was murdered to keep the secret. It's more likely that old man Mahoney was the shooter. And even if it was Buxter, why would he take up the mission again after so many years?"

"Someone told him to."

"Who?"

Penelope turned to Cricket. "You knew Buxter. Can you think of any place he might go to hide out?"

"Now who's changing the subject? You want to hear the other tape?"

"I was right?" Penelope asked. "There was something on it?"

"You were right, but they couldn't get

311

much." Dutch switched cassettes and hit the play button.

"Arooo, Kingman, Kingman."

"That's it?"

"Yep?"

"Now, what in the hell does Kingman, Arizona, have to do with anything?"

"The weirdo who blew up the Federal Building in Oklahoma City hung out there for a while. Maybe someone told Mahoney to go live in Kingman for a while."

"You think some militia group is branching out into dinosaurs?"

"Finance a lot of fertilizer bombs with the proceeds of an illegal dinosaur sale."

"That's just too strange."

Penelope sat in the Jeep, feeling a little like Humphrey Bogart on a stakeout and thinking, This is where the private eye lights a cigarette to help him ponder the imponderable. She watched the rain streak the windshield on the outside and her breath steam the inside, waiting for a crime-fighting inspiration. No wonder private eyes always smoked. It gave them something to do while waiting for that key revelation to wander up from the subconscious or wherever it happened to be hiding out. She drew a smiley face with her finger in the steamed glass, hoping that a cheerful attitude would stimulate her subconscious. All that did was leave her forefinger wet and smudged with dirt and remind her that it was time to give the Jeep a good scrub down fore and aft — when the rain stopped.

A game of tick-tack-toe — she won — occupied another minute and dirtied her fingertip again, but brought her no closer to a prophetic vision. Three games later, Penelope decided she was making her head hurt. She dampened her fingers with the moisture on the windshield and held them to her temples. It was cool and refreshing and eased the warning pain. She started the Jeep and turned the defroster on full blast. That was a good thing about the Jeep. The heater blasted away and quickly obliterated the windshield of all signs of frustration. She pulled out of the parking lot and headed for the Double B, seriously considering her retirement from sleuthing.

" 'The more cunning a man is, the less he suspects that he will be caught in a simple thing. The more cunning a man is, the simpler the trap he must be caught in.' " So much for cooling the Dostoyevsky. Boris tossed back a straight shot of vodka before pulling out the chair for Penelope.

"Don't you ever say good morning or good afternoon?" Penelope asked. Because of the rain, Big Mike had declined the invitation to cross the street to the Double B. It was probably just as well. As a young cat in Ethiopia, Mikey had developed a distaste for Russian novelists generally and Dostoyevsky in particular, when the manuscript of a translation of *The Brothers Karamazov* from English into Amharic fell on his head. The fact that Mikey had caused the unfortunate incident mattered not a whit. Big Mike had never forgiven the Master.

"Too mundane. The Master has said it all. Do you know the quotation?"

"Too easy," Penelope said. "*Crime and Punishment.* 'There is, if you recollect, a suggestion that there are certain persons who can . . . that is, not precisely are able to, but have a perfect right to commit breaches of morality and crimes, and that the law is not for them.' "

"You see."

"Hi, Penelope. The usual?"

"Hi, Debbie. You're looking perky today."

"Sam agreed to pose for the calendar, so he got a reward last night."

"When you come back from memory

land, I'll have the usual and a cheeseburger with fries. I'm starved."

"Okay. Another milk shake for the lady?"

"Could I please have chocolate this time?" Katerina asked.

"She's already had vanilla and cherry," Debbie said with admiration. "She has to keep her strength up. She's going to enter the wet–T-shirt contest. She also has a date with Riley."

"Good for you," Penelope said. Old Riley sure had found an interesting way to court a lady.

"I shall get a gold medal yet and give it to Riley."

"Another vodka too, please, dear lady."

"I'll be right back."

"Well," Penelope said. "Thank you for inviting me."

"We are delighted," Katerina said. "It is our honor. We hope you can help us."

" 'Nobody knows anything,' " Penelope said.

"That is not the Master," Boris protested.

"No, but he is a master," Penelope said. "William Goldman, author of *Adventures in the Screen Trade*, from which the quote comes. He was talking about the film industry, but it holds true for detecting. 'Nobody knows anything,' " Penelope repeated, "until they do, of course. He also wrote *The Princess Bride* and *Butch Cassidy and the Sundance Kid.* Definitely a master."

"I do not understand," Boris said.

" 'Raindrops Keep Falling on My Head,' " Katerina said. "You should get a bicycle and give me a ride on the handlebars like Paul Newman."

"It would give me a heart attack."

"Good. Then you could get a heart transplant. You need a happy heart."

"I have my vodka. That makes my heart happy. The Master says . . ."

Fortunately, Debbie arrived at that moment, forestalling another quotation from Dostoyevsky. Penelope was beginning to agree with Mycroft about the Master.

With drinks and milk shake distributed, Penelope took a sip of her Chardonnay and asked, "How can I help you?"

"We know that Cohen is cousins to what you call the Russian Mafia."

"But we don't know that he has your missing fossils, nor do we know who killed Cornelius Hacker and Millicent DeForest, blew up a hillside, and took a shot at a balloon in which I happened to be riding at the time."

"What does this have to do with fossils

taken illegally from Mother Russia?"

"Perhaps nothing," Penelope answered, "perhaps everything."

"We want you to meet Cohen and offer to sell him a dinosaur. It is the simple trap, you see, for the cunning man."

"But I don't have a dinosaur."

"He doesn't know that. You will ask to see his bona fides."

"Which are?"

"The missing fossils, of course."

"This is beginning to sound awfully complicated. Why should the buyer show the seller anything but money?"

"There are certain details to be worked out."

"I should say so. Where is Mr. Cohen anyway? Shouldn't you be skulking about in an alley, keeping tabs on him?"

Boris smiled. It was the first time Penelope had seen a hint of anything other than melancholy about the Russian policeman. "Mr. Cohen kindly accepted Katerina's offer of hospitality."

"Then shouldn't he be with us?"

"He's waiting in our suite."

"Willingly?"

"Not exactly. He's tied up in a chair."

"That's kidnapping, and not a simple plan at all. The Master would call it stupid."

"We didn't want him to disappear while we talked with you."

"We left the television on," Katerina said, "and gave him a choice of detergent operas or CNN. He chose detergents."

"Soaps," Penelope corrected Katerina automatically, "but it's still illegal. I think we'd better go release him."

"First we ask him some more questions. He is rockwalling."

"Stonewalling. No, we release him," Penelope said firmly, "and *then* you can ask your questions. *If* he doesn't press charges."

"But what about our plan?"

"Your plan," Katerina said. "Mine was better."

Penelope wasn't sure she wanted to know but asked anyway. "And what was that?"

"I was going to make him drink ten gallons of caffe latte. Russian Mafia hate coffee with milk. It is not masculine."

Ordinarily, Penelope might have taken the opportunity for a pleasant walk in the rain, but under the present circumstances she bundled Boris and Natasha into the Jeep and sped down Empty Creek Highway, waving at Guido with a cheerfulness she did not feel. What *were* they thinking? You couldn't just abduct someone, tie him up, and give him a choice of soap operas or CNN. And if you were determined to do such a thing, the very least you could do was offer one of the racy movies on cable, even if it did put a crimp in a tight budget.

"What room?" Penelope asked when she pulled into the parking lot.

"The Jacaranda Suit."

"Suite."

Familiar with the labyrinthian sprawl of the Lazy Traveller, Penelope led the way past the Olympic-sized swimming pool and up the stairs to the adult suites. When she reached the door of the Jacaranda Suite and the Do Not Disturb placard hanging from the doorknob, she stepped aside and motioned for Boris to open the door.

A soap opera theme song thundered when Boris pushed the door open. The adult suites were soundproofed so consenting adults could squeal and frolic without disturbing the other guests.

Boris frowned. "We did not leave the volume so loud." He pushed Penelope and Katerina out of the way and entered the room.

Penelope looked past him at the bound figure slumped in the chair.

It seemed that Yitzhak Cohen had peddled his last fragment from the Dead Sea Scrolls.

CHAPTER SIXTEEN

Penelope was unfamiliar with daytime television except for weekend or holiday football games. She could not recall ever seeing one of the network "Howdy, America" shows or any of their local counterparts. Even on the rare occasions when she was sick and took to her bed, she preferred the soothing, even medicinal company of Big Mike and a good novel — even a bad novel was preferable to sitcom reruns or the tortured machinations of soap operas and their tangled interpersonal relationships. But Penelope would always associate soap operas with death now.

The melancholy, haunting theme of whatever soap was drawing to a close filled the room. She stood between Boris and Natasha, looking down at Yitzhak Cohen. He had seen his fate clearly. His eyes were wide and the fear remained, even in death. The dead eyes were glazed and Penelope forced herself to meet the blank stare, as though she might see the last image recorded there. But the dark eyes revealed nothing. She turned away then, steeling herself against the sickness she felt, and took charge, but the memory of the bullet hole in Cohen's forehead and the trickle of blood were burned into her consciousness for so long as she might live.

She pulled her sweater down over her hand to preserve any fingerprints the killer might have left and gently turned the volume down. The program seguéd silently into commercials.

For once Boris lacked an apt quotation from Dostoyevsky. Nastasha shook her head sadly. "What do we do?" she asked. "What is the procedure in your country?"

"Probably the same as Russia. We don't touch anything and we call the police. I'll use the pay phone downstairs. You better come with me."

Penelope called Dutch's private line rather than 911. There was no use in having the cavalry arrive with red lights and sirens. Cohen was past caring, and she could see the door to the suite. The scene would remain undisturbed while they waited.

"I was just leaving, darling," Dutch answered. "Go ahead and get naked in front of the fire. I won't be long."

"I'm afraid you will," Penelope said. "I've got a situation here."

"Oh, no."

"Oh, yes."

Penelope explained quickly. "And, Dutch?"

"Yeah?"

"Stop by the store and pick up Mikey for me. You know how he'd hate being left out."

"Good God almighty."

The phone went dead in Penelope's ear. But he didn't slam it down. That was a good sign. She needed Big Mike for a little companionship in the face of violent death. She replaced the receiver in its cradle. Less than a minute later she heard the first siren wail. So much for remaining discreet. In two minutes, black and whites were screeching to a halt. Police officers leaped out, loosening the straps on their holsters. His hand on the butt of his service weapon, Sam Connors was ready for a little action. "Where is it, Penelope?"

"Up there." She pointed to the Jacaranda Suite. "But there's no one there except the deceased. He was shot in the forehead."

The Fourth Estate checked in. It was a standing rule of Empty Creek journalism to chase ambulances and police cars. Penelope gave Andy a kiss on the cheek and quickly filled him in.

The light but steady rain did not keep guests indoors. A group of curious on-lookers quickly gathered, standing under overhangs and the awning that covered the bar that served sunbathers at poolside, watching as the police secured the scene.

Dutch — and Big Mike — arrived with his Kojak light flashing on the top of his car. Penelope supposed a little Code Three might help dampen impending ardor and hoped he had remembered to call Stormy and tell her to get dressed again. Her sister could be so susceptible to colds.

"I'm thinking of taking up the bagpipes," Dutch said. "Something soothing for my retirement."

"If this keeps up," Penelope replied, "I'll join you. I've always wanted to play the bagpipes."

Big Mike mewed loudly. Bagpipes be damned. Where's my umbrella? Penelope smiled. He could be so expressive.

The facts of the case, such as they were, seemed clear. Yitzhak Cohen had been shot once in the forehead with a handgun, probably a .22 or .25 caliber, by a person or persons as yet unknown who had ignored the

Do Not Disturb sign. The killer had used the volume of the television to mask the sound of the shot. The window of opportunity had been one hour and fifty-seven minutes. There was no sign of forced entry. Rigorous questioning of hotel staff — maids, bellhops, room service waiters — revealed nothing. No one had seen anyone or anything out of the ordinary.

The search of the suite shared by Boris and Natasha — she had the bedroom; he slept on the couch in the living room — revealed little except that the Russians traveled sparely, with a minimum of luggage. Penelope supposed rubles were at a premium for field trips. Boris used the bar to keep a bottle of vodka and the two most recent issues of *Playboy*, both well perused. Natasha had apparently used a good portion of her per diem to purchase American cosmetics and flimsy underwear.

There were fingerprints galore, but they'd belong to Boris and Natasha, and perhaps Cohen if he had managed to touch anything before getting tied up. Anyone clever enough to enter a locked room in a large motel without being seen and commit what was beginning to look like a pretty flawless murder would be smart enough to wear gloves.

Tweedledee and Tweedledum entered Cohen's suite with a passkey provided by a very nervous day manager. "Hey, boss, better take a look."

Penelope beat Dutch to the door.

Cohen's suite had been tossed, but good.

"Damn!" Dutch said. "All right, leave it until we get photographs."

"Well, what did you expect?" Penelope asked. "Whoever killed him was looking for something. Presumably, he found it, because he didn't need Cohen anymore."

"Boris and Natasha could have found what they were after and killed him before they met you for lunch, using you as their alibi."

"I don't think they did it."

"Why not? They had motive and opportunity. That would explain why no one saw anything out of the ordinary."

"Mikey likes Natasha."

Big Mike was, indeed, curled up in Natasha's lap, consoling the distraught woman in his very best bedside manner — purring incessantly.

"He's been wrong before."

"Only once, and that didn't really count."

"The time of death, then, would seem to be important."

"*If* we can narrow it down far enough."

Penelope frowned. The only good thing she could see about the day so far was that no one was shouting Fire in the hole!

Yet.

"Come on, Mikey, let's go help the nice detectives sort out Mr. Cohen's room."

"Don't pick on them, dammit," Dutch said.

"You sure get out of sorts when you're deprived of an afternoon tryst."

Tweedledee and Tweedledum searched the late Yitzhak Cohen's room by cleaning up the mess and restoring order, putting drawers back in the dresser and desk, replacing clothes on hangers, picking up toilet articles, sifting through the bed coverings without bothering to replace them.

Penelope's contribution was to play the role of interested observer and to gather up far-flung fragments of the Dead Sea Scrolls and pieces of the true cross.

The search revealed that Cohen's taste in liquor and magazines ran to cheap scotch and *Penthouse*. A copy of Nora's guide to Empty Creek — the first edition, not the second — and *The Maltese Falcon* appeared to be his only reading material. Apparently he had memorized the guidebook, for the pages were well thumbed. Thankfully, there was no evidence of Dostoyevsky anywhere in the suite. He wore boxer shorts and his socks were all black or brown. There were three ties.

With the room more or less restored to order, Tweedledee and Tweedledum started through it again, more to stay away from Dutch's wrath than in the hope of finding anything resembling a clue.

"I've never heard of anything so stupid," Dutch shouted for about the umpteenth time. With the doors open for a steady stream of officials, the soundproofing was not working.

If Boris or Natasha replied, Penelope could not hear it. She sat at the small desk in the late Mr. Cohen's suite, idly playing with fragments purportedly from the Dead Sea Scrolls. She had to admit that they looked authentic. The largest measured about four inches across. The smallest was about the size of a man's thumbnail.

"Dumb, dumb, dumb!"

Penelope agreed with Dutch's assessment. She moved the parchment fragments about like chess pieces, remembering idle summer afternoons looking up at cloud formations to discover duckies and horseys in the billowing shapes. One of the pieces actually *did* resemble a ducky. With a little imagination, one oddly-shaped fragment managed to become a skunk in her mind's eye.

While Penelope jumbled the Dead Sea Scrolls, Big Mike played pick-up sticks with the toothpicks that the late Mr. Cohen had represented as having come from the true cross.

With just a bit more inventiveness, the parchment became a Rorschach test. "Good God," Penelope said, "I wonder what Nicole would make of *that?*"

"What are you doing?"

"First, I saw a ducky and a little skunky and then I took the Rorschach test, but I'm not going to tell you what I saw there."

"That's definitely a phallic symbol," Tweedledee said, pointing to a fragment that did, indeed, take after a phallic symbol if your symbols came shaped rather like a fat jelly doughnut on a stick. "And looky there." He smirked. "I know what that is. . . ."

"Oh, never mind. I'm sorry I brought it up."

Mikey was bored with pick-up sticks and looked over to see what Penelope was doing. He pushed the jelly doughnut and the oh-never-mind together, mewing softly to ask if that was how this particular game was played.

Penelope stared at the two fragments. They fit together like . . . like . . . a jigsaw puzzle. Penelope quickly scattered the fragments again, glancing over her shoulder at Tweedledee. He was engrossed in a close examination of the skunk fragment.

Catching on to the rules, Big Mike batted the pile of fragments across the smooth surface of the desk. Several dropped to the floor.

"Furball's always making a mess." He tossed the skunk toward the desk. Big Mike caught it in midair and sent it flying into the left field corner — ground rule double, at least. Leaping off the desk, he pranced sideways across the room and whacked it again. One mighty bound later, he had recovered the fumble on the ten-yard line. Penelope wondered what the Essene monks would think of that. Footbaseball enlivened the boring national pastime. That's what Mikey thought.

"A gentleman would pick them up," Penelope said.

"That's right," Tweedledee agreed. "A gentleman would."

"Forget it. I'll do it."

Penelope pinched the Dead Sea Scroll fragments then. For good measure she threw in the pieces of the true cross and

Nora's guidebook.

The motel manager knocked timidly on the door. "I have the telephone records you asked for."

"I'll start calling them," Penelope said.

"Who's gonna pay for it?" Tweedledee asked. "Dutch won't want to do the calling from here."

"We'll tell him later. There aren't that many. Only a couple of pages." And speaking of guidebooks, Penelope punched in a familiar number listed on the second page.

"Hi, Nora, why was Yitzhak Cohen calling you from his motel room?"

"He thought the president of the historical society might know where to find fossils."

Good God, Penelope thought. Did Cohen spend his time cold-calling like a real estate agent? Hi, want to sell your house? Shalom, any fossils for sale today? Well, then, how about something in a Dead Sea Scroll or a bit of the true cross? Penelope was surprised he hadn't gotten around to hawking the Shroud of Turin. Perhaps he would have if he had lived.

"Penelope? Are you there?"

"Just thinking. What did you tell him?"

"That the only fossils I had weren't for sale."

"You have some fossils?"

"Of course not. Just what's in the museum. He hinted there might be a profit for me if the fossils suddenly disappeared."

"Why didn't you report it?"

"He didn't come right out and make an offer. He just danced around the subject. There was no proof. What's happened?"

"Mr. Cohen has met an untimely demise."

"Oops."

"What does that mean?"

"I was going to meet him. See if I could trick him into making a real offer."

"That's entrapment."

"Oh."

Penelope went through the rest of the numbers quickly. One equally familiar number was the reference desk at the library. Cohen had asked Noogy what dinosaur materials were on hand. He had also called the drugstore — no one remembered the call — Delta Airlines — ditto, of course — and Hayden Chudnik. "He wanted fossils. I told him I couldn't help him."

Penelope reached an answering machine with the last number. "Hi, this is Schyler. Leave a message and I'll return your call as soon as possible."

Penelope hung up and looked at the

sheet. Cohen had made the call the previous evening and talked for eleven minutes. But that wouldn't be unusual, Penelope thought. Schyler did have an interest in dinosaurs. She wondered if Schyler had a larcenous heart as well.

A glum Boris and Natasha were listening to their rights when Penelope and Big Mike returned to the Jacaranda Suite. "Do you understand these rights as I have explained them to you?" Sam Connors asked.

Boris nodded.

"But I have a date," Natasha wailed when Peggy Norton put the handcuffs on her wrists. Big Mike rubbed against the Russian woman's legs in an expression of sympathy. Or he might have been doing *his* Humphrey Bogart imitation. Don't worry, sweetheart, we'll bust you out of the slam tonight.

"With a cell," Dutch said.

"But Riley . . ."

"What are you charging them with?" Penelope asked.

"Congenital stupidity."

"That's not a crime."

"It should be."

"I want to call my embassy," Boris said.

"That's a conversation I'd like to hear," Dutch said. "Mr. Ambassador, dumb cop here. I kidnapped an Israeli national on American soil, tied him up, questioned him without an attorney present, and then went off to lunch so he could be murdered in my hotel suite. Go ahead. Drop a dime or two. How do you spell Siberia? Siberia *is* still there, or did you lose that with the rest of the Evil Empire?"

"You've got their passports. Where are they going to go?"

"I've got two Russian cops too, and I'm keeping them until this mess is straightened out."

"Don't worry, Katerina, I'll tell Riley where you are. He can visit you. Maybe he'll bring a pizza."

"With everything?"

"Sure, with everything."

"Even anchovies?"

"A double helping if you like," Penelope said, smiling, hoping Riley liked anchovies on his pizza. But, then, love conquered all — even the dreaded anchovy pizza.

Penelope watched as Boris and Natasha were put in separate units and driven away. Having been handcuffed and in the back of a police car once — Tweedledee had overreacted, as usual — Penelope knew that Natasha would find the ride to the local pokey uncomfortable. With your hands handcuffed behind your back, there was no way to ease the awkward position. It would be doubly so for such a large woman.

"I'm going back to the office and write this while it's all fresh," Andy said.

"I'll see you later, sweetie?"

"Of course."

Soon, Penelope was standing alone. Big Mike was already in the Jeep. The rain had turned into a light drizzle. She looked around the empty courtyard and then up at the crime scene tape that sealed the Jacaranda Suite.

What a wretched and forlorn day to die, she thought, turning away at last to walk to the Jeep. She did not see Hiroshi Ishii watching her go.

Having tampered with potential evidence — she admitted to herself that *stealing* evidence was a more appropriate description — Penelope set course for the solitude of home.

With Big Mike's assistance, she quickly fit the Dead Sea Scroll fragments together. When she had finished, a large parchment with curling edges on many of the pieces covered the kitchen table. The outer edge of the puzzle was ragged. There were several gaps, including one big hole right in the center. The missing pieces probably represented what Cohen had peddled before his death. Cricket's brother had one of them.

"Now, isn't that interesting, Mikey?"

They both stared at the puzzle before them.

"But so what?" Penelope said finally.

Obviously, Cohen had used an animal skin to make his bogus scrolls, tearing it apart to provide any number of potential sales to the gullible. Of course, the skin would fit together like a jigsaw puzzle.

She turned to Nora's guidebook, letting it fall open where it may. It was Driving Tour Number Four — to the backcountry beyond Lonesome Bend. She leafed through the pages. Like any well-read book, it opened naturally to sections that had been examined over and over again. Considering Driving Tour Number Four, Penelope was not surprised to find that the book also opened to the corresponding map in the appendix.

"So what?" Penelope repeated. "A dinosaur was found at Lonesome Bend. Therefore, Yitzhak Cohen, a man interested in fossils and suspected of possessing stolen fossils, would find the Lonesome Bend sections of the guidebook required reading."

There were just too damned many "sowhats" in this case.

"And how does it relate to 1973, Millicent DeForest, and Yitzhak Cohen? Who is killing the fossil people?"

Penelope went to the refrigerator and pulled out a bottle of wine. Then she put it back without opening it. A refrigerator magnet — a movie poster of *Chinatown* — fell off. She picked it up and replaced it. It fell off again when she retrieved the bottle of wine. Jack Nicholson was getting on her nerves.

"We need a plan, Mikey."

Doubtless, Big Mike agreed, because he said, "Grr." It was his soft God-I-love-lima-beans growl.

"A simple plan," she quickly amended, recalling Boris's lunchtime recitation from Dostoyevsky. "But what?"

What indeed?

She left the wine on the counter and dialed Schyler's number again. This time she left a message.

Big Mike growled with greater urgency and then leaped to the floor when Penelope played the magic tune on the electric can opener and doled out a generous portion of lima beans. With Big Mike happy for the moment, Penelope finally poured a glass of wine and sat at the kitchen table. She began to read Nora's guidebook.

"Beyond Lonesome Bend are the fabled badlands, which have contributed so much to western lore and legend. At mile two there are the ruins of an adobe house where Bad Jack Burke lived with three Mexican mistresses after his release from the territorial prison in 1907, where he served seventeen years for bank robbery and murder. Burke died in 1913. Stop at this landmark in the late evening and listen carefully. It is said that his mistresses can still be heard lamenting his passing. Apparently, Bad Jack was a much better lover than he was a bank robber.

"Once beyond the old Burke place, the wild desert rules. The uninitiated should not stray from the dirt road. . . ."

Penelope closed the book. If Buxter Mahoney lived out there, he was certainly initiated in the ways of desert survival. But why would he come into town and kill Cohen and search his room? If Buxter *was* out there, how would he even know Cohen existed?

"All right, Penelope, go back to the beginning and look at this logically. Millicent DeForest was presumably murdered because voices told Buxter Mahoney to protect the dinosaur at all costs, duplicating the twenty-five-year-old murder of Cornelius Hacker. The news of the dinosaur's discovery brings a horde of foreign dinosaur seekers, who were already nearby for the annual gem, mineral, and dinosaur show, into Empty Creek. An Israeli lowlife suspected of stealing or, at least, being in the possession of stolen Russian fossils, is then murdered."

Penelope sipped her wine. "This isn't logical, Mikey, it's madness."

Fortunately, Penelope was saved from further descent into lunacy by the sound of Andy driving up. She poured him a glass of wine, thinking that he had really ripped through the story. She also contemplated a quick striptease to test his vital signs, but was glad she had refrained, when the doorbell rang. Andy never rang the doorbell. Oh, well, whatever weary traveler was at the door would probably welcome alcoholic refreshment — unless the Temperance Society had come calling.

Penelope flung the door open. "Welcome, weary traveler," she said.

Hiroshi Ishii stood there with a bottle of sake cradled in his arm and a troubled expression on his face. So much for the inscrutable and implacable face of the Orient.

CHAPTER SEVENTEEN

While Penelope was skilled in the art of providing light-hearted and entertaining company for her man and her friends, she was fairly certain that a proper geisha girl would rather die than be caught heating sake in a microwave oven, but Hiroshi-san did not seem to mind. After several bows to Penelope and Big Mike, he had left his shoes on the porch and, as a result, seemed to have caught a chill. He was now sneezing at regular intervals, apologizing after each "gesundheit" or "bless you" uttered by Penelope. Since he refused to put his shoes back on, Penelope trotted out a space heater. It was either that or waste perfectly good sake by pouring it over his feet.

Nor did Penelope believe that a well-trained geisha would serve sake in coffee mugs or prance like a demented Clydesdale across the kitchen to bang the mugs down on the table, hissing, "Ow, ow, damn, that's hot!" But that's what came of improvisation. Had she anticipated a Japanese gentleman, late of the Yakusa, coming to call with a bottle of sake in arm, Penelope might have purchased a complete sake serving set, some bamboo mats, the handbook for geishas — surely, such an ancient profession had managed to produce an instructional manual for all occasions — and, given enough notice, even the proper clothing. As an apprentice geisha, however, Penelope made do with the materials at hand but drew the line at washing his back.

Still, while her sake ceremony may have lacked certain qualities of grace, style, and tradition, there was compensation in effectiveness — the sake was served quickly and it was hot. A grateful Hiroshi Ishii bowed, even though he was seated, and murmured his gratitude before sipping.

"Ah," he sighed.

Penelope joined in the solemnity of the occasion, raising her mug to her lips, and tasting of the fiery liquid. "Ow," she repeated, thinking the extra minute in the microwave had been a little too much. That was just about the fourth or fifth strike in her geisha career.

"You are most kind," Hiroshi-san said.

"You are welcome in our home," Penelope replied.

"Thank you. I have never been in an American home, only the motel."

"You were there this afternoon? You know about Mr. Cohen?"

"Yes. It is most sad. I must now commit hara-kiri."

Now, that was a showstopper if Penelope had ever heard one, and she had, ranking right up there with "Frankly, my dear, I don't give a damn." It was also a ceremony she had no wish to participate in. Think fast, Penelope told herself. Where was that damned manual when you needed it?

She glanced around, looking for a sword. Her knowledge of hara-kiri was sadly lacking in many respects, but she believed the sword was traditional, although she supposed any sharp instrument would do. I suppose it's too late to lock up the kitchen knives, she thought.

"Why?"

"I am a failure, I have brought shame upon my family, and I have dishonored my ancestors."

"Is that all?" Penelope said. "We do that every day in the United States. Just look at Bill Clinton and Newt Gingrich."

"But they are politicians. It is what they do."

"You've got me there," Penelope said,

"but before you kill yourself, tell me what you were really doing here in Empty Creek."

"Truly, I was looking for fossils in my new career, but I failed miserably."

"How?"

"It was my job to protect Cohen-san. He was to deliver fossils to me. I had already paid him a substantial down payment."

"How much?"

"Ten thousand U.S. dollars."

"That's a lot of yen. You didn't happen to buy any Dead Sea Scroll fragments, did you?"

Hiroshi-san shook his head. "Only fossils. He was to deliver them the day after to-morrow, but I think he was looking for a higher bidder."

"Were they Russian fossils by any chance?"

"Yes, but they were to have a new pedi-gree. That's why he was waiting."

Well, I'll be damned, Penelope thought. Fossil laundering. "What were you going to do with them?"

"Sell them at a profit when the mineral show opens next week."

"You're still a crook," Penelope said, wondering if geishas practiced tough love.

"But not a very good one. That's why I

left the Yakusa. All I ever wanted to do was open a sushi bar. Now it's too late."

"Oh, I don't know. We could use a good sushi bar in Empty Creek."

"You think so?"

"After you do something for me. It's very simple."

"I shall do anything to redeem my honor."

"It could be dangerous."

Hiroshi-san leaped to his feet, knocking over the chair, and assumed a martial arts position. "Hai!" he shouted.

A startled Big Mike assumed his own karate position. You want to commit hara-kiri, dude, come on.

"Please," Penelope said, "don't break my table."

"Solly, Penelope-san, solly Samurai Cat. Jackie Chan is my hero."

"I can see that."

"Please, could I have more sake?"

"If you forget that hara-kiri nonsense. It's too hard to mop blood out of the linoleum cracks."

By the time Andy arrived, Penelope-san and Hiroshi-san were pleasantly soused and singing a ragged version of "Home on the Range."

"He's staying for dinner," Penelope said.

"Good," Andy said. "Mr. Ishii, there's something I've always been curious about."

"Grad to herp, if I can. Have some sake. Then, we sing arong some more." With the possibility of redemption eliminating the need for hara-kiri, and thoughts of Arizona rolls dancing in his head, Hiroshi-san was in quite a pleasant mood.

"Thank you."

"I'll get it, honeybunch."

"Thank *you*." Andy sat across from Hiroshi Ishii. "Tell me, why did kamikaze pilots wear helmets?"

Andy cleared the kitchen table of sake mugs, Dead Sea Scroll fragments, and the remnants of the true cross in preparation for setting the table. He held a fragment up to the light. "They certainly look real."

"How would you know?"

"I saw one once. Interviewed a fellow whose specialty was photographing fragments like these. He used all sorts of infrared camera techniques to bring out the writing. The one I saw was no bigger than a thumbnail. 'These are the words of Noah.' That's what it said. He was the first person in two thousand years to read it. Impressive."

"I should say so, but Cohen conjured these up last month."

"Mrs. Burnham had a fragment," Andy said.

"What do you mean, she *had* one? What did she do with it?"

"Apparently, it was stolen. She claims that aliens took it. It's all in the crime report."

"Did she happen to see the aliens? Could we get Dave Macklin to do a composite sketch? That would be worth-while." When he was not busy painting for calendar illustrations, Macklin doubled as a police artist.

"I doubt it," Andy said. He put the parchment on the kitchen counter and took plates from the cupboard.

After seeing Hiroshi-san off on his mission, and then snuggling and kissing and fooling around for a while, the morning person drifted off to slumberland while the night person was wide awake. Penelope gently disentangled herself from Andy's embrace and crept out of bed. Big Mike watched her ease into the big, fluffy bathrobe and then loyally padded after her into the kitchen and settled on the table to doze while awaiting developments.

Although she had pretended drunken joviality with Hiroshi-san, Penelope had far less sake than it appeared, believing that proper geishas would lead their charges in whatever direction they might want — within reason, of course — without ever losing control of their own faculties. And so Penelope had jollied Hiroshi-san along, tempering his initial gloom with kind ministrations and hopes for honorable redemption. The fact that he was still of a criminal mind bothered Penelope not a whit. A good con man was refreshing on occasion — and useful.

Since she had partaken sparingly of the sake and the wine at dinner, Penelope figured a nightcap wouldn't hurt, and a nice cup of sake — lukewarm this time — would be just the thing to settle a racing mind. The fact that Cohen had arranged to provide new papers for old fossils certainly added a little more zest to the puzzle.

"Question, Mikey: Who was in a position to launder official descriptions of stolen fossils?"

Mikey twitched an ear but didn't open his eyes.

"Answer: Millicent DeForest or Hayden Chudnik. The fact that Schyler downloaded the documents from the Internet suggests Millicent DeForest might not have been averse to a lucrative part-time job after school. And, Cohen called Schyler, who has not yet returned my call."

Penelope swirled the sake in her cup and raised it to smell gingerly. "This sake is just right, as Goldilocks would say if she were a drinking girl." Penelope sipped. It filled her with a pleasing warmth.

"But . . ."

Still swirling the sake around, Penelope went to the back door and opened it. Mycroft cracked one eye and followed her movements until he was satisfied that she wasn't about to run off on some adventure without him.

The rain had stopped somewhere between "Home on the Range" and dinner, and the chilly air was filled with that fresh, sweet scent of renewal and rebirth. Stars peeped brightly between the wisps of overcast that was rapidly breaking up. Tomorrow the skies would be clean and bright. But . . .

Penelope returned to the table and stroked Mikey softly. "Good old friend," she whispered. "Whatever would I do without you?"

Big Mike apparently shared the sentiment, for he started purring instantaneously. He might have been saying,

"You're not so bad either — for a non-cat, but everyone can't be so fortunate."

Penelope took it as a compliment.

But exchanging affectionate pleasantries with Big Mike wasn't getting the Fat Lady anywhere near the stage. She was probably still lounging around her dressing room, gargling with warm saltwater to keep her vocal cords in shape, or whatever a Fat Lady did in preparation before going on. "Hell, Mikey, our Fat Lady hasn't even been cast yet. She's still at home eating chocolate bonbons."

The stroke of midnight found Penelope and Big Mike in front of her computer. It was actually one a.m., because the computer had been a gift from her parents and had been set up in California during daylight saving time. Since Arizona didn't subscribe to DST, the computer's clock was an hour off and Penelope hadn't bothered to learn how to correct it. At least, it was something like that. Penelope ranked DST right up there with the international date line, Greenwich mean time, algebra, and the sound of one hand clapping among the incomprehensible mysteries of the universe. Besides, as Penelope understood it, the computer world was coming to an end when

1999 slid into 2000, because someone had forgotten to account for the new millennium. She didn't think it was such a bad thing either. Life was far too complicated anyway. Penelope planned to spend New Year's Eve 1999 watching her computer go berserk, or whatever it was going to do while learning to tell time all over again.

With that propitious moment still more than a year away, however, Penelope rapidly began typing a summary of events since planting Guido, which was just about the last useful thing anyone had accomplished in Empty Creek.

An hour later, after much cutting and pasting, Penelope was sure of several things. It was probable, even likely, that old man Mahoney and/or his eldest son, Buxter, a diagnosed schizophrenic, had killed Cornelius Hacker and buried the evidence with an explosion. Twenty-five years later, the modus operandi suggested that Buxter Mahoney, his father having dropped dead, had committed a copycat crime because Millicent DeForest had discovered the dinosaur that Buxter's electronic voices told him to protect at all costs.

At that point, it got more than a little hazy, complicated by DeForest's two boyfriends, the Desert Development Company, foreign fossil hunters, restraining orders, and dueling paleontologists.

Penelope tried to put herself in the mind of a schizophrenic to see if she, given the proper circumstances, would kill Yitzhak Cohen. But there was no good reason for Buxter Mahoney to sneak into town and knock off Cohen after searching his room. Cohen's involvement was limited, so far as anyone knew, to stolen Russian fossils unless the Israeli had seized upon Corny-Milly as a target of opportunity. But that made little sense. The newly unearthed fossil was too well known and too well guarded. And that meant the Cohen murder was unrelated to the Hacker and DeForest killings.

Or did it?

And why would someone steal Mrs. Burnham's fragment of the Dead Sea Scroll? Surely, any alien visitations to Empty Creek would focus on the social and sexual mores of the local inhabitants rather than bogus parchment. Therefore, the jigsaw puzzle with its missing pieces had some significance.

But what?

Penelope turned everything off and headed back to the kitchen. The parchment fragments had been left on the counter. She quickly rearranged the pieces on the table. The gaps were still there. Why steal a piece of fragment that by Cohen's own admission had been made only a month or so ago?

"Why?" she asked. Penelope took a deep breath, closed her eyes, and waited.

There was no reply — not from Big Mike, not from the parchment, not from the kitchen walls.

"All right," she said, opening her eyes and looking around. "Be that way. I'm going to bed."

Andy barely stirred when she snuggled close to his warm body. Penelope sighed and tried to relax. But sleep was elusive. She couldn't get rid of that nagging feeling that an answer was close at hand. Her mind already possessed the information that would make everything clear. She was sure of that. It was rumbling around somewhere in her subconscious. Her quarry was close, just beyond the next little bend in the road.

Perhaps the simple little plan that Hiroshi-san would begin in the morning would spook someone from cover. It was also possible that her plan was not simple at all, but rather just plain old simpleminded. And if it didn't work, what then?

Several possibilities came to mind — none of them good.

Penelope fell asleep, only to dream of the bogeyman. He was out there somewhere, looking a lot like Freddy Krueger.

The rain had done a most excellent job. The morning was bright and clear, the air fresh and crisp, and it seemed silly to take the rifle on such a beautiful day, but take it Penelope did. If Freddy Krueger disturbed anything more than her dreams, he was going to get a good what-for.

Hiroshi Ishii had apparently done a good job, utilizing the desert telegraph beginning with the gang at the coffee shop to let it be known that he was willing to pay top dollar, no questions asked, for certain fossils. By the time Penelope and Big Mike arrived at the bookstore, she had three messages waiting — Laney, Nora, and Noogy. All had the same information — that little Japanese fellow was up to no good.

"What are you going to do about it?" Laney asked.

"Nothing."

"You're certainly a woman of action today."

"Trust me."

"That's what the scorpion said to the frog."

"It's my nature."

"You're up to something," Nora said when she answered the telephone. "I know you."

"Ah, the beautiful Penelope plots prettily," Noogy said. "I love a woman with a devious mind."

Penelope laughed. "You're just trying to seduce me."

"But of course, dearest Penelope, using all of the weapons at my disposal — an alliterative tongue, immense charm, brilliant mind, sparkling wit . . ."

"All right," Penelope interrupted. "Ten minutes. My place or yours?" She allowed the stunned silence to continue. Ten seconds. Twenty. Thirty.

Finally, Noogy said, "Alas, duty demands my presence at the reference desk."

"I knew it. You're chicken."

"Precious Penelope?"

"Yes, Neat Noogy?"

"What would you have done had I accepted?"

"Run like hell."

"A pity."

"Yes, isn't it? Oh, well, perhaps in our next lives."

Tweedledee and Tweedledum made a rare appearance at Mycroft & Company.

"What happened to those fragments and sticks?" Tweedledee asked without preamble. "They've disappeared. Guidebook too."

"I thought you had them," Penelope replied, hoping she didn't look quite as guilty as she felt.

"Nope. Ain't seen 'em since you and the fur ball was playing with them."

"I can't imagine what could have become of them. Would you like some coffee?"

"Well, dammit, they've disappeared. You sure you don't have them?"

"Of course not," Penelope said, mustering her indignation while making a note for her next confession, whenever that might occur.

"Dutch is gonna be mad. Evidence disappearing like that."

And I'm not telling him, Penelope thought. Mother always told me I'd come to no good if I did things like that.

At the screech of brakes, the strident blare of a horn, and an angry shout, Penelope ran outside to find Alyce standing in the middle of Empty Creek Highway with an angry driver shaking his fist. "What's wrong with her? She just walked in front of me. I could have killed her."

"Just a little trance," Penelope said. "I'll take care of her." She led a blinking Alyce to the sidewalk. "What is wrong with you, Alyce?"

"Something told me to come and see you. And then . . ."

"At this rate, we're going to have to put up an Astrologer Crossing sign as well."

"Something's happening at Lonesome Bend."

"What?"

"I'm not sure. It may not have happened yet. I just have real strong feelings about it. I was trying to focus on it. That's why I went away like that."

"Concentrate, but do it inside. And let me know if you come up with anything."

"Oh, I will. And I'm supposed to tell you to be careful."

Penelope felt the chill immediately. This time they were dancing an Irish jig on her grave.

Penelope and Big Mike drove out to Lonesome Bend but found nothing but a paleontologist, two graduate assistants, and a bored Sam Connors watching them work. Alyce's vibes must have been out of kilter. With Sam present, Penelope left the rifle locked in the storage compartment of the Jeep.

"Hi, Penelope," Sam said. "What's going on?"

"Not much. Thought I'd come out and see if anything was going on around here."

"Not unless you want to know all about dinosaurs. It's pretty interesting, I guess. Did you know there was a whole field of forensic paleontology?"

"Makes sense. The doc there thinks that the Diplodocus was the victim of scavengers. An Allosaurus probably got it after it got sick or something."

"Wish we could get an Allosaurus to confess."

"Yeah. This is a tough one."

Penelope wandered over to the excavation where Cornelius Hacker's truck had been found. Big Mike was staring down a lizard on the back wall of the big blemish on the desert floor. With the old truck hauled off to the impound lot behind the ECPD, it was like standing in a dirt garage. Penelope tried to tune her psychic powers into Alyce's feelings about Lonesome Bend, but nothing came to her. She wasn't surprised. Her psychic abilities were limited largely to knowing, more often than not, who was calling when the telephone rang. "Come on, Mikey, let's go check out the other Lonesome Bend. Alyce *might* have meant Cricket's ranch."

But nothing was amiss at Lonesome Bend Ranch either. Cricket offered refreshment, but Penelope refused, saying, "I need to get back to town. I'm hoping for an important message."

"I'll see you at the council meeting tonight, then."

"Damn, that's right. With everything that's happened, I forgot about it. Well, it's our civic duty, so we'll be there."

"Good," Cricket said. "I'm going to make an announcement."

"What is it?"

"It's a secret," Cricket replied with a broad smile on her face. "You have to wait."

"I hate secrets. Unless they're mine, of course. Tell Mikey," Penelope said, intending to eavesdrop.

"Absolutely not. He'd blab the minute you were gone."

"Oh, well, I tried."

Penelope drove off, looking back at Cricket waving goodbye in the rearview mirror. Penelope returned the wave with a beep on the horn.

"Any messages for me?"

"Nope," Kathy said. "It's been very quiet."

Damn. Penelope had been positive Hiroshi-san would have called by then. Double damn. So much for simple plans.

CHAPTER EIGHTEEN

Penelope masked disappointment by performing a good deed — sending Kathy home early. "Jump Timmy's bones," she suggested. "It'll be good for morale."

"What are you going to do?"

"Work for a change. I've gotten absolutely nothing accomplished since this all started. You've been great filling in for me, and I appreciate it."

After Kathy departed, Penelope resisted the urge to call Hiroshi-san. He would report if anyone took the bait. Or he would double-cross her for the potential profit in Russian fossils. She wondered if the temptation would be too great.

Andy joined her at the Double B for dinner. He looked rather wan. Penelope immediately put her wrist to his forehead. "You're clammy," she announced.

"I don't think sake agrees with me."

"It is rather an acquired taste. Have

some chicken soup."

"Is that good for hangovers?"

"No, I think it works only on colds and the flu."

"I don't have a cold or the flu."

"Pretend."

Since the soup du jour was minestrone and lacked the mysterious curative powers of chicken broth, Andy was sent home to bed with a promise from Penelope. "If you don't feel better in the morning, *I'll* make you some chicken noodle soup."

Attendance at an Empty Creek City Council meeting was always good, not from any sense of civic pride or involvement, but rather because it was the best sitcom in town, with the free-spirited and independent citizenry in constant opposition to their elected officials, who seemed to think that the winners of baby-kissing contests were then obliged to meddle in the lives of their constituents.

Penelope's own favorite highlight of a council meeting was the night an irate homeowner, told he had to move his hundred-foot-long fence one inch to conform with city setback regulations, mooned the council to express his displeasure at their decision. That moment was closely followed by the Gay Pride Coalition protesting the denial of a parade permit by holding their parade in council chambers. The men's drill team, resplendently clad in pink hot pants, marched back and forth between the lesbians on motorcycles gunning their engines. The council, on the verge of carbon monoxide asphyxiation, hastily convened in executive session, and emerged some short time later with their previous decision permanently rescinded.

There was also the time Councilman Dignan Dimwoody, in a misguided attempt to live up to his nickname, attempted to ban a certain cat from participating in the American political process. Penelope, not about to have Big Mike disenfranchised, presented an impassioned defense of his constitutional rights and, when that failed to move the three-two majority, organized a massive animal lover's protest, flooding the council chambers at the next meeting with seventeen cats, twenty-three dogs, two parrots, a goat, a canary, and an iguana. The resulting hubbub convinced two members to change their votes if everyone would just please take their animals home. Dimbulb Dimwoody refused to change his vote, however, and he was soundly trounced at the next election, thus learning the wisdom of several political maxims — all politics is local, vote early, vote often, and never mess with the cat lobby in an election year.

Penelope and Big Mike hung out at the coffee urn. It was the first stop for all those in attendance. As one long-time council watcher said, "It's the only time we get anything useful from the city."

"Hello, Penelope."

"Hello, Mrs. Burnham. How are you tonight?"

"Frazzled. Simply frazzled. We really have to do something about these aliens. They're getting bolder, you know. The next thing you know, they'll be moving right in and driving up property prices."

"I heard you had a visitation."

"And it was such a nice Dead Sea Scroll too. I was going to have it framed."

"I wonder if you could draw it for me. The shape, I mean."

"If you like, dear."

Penelope provided pencil and paper and watched as Mrs. Burnham pursed her lips, frowned, and drew a squiggly line that upon completion looked like an amoeba squished by a passing truck. But it did resemble the large gap in the parchment puzzle.

"What's that?" Dutch asked, looking over her shoulder.

Penelope started guiltily, trying to decide if she should eat the piece of paper and the incriminating shape. She opted to crumple the sheet in her fist and shove it into her purse. "Oh, just a note to myself."

"Good evening, Sheriff."

"I'm the police chief, Mrs. Burnham."

"I know *that*. What I don't know is what you intend to do about the aliens. They're getting out of hand."

Dutch put a finger to his lips and looked around furtively. "Not a word to anyone, Mrs. Burnham," he whispered. "We have a new alien detecting device. We call it ADD for short."

"For alien detecting device?"

"Exactly. I'll send a trained officer by in the morning. If there's an alien within a thousand yards of your home, we'll zap it."

"Oh, my goodness, I don't want to hurt them. I just want them to go away."

"That's what the ADD is all about. It emits an odor that only the aliens can smell. It's very repugnant and they run from it. The ADD, you see, works on the same principle as the spray that keeps a dog from wetting your carpet."

"Ah. Isn't modern technology wonderful?" Mrs. Burnham wandered away happy.

"How are you going to get out of that whopper?"

"Wrap some tinfoil around Tweedledee's head, stuff an antenna in it, and give him a remote control to stick under her bed. 'Nope, no aliens here, Mrs. Burnham.' Piece of cake."

"Send Tweedledum along with a camera. This moment must be recorded for future generations."

"Good idea."

Dutch had such an evil grin at times. "By the way," Penelope said. "What have you done with Boris and Natasha?"

"They're safe. I don't want any more dead civilians."

"I hope you let Riley visit Natasha, at least."

"She really does like anchovies. Disgusting."

The council members were still in executive session going over legal matters with the city attorney when Schyler Bennett entered the council chambers and looked around with a bewildered expression.

Penelope sympathized. The Empty Creek City Council had that impact on newcomers. "What are you doing here, and why didn't you call me?"

"I saw the agenda posted in the library and wanted to support fossil preservation, and I *did* call you. Your answering machine isn't working."

"I don't have one."

"Everyone has an answering machine."

"Not me, but never mind. You're here now. Why did Yitzhak Cohen call you?"

"He kept thinking I knew where he could get fossils because of my relationship with Dee. He wouldn't leave me alone. I finally told him what he could do with the first fossil that came along. He had no respect for my grief over Dee."

"Please, don't think I mean any disrespect for Dr. DeForest, but I have to know. Was she involved in laundering stolen Russian fossils for Cohen?"

"Laundering? I don't know what you mean."

"It would be like laundering money for the mob. Hypothetically, Cohen might approach Dee, give her a description of the fossils, and ask her to change them slightly. New papers from a college professor would give them legitimacy, and Cohen could sell the fossils. By the time anyone discovered the papers were bogus, he would be back in Israel, selling Dead Sea Scroll fragments."

"Dee wouldn't be involved in anything

like that. She just wouldn't."

"Why did she ask you to download those particular materials from the Internet, then?" She wanted to see if his story remained consistent with what he had said on the drive back from Palm Springs.

"She didn't. She was interested in anything about dinosaurs. That just happened to be what I found for her on that occasion. It couldn't have had anything to do with her death. She didn't even know what I was bringing her. It was just some weird coincidence."

"You must be right," Penelope said reluctantly. Damn, she thought, I hate consistency.

"There's no other explanation."

Big Mike wandered off to find a good front row seat. Penelope followed and put her purse on the chair next to her to save a place for Cricket. Looking over the agenda, she found that fossil preservation was the fourth item, following the consent calendar and two home expansion items sent on to the council by the planning commission. The council members, being politicians, would rehash every minute detail of the plans before sending them back to the planning commission for additional study.

"We'll be here all night, Mikey."

"Nice sweater, Penelope," a familiar voice with the timbre of a fingernail scratching a blackboard said.

Besides being a contemporary of Daniel Boone's and chief of security at the Burning Cactus Condominium and Golf Club, the local retirement community, Cackling Ed had a propensity for looking down the blouse of every woman he met.

"I wore it just for you," Penelope said.

"Too bad. Wanna autograph my calendar?"

"No."

"How about if I pose for the men's calendar, then?"

Penelope flirted with an age discrimination lawsuit. "We're full up," Penelope lied. "But I'll put you down for next time."

"Okeydokey." Cackling Ed headed off to see the city clerk. She *was* wearing a blouse.

With the video cameras rolling, Mayor Nicole Pagliero called the meeting of the Empty Creek City Council to order. Each council meeting was recorded on tape — once by the official city volunteer camera crew from the Ham Radio Club and again by Dr. Victorio Pagliero, along with a whispered commentary, for his home movies.

"Here's Nicole calling the meeting to order," he said despite the fact that it was fairly obvious she had just called the meeting to order. He was very proud of his wife's official position and planned to have each boring moment on tape to show their grandchildren.

The city clerk called the roll. The five council members testified that they were, indeed, present and even awake by answering to the sound of their name. The mayor asked the city attorney to lead city staff and the audience in the Pledge of Allegiance. "Nicole has just asked the city attorney to lead the Pledge of Allegiance," Victorio whispered.

Duly recited, everyone took their seats again. Mayor Pagliero turned to the city clerk. "Are there any speakers to the consent calendar?"

"Two, Madam Mayor."

"Please call them to the podium."

"Agnes Mainwaring."

The resident council watcher and gadfly strode purposefully to the podium, tapped the microphone, smiled at the answering squawk — she knew it irritated the immediate past mayor, Tiggy "Anything for a Vote" Bourke — and launched a tirade against mandated green waste collection.

"This is the desert," Agnes thundered.

Penelope sighed and tuned out, although conceding that Mrs. Mainwaring had a point. There wasn't all that much green waste to collect in a desert, since most people preferred to keep their yards like Penelope's — in a natural state. She looked down at the agenda. Fossil preservation was *still* the fourth item on the agenda.

Agnes went over her allotted three minutes of public comment, a rule instituted by the council to keep council meetings from running until three a.m., but finally sat down.

"Mr. Ed," the city clerk intoned.

Cackling Ed shuffled to the podium, clicked his heels, and saluted each of the council members in turn. With the formalities completed, old Ed said, "At ease."

"Thank you," Madam Mayor replied with a smile.

"Memorials. That's what we need. Memorials."

"Excuse me, sir. There are no memorials on the consent calendar."

"Well, there oughta be. Got memorials all over town. You got your snake memorials, you got your deer memorials, you got your raccoon memorials. . . ."

"Those are animal crossing signs, sir, and

they're coyotes, not raccoons."

"Look like beavers to me."

"He's out of order," Tiggy Bourke said.

"Out of order?" Cackling Ed screeched. "Out of order? You some kinda pinko commie nut?"

It was the mayor's turn to sigh. Representative government was flourishing in Empty Creek. "Let him speak," she said. "You have three minutes, sir."

"All right, then. Civil War memorial. We need a Civil War memorial."

"Our community wasn't founded until after the Civil War," Bourke interjected.

"Carpetbagger," Cackling Ed sneered. "Shows what you know. If we got memorials to beavers, we got to have memorials for our Civil War vets."

Big Mike took that moment to indulge himself in a good stretch. He reared his butt, elongated his front paws, swished his tail, and yawned cavernously. How Mrs. Burnham interpreted that to be the beginning of the wave was somewhat unfathomable, but she stood and flung her arms in the air. The person next to her followed suit. And the wave rippled through the audience — twice. Penelope shook her head, and for about the hundred millionth time since taking up residence in Empty Creek thought there had to be some mysterious element in the local water supply that induced more lunacy than a full moon. Still, when it was her turn, she stood and threw her arms up.

The mayor stared at her constituents in disbelief. Surely, the Founding Fathers had not considered the wave when drafting the Constitution of the United States. She could bang her gavel and ask the police chief to clear the room — he was participating enthusiastically — or she could wisely take the path of least resistance. Besides, doing the wave *was* fun.

Unaware of the wave behind him, Cackling Ed returned the mayor's salute.

When Big Mike had loosened his muscles to his satisfaction, he curled up and closed his eyes. Mrs. Burnham took her seat demurely, and the wave ended.

Nicole took advantage of the lull to appoint Cackling Ed chairman of the Civil War Memorial Study Committee. "Are you willing to serve, sir?"

"Damned straight," Cackling Ed cackled. He winked at the mayor. "You wanna go dancing sometime?"

"Mr. Ed has just asked Nicole for a date," Victorio whispered. "No, wait, erase that."

Democracy could be *so* trying at times.

The consent calendar was approved.

"Call the next item."

Penelope pulled out back issues of *Publishers Weekly* and started reading reviews of novels, ticking off those she wanted to order for the shelves of Mycroft & Company.

"Why do you need a five-car garage?" Penelope heard Tiggy Bourke ask before she tuned out completely.

At the break, Cricket had still not arrived. Penelope wondered what had happened to her big announcement. She left Big Mike asleep on his chair and went out to stand in line at the snack machine, but when her turn came she decided against cheese-filled crackers, M&Ms with peanuts, or a Hershey bar with almonds, and went to do what she really wanted to do all along — call Hiroshi Ishii.

There was no answer in his room. Double diddly damn.

"In light of the major discovery last week," Nicole said, "it is my belief that we should come to some sort of consensus on fossil preservation. My colleagues and staff concur."

Cricket slid into the seat next to Penelope. "Am I too late?" she asked sotto voce.

"Just started."

"Whew."

Dr. Hayden Chudnik, as the city's paleontology consultant, was the first to speak to the issue. "Of course, as an academic, I am vitally concerned that any and all fossils in and around Empty Creek be treated with the utmost care. As the city's consultant in such matters, however, city financial interests must be considered. Reasonable investigation should be conducted, but private property rights must also be taken into consideration. I will be available to answer any questions."

"That was certainly wishy-washy," Penelope said.

Dr. Chester Handley was the next to speak. He reported on excavations to date, the significance of the find, and the necessity for preserving all lands where additional dinosaurs might be lurking beneath the surface.

Save Our Desert members in the audience applauded.

A defeated Albert J. McCory took the podium. "If you folks delay the beginning of the Lonesome Bend construction much longer, we face severe financial penalties and hardship. In order to protect our interests, we must consider legal action against the city of Empty Creek, SOD, and we're gonna throw in a hundred or so John Does and Jane Does, just in case."

SOD members booed.

Cricket was the last to speak. "For the record," she said, "my name is Cricket and I own and live at Lonesome Bend Ranch. The dinosaur known informally as Corny-Milly was discovered on my property and therefore I believe I have the legal right to dispose of the fossil as I see fit. When Dr. Handley has finished his excavation, it is my intention to donate Corny-Milly to the Empty Creek Historical Society and Museum in memory of Cornelius Hacker, my father, and the late Dr. Millicent De-Forest, who died so tragically after discovering the fossil in question."

Almost everyone in the room rose and applauded a blushing Cricket enthusiastically.

Now, *that* was a worthwhile surprise.

Penelope and Big Mike arrived at an empty house. It just wasn't the same without Andy hanging around for a good snuggle. Penelope decided it wasn't too late to give him a quick call and make sure he was okay. It wasn't like him to get sick. He answered on the second ring.

"How are you feeling, sweetie?"

"Still a little queasy, but I'll be fine in the morning."

"I miss you."

"I miss you too."

"Sleep tight."

Reassured, Penelope poured a glass of wine, and took the crumpled sheet of paper with Mrs. Burnham's amoeba on it and flattened it as best she could. With the parchment fragments quickly assembled, the shape of her drawing did, indeed, fill the hole in the parchment rather nicely.

But so what?

Penelope was still pondering the answer to this question, when the telephone rang.

"Hello."

"Ah, Penelope-san."

Penelope sensed Hiroshi-san's bow even over the telephone and returned it. After all, politeness was a virtue.

"I called you earlier. You weren't there. I was worried."

"That is most kind of you, but there is nothing to worry about."

"Has anyone made contact?"

"That is where I went when you called. I have opened negotiations."

"With whom?"

"It is most curious. I met him in the desert. He wore a Donald Duck mask. Most curious."

"Yes, I wonder what the mouse factory thinks of that."

"Mouse?"

"Disney."

"Ah, yes. I am going to Disney World."

"You are?"

"No. Isn't that what they say after sporting events? I am a baseball fan."

"I believe you're correct. The most valuable player gets to go to Disney World."

"Good. I am pleased I was correct. I must learn American ways if I am to have a sushi bar in Empty Cleek."

"Do you have any idea whom you met with?"

"Oh, yes. I have heard that voice before, when I was in Bathsheba that afternoon."

"Yes?"

"He called himself Curry Mahoney."

CHAPTER NINETEEN

Such a simple plan. Such a sweet, delicious, simple plan, worthy of the Master. It was beautiful in its precision, its clarity, its austerity — its naïveté. We just better damned well pull it off or Dutch will rescind my status as an honorary police officer. Big Mike's too.

"It'll never work, boss. I say we just pick him up and grill him. He'll talk."

"Oh, sure. What are you going to do? Feed him jelly doughnuts until he confesses?"

Dutch's office was crowded. Tweedledee paced. Tweedledum leaned against the wall. Penelope and Big Mike were in the two comfortable chairs in front of Dutch's desk. Dutch had his feet on the desk and stared at Stormy's movie posters.

"They're here, boss."

Boris and Natasha shuffled into the office, the body chains they wore clinking.

"Why'd you put 'em in that, for crying out loud?"

"They're prisoners," the offended jailer replied. "It's *your* standing orders."

"They're colleagues, for God's sake," Dutch said. "Get 'em out of that."

"Well, jeez, make up your mind."

"How was your date?" Penelope asked.

"Dreamy," Natasha replied. "Riley is such a gentleman."

"And the pizza?"

"The best."

Dutch grimaced. "We're going to have to teach you American ways," he said.

"Oh, Riley has promised to do that. He is taking me riding on horseback. When I get out of here, of course."

"You're almost out," Penelope said. "We think we know who has your fossils."

"Oh, no," Natasha cried. "Then I will have to go back to Moscow before I see Riley again."

"The Master says —"

"Oh, stuff your master. I want to go picnicking with Riley."

"I still say we haul him in," Tweedledee said.

"Put a sock in it," Penelope said. "He'll just keep his mouth shut and what do we have? Zilch."

"Mahoneys ain't that smart."

"Both of you, zip it," Dutch said. "I'm

trying to think here."

"What is going on, please?" Boris asked.

Under the circumstances, even Dutch thought it was a reasonable question. "You tell him, Penelope. It's your idea."

Penelope wondered if that meant he thought it was a *good* idea. It was difficult to tell when he stared at Stormy like that. "You're not thinking at all," she said, "at least about the matter at hand. You're mooning over my sister, conjuring naughty thoughts, and you're not even married yet."

"Penelope!"

"What is naughty?" Natasha asked.

"What you're thinking about doing to Riley."

"Ah." Natasha beamed. "That."

"The Master says . . ."

Penelope hurriedly interrupted. "It is the Master's 'simple plan,' " she said.

The morose Russian nodded and almost smiled.

"After I talked Hiroshi Ishii out of harakiri, he agreed to put out the word that he was willing to pay big bucks for any fossils, no questions asked. He had a clandestine meeting with Donald Duck. . . ."

"Donald Duck is a crook?" Boris asked. "It cannot be."

"Only in the prices they charge at Disneyland. At any rate, Hiroshi-san recognized his visitor's voice. It was Cully Mahoney."

"That moron at Bathsheba?" Natasha asked. "The one who wanted to teach me the French kiss?"

"The very same. He's meeting Hiroshi-san again tonight to exchange fossils for money. I want to put a wire on Hiroshi-san and stake out the meet. Once we have Mahoney on tape, we'll have your fossils and the man or men who killed Millicent DeForest and Yitshak Cohen. I'm not sure how many of the Mahoneys are involved."

"You think the same people who have our fossils killed these people?" Natasha asked.

"It's the only thing that makes sense. I called the development company and asked if any Mahoneys were on the payroll. The night watchman is a cousin."

"I still say we go out to Bathsheba and pick 'em up," Tweedledee said. "Arrest the whole damned bunch. They'll talk."

"I agree," Tweedledum said.

"All that does is fill your jail with mouths to feed. They'd probably look on it as a vacation. We have no hard evidence. Everything is circumstantial. Sure the Mahoney cousin had the opportunity to steal the dynamite, but how do we prove it? Sure Cully Mahoney set up a meeting to sell some fossils, but we're not sure they're the Russian fossils. Yet. He could be pulling some scam of his own. Perhaps he even has some fossils of his own to sell. Maybe he just likes to wear Donald Duck masks. There's no law against that. Yet." Penelope looked at Dutch. "How say the High Mucky Muck?"

"Natasha's put our food budget out of whack, even with Riley bringing pizzas."

"I'm a big girl. I have to keep my strength up for Riley."

"You should have seen her when she was a shot-putter. She could really eat then."

"Fyodor, I was in training."

Penelope thought she was still in training. Poor old Riley had better be taking his vitamins. He was about to encounter a Russian woman with strong appetites.

"I agree with Penelope," Dutch said. "Too circumstantial. Burke, Stoner, get Ishii over here, and don't let anyone see you do it."

"How we gonna do that?"

"Put him in the back of a laundry truck or something. I don't care. Just get him here." Dutch turned to Penelope. "Good job."

"Thanks, Dutch."

"But next time let me in on it first."

"Yes, sir."

★ ★ ★

The meeting was set for nine p.m. Hiroshi Ishii agreed to Cully Mahoney's conditions after some brief argument over why he had to purchase a Giant Mushy at the convenience store first.

"It's so I'll recognize you," Mahoney said.

"You have already seen me," Hiroshi-san pointed out. "How many Japanese do you expect in the park behind the convenience store at that hour?"

"Better be just one," Mahoney warned.

"And I will recognize Donald Duck," Hiroshi-san persisted. "I still do not see why I must have a Giant Mushy."

"It's the way things are done, for God's sake. Haven't you ever been to the movies?"

"I am fond of Godzilla. I should like to see Steven Spielberg remake *Godzilla*. I can imagine it would be quite good."

"Just get the Giant Mushy or no deal. And come alone."

When Hiroshi-san related the conversation, Penelope had some doubts about her simple plan. Cully Mahoney *was* a moron. Well, no one ever said criminals had to be smart. If they were, they'd go to law school and learn to steal legally. Still . . . if things

382

went well, this case would be history to-night.

"Did anyone see you?" Dutch asked.

" 'Course not. You said to do it on the QT. So we did."

"What'd you use?"

"We couldn't find a laundry truck, so we got an ice-cream truck. Sold forty bucks worth of ice cream on the way over. Elementary school just let out."

"You used an ice cream truck? With music and everything? And you stopped along the way? Good God, why didn't you just put up a sign saying police operation under way?"

"Couldn't disappoint the kids, could we?"

"Nobody saw him. He was under the counter the whole time."

"Get the paramedics to take him back."

"You want us to use the siren?"

"No, I don't want you to use the siren. Just slip in the back and let him out."

"Okay, what time do we meet?"

"You're not going, Penelope."

"Oh, yes, I am."

"Oh, no, you're not."

"And why not?"

"Same reason Boris and Natasha aren't going. I don't want an international incident with more foreigners getting killed."

"I'm an American citizen, and you can't stop me. I have rights."

"Better let her go, boss."

"Yeah, otherwise she'll just show up. This way we can keep an eye on her."

"Oh, all right," Dutch said. "God save me from ice-cream trucks and future sisters-in-law."

"And Andy. He'll need pictures of the arrest."

"Why don't you invite your mom and dad? They don't get out much."

"Big Mike too."

"Don't push me."

"I ain't locking that cat up," Tweedledee said.

"I'll get my rifle out of the Jeep."

"You-are-not-taking-a-rifle," Dutch said, staccato voce.

"You can have my backup," Tweedledee said. He pulled his pant leg up and removed the ankle holster with its .38 snubnose.

"Why, thank you, sir." She checked the revolver before pulling her pant leg up to fasten the holster on her ankle. "Pretty cool," she said. "I'll have to get one of these."

"Nice calf," Tweedledee said. "Too bad we're not wiring *your* chest."

"Don't push your luck, buster."

★ ★ ★

It was worse than waiting for the opening game of San Diego State's football season. At least the off season offered any number of collegiate football preview magazines, World League games from Europe, NFL preseason games, and finally, near the last week of August, real college games from the various classics. There was something for the impatient fan to do while waiting for SDSU's first game, even if it wasn't a very productive use of time.

Still, Penelope always said that fans had to get their training in too. Skills honed during the season grew rusty from disuse during the tedious months between the last kickoff and the first — timing routes from the couch to the bathroom and the refrigerator had to be practiced, stiff fingers needed limbering for quick and dexterous use of the remote control in switching from one game to another. Nor was it easy to listen to one game on the radio while watching another on television without preparation. Entire chapters had to be read during commercial breaks. And, perhaps of greatest importance, the shovel-scoop play had to be perfected in order to get Big Mike from lap to cushion without ticking him off too much.

But that was easy in comparison to

waiting for the stakeout to go down, and Penelope vowed never to complain about the football off season ever again. But it was a source of irritation that everyone else seemed to be coping with the wait very well indeed.

Dutch was napping in his office.

Tweedledee and Tweedledum were in the process of devastating another vat of dough and jelly.

Hiroshi-san was planning his menu for the sushi bar.

Andy was editing a long article by the *News-Journal*'s version of Lois Lane on the history of foundation garments.

Big Mike snoozed and dreamed of Murphy Brown.

With better anticipation, Penelope might have brought a kite to fly. She had found kite flying at the beach to be very therapeutic during her undergraduate days at SDSU. Of course, Empty Creek didn't have a proper beach, but there were tapes of waves crashing. A little ingenuity could solve almost any problem — except what to do while waiting for a stakeout.

Lacking kite, beach music, and ingenuity at the moment, Penelope screamed.

"Arrggh!"

Screaming was also very therapeutic, although it tended to disturb the hired help and customers.

Kathy rushed into the back of the store brandishing a ceramic figurine of Mycroft Holmes, the elder, smarter, and stouter brother of Sherlock. Penelope always thought of Big Mike's namesake as stout whether the Holmesian Canon supported it or not. She was followed by Nora Pryor, unarmed but ready to wade in if necessary.

"What's wrong?" Penelope asked.

"What's wrong?" Kathy cried. "Good God, you emit a shriek worthy of *Friday the 13th, Part 12*, and you ask *me* what's wrong?"

"I was releasing tension," Penelope said. "Don't you ever feel the need to get rid of a little tension?"

"Only around here," Kathy said, retreating to the safety of the bookstore proper.

"Next time bring the poker from the fireplace," Penelope suggested. "We don't want to break the merchandise."

"Next time," Kathy hollered, "I'm bringing a straitjacket."

"That might be fun," Nora said.

"It might at that. I'll have to suggest it to Andy. Let's see now, the beautiful young heiress is wrongly committed to an institution by the wicked uncle, where she falls in love with the dashing young psychiatrist."

"Shrinks are always old and grumpy."

"I'll have to work on that part."

"And why are you tense?"

"Football season." It wouldn't do to get the plan out on the desert telegraph. A Mahoney might be listening.

"It just ended."

"That's why I'm tense. Withdrawal symptoms."

"You should take up a hobby. Needlepoint, perhaps."

"Ugh."

"Pornographic needlepoint."

"That has possibilities. I could illustrate scenes from the great erotic classics."

"It would be more fun to do your own."

"That's what I was referring to."

"I should have known."

"By the bye, Nora, you should be pleased about Cricket giving the dinosaur to the historical society."

"Oh, we are. It was very kind and generous of her."

The park was surreptitiously sealed off as soon as darkness fell. The vehicles took their assigned spots, their drivers slumping below the windshields to hide.

There was still nothing to do but wait.

Penelope offered to play a game or two of literary twenty questions but gave up after Tweedledee and Tweedledum couldn't come up with Jane Austen even after she spotted them the initials and gave the clue, "Her books are very popular now. Several of them have been made into movies recently."

Andy knew better than to play literary twenty questions with his beloved. She showed no mercy and once drove him crazy by an obscure reference to a cannonball in Mark Twain's essay on the literary offenses of James Fenimore Cooper. Big Mike also refused to play unless it involved the superior species — cats.

"We could play spin the bottle instead," Tweedledee said hopefully. "That ain't so complicated."

"How about Jane Austen, you doofus? That wasn't so hard."

"Okay, I'll play, but it's my turn this time."

"Get it on. What's the clue?"

"Twentieth century male literary figure."

"Hugh Hefner," Penelope said. "And he's hardly a literary giant."

"Aw, for Christ's sake, you don't play fair. How'd you know?"

"*Playboy* is the only thing I've ever seen you look at."

"Come on, I read the articles too."

"Name one."

"Miss February's ambition is to be a race car driver."

"I rest my case."

" 'Sex After Sixty.' I read that one."

"Naturally."

At eight forty-one p.m., Hiroshi Ishii emerged from his room at the Lazy Traveller Motel.

"Moving," Sam Connors whispered into his microphone. He then turned his black and white away from Hiroshi-san's destination.

" 'Come, Watson, come!' " Penelope said. " 'The game's afoot.' "

"I know that one," Tweedledee said. "I just can't think of his name at the moment."

"Larry Flynt."

"Aw, it was not."

At eight forty-nine p.m., allowing for customers ahead of him, Hiroshi-san entered the convenience store.

Six minutes later he emerged holding his Giant Mushy and walked into the park, disappearing in the darkness.

"Cue the zither," Penelope said.

"Huh?"

"Haven't you ever seen *The Third Man?*"

"Nope."

"Great zither music. You should rent the video sometime. Orson Welles is Harry Lime and —"

"Cut the chatter," Dutch ordered. "This isn't Movie Appreciation 101, dammit. I want radio silence."

"Grump."

Hiroshi-san whistled "Amazing Grace." It was more of a wheeze than a whistle, but recognizable. It was the code that signaled his arrival at the park bench and indicated that Mahoney was not yet there. He would switch to "Hey Jude" when Mahoney arrived. That would trigger the tape recorder.

If they expected a quick rendition of the famed Beatles song, they were disappointed. They waited. Ten minutes. Twenty.

"What's going on?" Penelope asked. "Where is he?"

"Dunno."

"Has he seen us?"

"Dunno."

"Is that going to be your epitaph?"

"Dunno."

"Call Dutch. See if he sees anything."

"Can't. He said to keep radio silence."

"What's his call sign? I'll shout at him."

"Jeez. What a pain. I'll call him. Dutch this is Larry. Over."

Penelope humphed. What kind of outfit didn't have decent and imaginative call signs? I have to do *everything*.

"Dutch."

Penelope started worrying when Dutch didn't jump on them for breaking radio silence. That was not a good sign.

"See anything?"

"Not a damned thing. We'll give it another half hour or so. Maybe Mahoney can't tell time."

Hiroshi-san stopped whistling.

Penelope stopped breathing. It was going down. Yes!

"What's that clacking sound?" Tweedledee asked.

"His teeth are chattering," Penelope said disgustedly. "He's cold." Dammit. Where is Mahoney, and why is he screwing up *my* stakeout?

For good measure, Dutch gave it nearly another hour before calling it off.

Hiroshi-san hotfooted it back to the Lazy Traveller bar for a hot sake.

One by one the other members of the surveillance team withdrew from their assigned positions, taking care to appear as though they belonged in the area. If he were observing, Penelope wondered what Mahoney would think when parked cars with no drivers in sight suddenly started, apparently of their own volition, and drove off. She hoped he believed in aliens like Mrs. Burnham.

Tweedledee and Teedledum dropped Penelope, Big Mike, and Andy off at her Jeep and headed out to Bathsheba. "If he's there," Dutch said, "bring him back."

"Bratwurst," Penelope said.

"I'm not hungry," Dutch said.

"I am," Tweedledee said hopefully.

"Next time, that will be your call sign. You definitely need a good call sign like 'bratwurst.' Larry can be 'sauerkraut' and Willie will be 'mustard.' "

"There ain't gonna be a next time," Dutch said.

What a spoilsport.

"Well, I think it was a good plan," Andy said.

"Dutch hates me."

"He'll get over it."

"Damn, I hate this waiting."

"We could fool around," Andy suggested.

Penelope smiled. "It would pass the time."

Penelope grabbed the phone. "Bratwurst

— I mean, Dutch?"

"Yeah."

"What happened?"

"No Cully Mahoney. His brother and mother swear they don't know where he is."

"Damn."

"We'll get him. He can't be too far away."

"What went wrong? There was no reason for him not to show."

"He probably made the ice-cream truck. Or the surveillance."

"He's not that smart."

"Smarter than we are at the moment."

For once Penelope was stuck for an answer and fooling around with Andy didn't help.

"Oh, Mikey, you can be such a klutz sometimes."

His expression said What do you expect in the middle of the damned night? It was the middle of the night somewhere, but not in Empty Creek, Arizona, where the sun was shining brightly and Penelope's alarm, rarely set, went off at the terrible hour of eight a.m., two hours after Andy's departure.

In stretching out for a prebreakfast nap, Big Mike had knocked two of Cohen's parchment fragments from the counter into his water bowl on the floor.

"To hell with it," Penelope said, rubbing her eyes. "Eat liver crunchies, and if you're thirsty, drink around them until I have my coffee and can stand the sound of the can opener."

That said, Penelope set about the important business of the morning — breathing the aromatic fumes of perking coffee, which was now said to have healthy benefits. That occupied her until there was enough coffee to fill a mug.

Two cups later, and with her eyes fully open, albeit reluctantly, Penelope fished the fragments out of the water bowl and dried them off with a dishrag. The dirt of two millennia came off on the cotton towel, revealing a series of detailed marks that looked suspiciously like part of a map of Empty Creek and its environs.

"Mikey, look at what you've done!" Penelope grabbed his front paws and did a little jig with him along the kitchen counter, to the sink and back. "You can have all the lima beans you want," she cried, "but later. First, I have to wash some Dead Sea Scrolls."

Big Mike probably thought it was a hell of a way to make a living.

An hour later, Penelope had washed dirt

from a multitude of fragments. While they did not reveal the words of Noah, they did have a pretty good representation of a map of the backcountry beyond Lonesome Bend Ranch.

She went to Cohen's copy of Nora's guidebook and let it fall open to the appendixes. It wasn't exactly precise, but it gave her a pretty good idea of where Mrs. Burnham's missing fragment happened to lie in the parchment map. It was a little like directions in the African bush. Go to the third baobab tree and turn left. Substituting a stately saguaro cactus for the baobab wasn't exactly precise, but it was close enough. What a clever way to disguise a map, Penelope thought, and I'll bet it shows where some missing Russian fossils are buried.

"Good work, Mikey. Let's saddle up. We have fossils to find." She reached for the phone to call for backup and then replaced it. Better check it out first, she thought. I'm not admitting to the misappropriation of evidence unless I've got something to trade. Otherwise, Andy will be bringing pizza to me in jail. Dutch would do it too.

CHAPTER TWENTY

The area outlined on the makeshift map was beyond Lonesome Bend Ranch and accessible by the Jeep, but Penelope had no intention of announcing her arrival to Buxter and whatever other Mahoneys might be hanging out at the X on the missing piece of the puzzle by blithely driving up to say howdy. This was a mission that called for silence and cunning.

But Cricket didn't answer her phone. Penelope thought she was probably still out feeding and caring for the horses or doing any of the myriad tasks associated with creatures who ate. No problem. *If she's not there, I'll just borrow a horse and leave a note so she won't think it's been stolen. Police officer on official business. I have to commandeer this horse.* That brought a smile.

Penelope went through a checklist that began and ended with a rifle and two fully loaded magazines. Unless the Mahoneys were having a family reunion out there, that ought to be more than enough ammunition. The list also included binoculars, a compass, and the ankle holster and the little snubnose she had forgotten to return to Tweedledee. It didn't fit inside her boot, however, so she dropped it in the pocket of her windbreaker, hoping Tweedledee wasn't going to be needing his backup piece today. That brought personal reinforcements to mind again, but she wasn't about to get Dutch involved in another operation until she had more details and facts.

Reconnoiter first. Gather information on the enemy position and strength. Then call for backup. Bratwurst, this is Cupcake, I have a fire mission for you, over. But how to communicate? There were times when Penelope wished she were more sympathetic to the devices of the twentieth century. There was nothing to do but to call Stormy.

"Hi, I need to borrow your cell phone."

"Sure, why?"

"I'm thinking of getting one and I thought I should try one for a day."

"You, Penelope Warren, my technology-challenged sister, wants a cell phone? I don't believe it."

"Can I stop by or not?"

"Of course."

"By the way, is Dutch there?"

"Nope. He's at work."

A Marine expeditionary force consisting of former Sergeant Penelope Warren and Corporal Mycroft Cat moved out in search of a murderer and some old bones. Ten minutes later they pulled into Stormy's driveway to find her waiting for them.

"I'm ready," she said, opening the passenger door. "Move over, sweetie," she told Big Mike.

"For what?"

"I'm going with you."

"No, you're not."

"I know you. You're up to something. No Stormy, no phone. *And* I'll tell Dutch."

Damn. Trapped by a little sister who had once been susceptible to any number of snipe hunts. "You always were a tattletale."

"How's my outfit? I didn't know where we were going, so I had to guess." Stormy wore snug designer jeans, an old and baggy pink cashmere sweater, cowgirl boots, and hat.

"Very chic."

"Oh, good. It's important to be well dressed for any occasion. Where *are* we going?"

"In harm's way, I hope. Better take this."

Penelope handed over the backup gun.

"Oh, goodie. Who do I shoot?"

"I'll let you know when we get there."

"The horses haven't been fed. I don't know where Cricket is. It's not like her. It's a good thing I decided to take the day off. I'm Roxanne, by the way."

"I'm Penelope Warren. This is Stormy, and the big guy is Mycroft."

"It's nice to meet you. Do you have horses here too?"

"No, but we're going to borrow a couple. If Cricket comes back, tell her we have them."

"Sure, I guess." Roxanne looked a little queasy when Penelope unpacked the heavy artillery and slung it over her right shoulder.

"Stormy, pick a couple of horses and saddle them. I'm going to look around."

The front door was unlocked, not at all unusual in Empty Creek. Stanley galumped to greet her, jumping up affectionately. "Hey, boy, where's Cricket?"

There was no sign of a struggle inside the house, but there was no indication that Cricket had been there recently. The coffeepot was cold and empty, which meant that Cricket hadn't spent the night at home or she had gotten up and gone off without coffee. Unlikely. Stanley's food and water dishes were empty. Penelope filled them and left the puppy gobbling his food. Roxanne was right. It wasn't like Cricket to leave Stanley and the horses unfed. The silence of the house was just too ominous. "I don't like it, Mikey."

Big Mike decided to ride with his favorite aunt. It provided a little variety.

Penelope thought it was appropriate that Stormy had saddled Ghostdancer for her. That's a good omen, Penelope thought. Millicent DeForest's horse should be in on the capture of the killer. Then it occurred to her that Millicent had been the last to ride Ghostdancer and she had died. Oh, well, it was a little too late to get superstitious.

With the makeshift map committed to memory, Penelope consulted her compass and pointed her hay-eating machine due north. There was a dirt track leading to their ultimate destination, but ten minutes out, Penelope veered into the desert.

"You *do* know where we're going?" Stormy asked.

"Yep," Penelope replied with a great deal more assurance than she felt. Cricket's disappearance was not good. Well, one thing at a time.

Penelope jumped when the cell phone rang. "Don't answer it. Can you turn it off?"

"Yes, but it's probably Dutch. He'll worry."

"We'll call him soon. Just turn it off."

"Okay."

A minute later, Stormy's beeper went off.

"Good God, you're a walking advertisement for every device known to mankind. Turn that off too."

"It's definitely Dutch," Stormy said, looking at the beeper. "He wants me to call ASAP."

"Later."

With technolgy muted, the party pressed on through the desert.

They reined in at the foot of a rise in the desert floor. "This should be it," Penelope whispered after dismounting and unslinging the rifle. "You hold the horses while I check it out."

It was truly uncanny how often life imitated fiction, even when the make-believe was set in old frontier Arizona and the reality happened in an Arizona galloping full speed toward the new century and the new millennium.

Penelope had read this particular novel. In *Savage Love*, Laney's ravishing heroine,

Jessica McDermott, a society belle late of Philadelphia, had been captured by Indians and taken to their mountain stronghold, where an unspeakable fate awaited her . . . unless the dashing Captain Walters (West Point, Class of 1862) arrived at the head of his cavalry troop or . . . Harry Scott, descendant of Leatherstocking and a pretty sexy Noble Savage in his own right, tracked the untrackable badlands. Since an inept scout guided Captain Walters down the wrong fork in the trail, it was left to Harry (always secretly Jessica's first choice, although Many Horses, the rugged Indian chieftain who looked exactly like Fabio on the cover of the novel, *had* stirred her curiosity) to bargain for Jessica's life.

The unspeakable rites had barely begun — Jessica was nothing if not plucky, and it took the Indians the better part of two pages to divest her of clothing and get her staked out on the ground next to a handy anthill — when Harry rode up, looked down at his spread-eagled ladylove, modestly averting his eyes from her ample charms, and said, "Howdy, Jessica."

The scene Penelope now observed in the clearing below bore a similarity to the events in *Savage Love* — with a little imagination. Actually, it was nothing like the novel. Cricket *was* spread-eagled, her wrists and ankles tied to stakes driven into the ground. But unlike Jessica, except for being barefoot, Cricket was fully clothed, there were no Indians, no anthill, and Penelope doubted that Harry Scott was going to appear out of nowhere to rescue Cricket from the man who looked like a refugee from either the Donner party or World League Wrestling. Penelope couldn't make up her mind. She was, however, pretty sure that she was looking down at the secretive Buxter Mahoney.

He was sitting, eyes closed, in the lotus position about ten yards from Cricket with a boom box in front of him. His hair, while tangled and unkempt, made Penelope envious. It was long, falling beneath his shoulder blades in back and over his eyes in front. His hair was matched by an equally disheveled full beard. He wore ragged and faded bib overalls — no shirt — and his toes protruded from tennis shoes.

"I guess it's up to us, Mikey."

But first Penelope decided to go over the rest of the scene from Laney's novel. It never hurt to have some prepared dialogue and other guidance.

"Good afternoon, Harry," Jessica replied, looking up at her hero. "I think they're going to torture me." (For a Laney heroine, Penelope always thought Jessica was a few debutantes short of a society ball.)

"Looks like it."

"I'd rather they didn't."

"See what I can do."

"Thank you."

Harry dismounted and squatted next to Jessica. Many Horses hunkered down on the other side of the young woman. She looked back and forth between them. Both faces were implacable.

"Give you two horses for her."

"Harry," Jessica cried. "Surely, I'm worth more than two horses."

Many Horses replied in his own language.

"What did he say?" Jessica demanded.

"Says you talk too much. You do too."

"Well!"

Penelope skipped the rest of it. After some prolonged negotiations, some ants intent on picnicking on Jessica, and a knife fight between Many Horses and Harry, Jessica was duly rescued with a parting gift from Many Horses, who handed Harry a switch cut from a scrub oak.

"What's that for?" Jessica asked.

"Many Horses says it'll cure Woman Who Talks Too Much."

Penelope backed down the hill.

"Now?" Stormy asked.

"Now," Penelope said, holding her hand out for the cell phone. "Cricket's there, tied down to stakes. There's a guy meditating too. I didn't see anyone else."

"Meditation is always good."

"Newsroom, Anderson."

"Get your camera and hit the road, sweetie. You're about to have a scoop."

"Good God, you stay undercover until I get there," Andy shouted after taking down the directions.

"Gotta go, darlin'," Penelope said. She punched the code that rang Dutch's private line automatically.

"Where have you been?" Dutch cried. "I've been calling for an hour."

It was too good to pass up. "Bratwurst, this is Cupcake."

On the rise again, Penelope saw that nothing appeared to have changed. Buxter Mahoney was either still meditating, or he was catatonic. Cricket was still tied to the stakes. And good old Harry Scott was nowhere to be seen. Rifle at the ready, Penelope assumed the role of the absent Noble Savage and went down into the clearing. Noble Cat dashed ahead. He always was a sucker for distressed damsels.

Stormy watched, peeping over the rise, ready to create a distraction if necessary before the cavalry arrived.

"Howdy, Cricket," Penelope said, covering Meditation Man with her rifle. He didn't appear to be armed. He didn't appear to be in this world, as a matter of fact.

"Hi," Cricket replied.

"You're supposed to say 'Good afternoon, Penelope,' but I guess you haven't read *Savage Love*."

"Actually, no. You better not get too close. I'm booby-trapped."

"Hmmm. That wasn't in the novel. How did you get here anyway?"

"Cully and Buxter came for me before dawn. Cully said he wouldn't kill me if I gave him the dinosaur."

"I assume from your present predicament that you refused."

Cricket nodded. "Then they brought me out here and dug up some fossils, replaced them with dynamite, and tied me down over it."

"Did they look like Russian fossils by any chance?"

"I couldn't really tell."

"Trust me. They were Russian all right."

"I'll take your word for it." Cricket paused. "Do I get rescued in, what did you call it, *Savage Love?*"

"Of course. Many Horses lives up to his name and sells you to Harry Scott — you're in love with him — for six horses, two knives, a revolver, and a set of pots and pans. And you live happily ever after."

"That's nice. I'll have to read it."

"I have several copies in the store." Penelope scanned the desert. "Where's Cully?"

"He took some fossils to his truck. He's been gone a long time. I tried to get loose, but I was afraid to move too much. I'm lying on about a ton of dynamite." Cricket wiggled her fingers and toes helplessly. "Considering my former profession, I'm a little embarrassed, but Mistress Juliana always was better with knots than me."

Penelope tried one of the knots, but her fingers slipped off. "Damn, that's tough. I didn't think to bring a knife. I should have reread *Savage Love* before starting out."

"Would you scratch my nose, please? It's driving me crazy."

"Better?"

Cricket sighed happily. "Thank you."

"Hi," Meditation Man said pleasantly. "Who are you?"

"Buxter," Cricket said. "This is Penelope. She's my friend. So is Big Mike."

"Hi, Penelope," Buxter said. "I like cats."

"It's nice to meet you," Penelope said. "Do you have a knife?"

"Whatcha want a knife for?"

"To cut Cricket loose. She's uncomfortable."

"Don't see no crickets."

"He thinks I'm still Sally Anne."

"Sally Anne's uncomfortable," Penelope amended.

"Can't."

"Why not?"

"We're all going for a comet ride. It'll be neat. Big bang and then we go to the comet."

"Hale-Bopp is gone and Halley's Comet won't be back for a long time," Penelope said.

"No comet?"

"Aoooo," Penelope said.

Big Mike twitched his ears. He didn't like spooky sounds. He would not have made a good witch's familiar.

"Aoooo," Penelope repeated.

Buxter Mahoney closed his eyes.

"Listen to me, Buxter," Penelope said, trying to imitate the voice on the tape. "Did you kill Cornelius Hacker?"

"Daddy did."

"Your daddy killed Sally Anne's father?"

"Yes." Twin tears squeezed past Buxter's eyelids. "I buried him though. Nice funeral."

"Did you kill Millicent DeForest, the woman at the dinosaur?"

"Don't like that voice," Buxter said. "Where is the nice voice." It was a plea.

"Who killed the woman at the dinosaur?" Penelope asked in her normal voice.

"The King Man."

The penny finally dropped. It was followed by a cascade of quarters from a celestial slot machine clanging away in a jackpot announcement.

The spooky voice on the tape hadn't referred to Kingman, Arizona, at all. It was King Man. Two words.

"Don't move," Cully Mahoney said, appearing out of the desert. He held a detonating device and his hand was poised on the plunger.

Penelope leveled the rifle. "I'm a very good shot," she said. "Believe that."

"Couldn't get me before I blow her up," Mahoney said. "You too."

"I'm willing to talk about it."

"Ain't nothing to say, but you can sit a spell, I reckon."

"I'll stand, thanks." Penelope kept Mahoney in her sights. Mycroft stepped

410

gingerly on Cricket's belly, turned around three times, and settled down, staring impassively at Mahoney.

"You mind?" Penelope asked without taking her eyes off Mahoney.

"He ain't heavy," Cricket said. "He's my friend."

Penelope smiled. It was always good to keep a sense of humor about these things. "I'll give you two horses for her."

"Ain't no Hacker ever worth two horses."

"It's too bad Laney isn't around to write some new dialogue," Penelope said. "Now I'll have to improvise."

"Don't matter what you do. She's gonna die. You too. Shoulda done it that first day, but I wasn't thinkin' straight."

"Why'd you warn us?"

"He did," Cully said, indicating his older brother. "Damn fool wouldn't listen."

"Supposed to yell," Buxter said. "Ain't polite not to yell."

"You killed Millicent DeForest on orders."

"Ain't you the smart one?"

"And your father killed Cornelius Hacker."

" 'Course he did. That's what Mahoneys supposed to do. Kill Hackers. Sally Anne shouldn't have given our dinosaur away

411

like that. Ain't right."

"I'm a Warren."

"Might as well be a Hacker."

"Why Yitzhak Cohen?"

"Who?"

Penelope frowned. This was getting confusing. "The police are on their way."

"Don't matter none. You be riding the comet before they get here." Cully giggled.

"Penelope?"

"Yes?"

"I'm tired and thirsty. Shoot the son of a bitch so we can go have some tequila and orange juice."

"You shut up . . . you . . . you Hacker."

"Mahoneys suck eggs."

"Don't you be talkin' like that."

"I'll bet that thing isn't even connected."

" 'Course, it is." He tugged on the wire, and a silver streak unburied itself from a light covering of dirt. It shimmered along the ground all the way to Cricket's waist.

During the course of conversation Big Mike had grown bored. It was one thing to recline on a warm tummy, but reciprocity was indicated and Cricket was not doing her part with the occasional scratch behind the ears or a gentle kneading just above the tail. So the rippling fuse with the light glinting from it was the perfect diversion for a big cat who often regressed to playful kittenhood.

Big Mike pounced, using Cricket's stomach as a launching pad.

"Oof," Cricket said.

Big Mike whacked the fuse, caught it just right, and reared and pranced away, seriously intent on what he considered to be no more than a string thoughtfully provided for his amusement, incidentally pulling it free of its connection beneath Cricket.

Way to go, Mikey.

Mahoney pressed the plunger and two female hearts stopped.

When nothing happened, he jammed it down again. And again.

Since Penelope's heart was now beating rapidly and since she didn't know that much about bombs — something about kinetic energy flashed through her mind — she decided enough was enough and cranked off a round, resisting the urge to shout Fire in the hole!

Dirt kicked up between Cully Mahoney's legs, and he dropped the detonator. The bullet ricocheted away, whining through the desert.

"Turn around."

Mahoney followed orders.

"I won't kill you," Penelope said, "but if you twitch without my saying it's okay, you'll be singing soprano in the shower from now on. Understand?"

Mahoney nodded.

Stormy started down the hill. Penelope waved her back.

"Empty your pockets."

Penelope smiled when the jackknife tumbled to the ground. "Now, back off and lie facedown, hands behind your head." She took the knife and cut Cricket's hands free and handed her the knife to finish the job.

"Mahoneys never were too bright," Cricket said. "Oops, I didn't mean you, Buxter. You were always my friend."

"Would you ask Mistress Juliana to restrain Mr. Cully Mahoney, please?"

"Certainly."

Mistress Juliana certainly did have a way with knots. When Mahoney was securely hogtied, Penelope picked up a stick and handed it to Mistress Juliana.

"Brings back many happy memories," she said, promptly whacking Mahoney across the butt.

"Ow, goddamn, what was that for?"

"You talk too much," Penelope said. "Now, I wonder where Mr. King Man is."

CHAPTER TWENTY-ONE

"It's hard to get good help," Schyler Bennett said, materializing out of the desert like a second-rate magician in a third-rate club. He seemed intent on sawing a lady or two in half before making them disappear. In this case, however, the saw looked suspiciously like a 30.06 and it was pointed at Penelope. The inherent problem there was that one of the ladies was also armed and was rapidly developing an attitude.

"Looks like a standoff to me," Penelope said. "And I've got help on the way."

"I didn't think you were dumb enough to come out here alone, but you'll be dead before they get here and I'll be gone."

Penelope didn't think that was true because a little spot in the sky behind Bennett was rapidly growing into a red, white, and blue balloon. It was discussion-group time.

"Before I shoot you," Penelope said, "I'd like to clear a few things up."

"You've got two minutes."

"Buxter didn't kill anyone. He was just here to take the fall for you. You wanted Millicent to launder the fossils, but she refused, so you had Cully follow Millicent and kill her while you established your alibi in Flagstaff. She was going to dump a boyfriend, but it was you, not Brian Abernathy. There was just enough truth in your story to throw me off."

"I thought I played the bereaved boyfriend rather well. I might have a future as an actor."

"Unfortunately for you and Cully, Red came along before Buxter could set the explosion."

"Cully screwed up. He wanted to play with the dinosaur for a while. He had plenty of time to get the job done."

"Like you said, it's hard to get good help. Then Cohen double-crossed you. He got a better offer from the Japanese contingent. So you killed him after he told you how to find the fossils. I'm not sure how you got into the suite."

"I used to work at the motel. I kept a passkey."

Penelope nodded. "But then Cully got greedy when he heard Hiroshi-san was willing to buy, and he went to him without your okay. Even worse, Cully thought he could force Cricket to give him the dino-saur."

"It's too bad you won't get to use all this. Time's almost up."

"I'm through," Penelope said. Okay, Stormy, she thought, you can step in here anytime now.

"Good. Buxter," Bennett said in the spooky voice from the tape, "King Man says take your stupid brother over to Cricket and then we'll make boom-boom."

"Buxter, King Woman says stay where you are." Stormy, what the hell are you waiting for?

"Sky, we're cousins. You can't kill me." Cully rolled away.

"Dammit, Buxter, do what King Man says."

"Pretty comet," Buxter said.

"King Woman says Buxter can have a comet ride."

"That's nice," Buxter said. "Can we take the cat?"

"Jesus, what a nutcase," Bennett said. "I have to do everything myself." His finger tightened on the trigger. "Do what King Man says, Buxter."

As a comet, Ralph's Romantic Balloon was pretty slow, but the stealth balloon swooped silently through the sky and Andy

417

was hanging over the basket with ballast in his hands.

Penelope waited.

All hell broke loose.

Stormy started blasting away from the hillside.

Finally.

Andy's aim, while not unerring, was pretty damned good. The ballast landed two feet in front of Bennett, scaring the bejesus out of him.

The sudden cacophony sent Big Mike about three feet in the air. When he landed, he went into a hissing and spitting fit.

The spirit of the bayonet was to kill in close hand-to-hand combat. Penelope lacked the bayonet but charged anyway, delivering a classic vertical butt stroke with her rifle right between Bennett's legs. Penelope was reminded of William Goldman's description in the screenplay of *Butch Cassidy and the Sundance Kid* when Butch delivered "the most exquisite kick in the balls in the history of American film."

Now, that was a *Master* at work.

"Good distraction, sweetie," Penelope said when the balloon landed and Andy dashed to her. "You, too, Stormy, but you sure took long enough."

"Critics," Stormy huffed. "I thought my timing was impeccable."

Big Mike rubbed against Penelope's leg. "You did good too, Mikey. You're the best cat in the entire world."

Damn right.

"Stupid plan," Dutch said when the helicopter landed.

"You oughta lock them two up, boss," Tweedledee said, climbing out of the Bronco. "They're a menace to society. The fur ball too."

"I'm thinking about it," Dutch said.

Stormy was right. Damned critics anyway.

"If you do," Stormy said, "I won't let you pose for the calendar."

Gotcha!

EPILOGUE

Buxter Mahoney was happy to guide them — with a little prodding from the *good* voice — to the makeshift lean-to where he had lived for two years, subsisting on canned goods provided by his brothers and, later, Bennett. Enough tapes were found to provide further evidence against the conspirators, including one that ordered Buxter to shoot anyone who trespassed after the police left the original crime scene. Penelope believed that Buxter had interpreted that to include balloons. The additional evidence was hardly necessary, since the rifle in Bennett's possession proved to be the weapon that killed Millicent DeForest (they found the .25-caliber semiautomatic that was the murder weapon in the death of Yitzhak Cohen in Bennett's vehicle). They also recovered nearly a case of dynamite.

They could not, however, link Sully Mahoney to the crimes.

In due course, Schyler Bennett and Cully Mahoney were convicted of first degree murder and sentenced to life in prison without the possibility of parole.

Buxter Mahoney was acquitted of complicity in the murders by reason of insanity and was returned to the hospital, where he is responding to treatment. Once a month on visitor's day, either Penelope or Cricket arranges for Ralph to take him on a comet ride.

The little group that originally planted Guido gathered to post a dinosaur crossing sign on Empty Creek Highway. "Just in case," Penelope explained, "they're not really extinct, but only hibernating." You never could tell, not in Empty Creek.

The long-anticipated wet–T-shirt contest was held, raising over a thousand dollars for the children. But it did not go smoothly.

"Men!" Laney huffed. "I'm going to take vows."

"You're just jealous."

"The judges were all drunk and cheated."

"How can you cheat in a wet–T-shirt contest?"

"Bribery. I don't know. I should have tied with those other two. And one of them a foreigner at that."

The foreigner in question applied for an

immigrant visa so she could marry the cowboy who had cheered her to victory and, incidentally, promised to clean any judge's clock who didn't vote for the voluptuous Natasha.

"I was proud of you today," Big Jake said after his two pair — tens and sevens — lost to Samantha's club flush. He unfastened another button on his shirt.

"I don't know what got into me," Samantha said, blushing for about the fortieth time that day. "I hope my board of directors doesn't hear about it."

"They'd be proud of you too. You beat everybody fair and square. There should not have been a tie either. And I know what I'm going to do."

"What's that, Jake?"

"I'm gonna start saving for one of them million-dollar bras like Cindy Crawford modeled for Victoria's Secret a couple of years back. The one with all the diamonds on it. You deserve it."

Samantha smiled. "That's a lot of diamonds, Jake," she said demurely.

"Yes, it is, and ain't it grand?"

Boris boarded a plane for the return trip to Moscow with the fossils safely bundled in the cargo hold. Waving goodbye to his American friends, the last thing he said was

"Hurrah for Penelope." He even returned her first edition of *The Maltese Falcon*.

And, yes, the men of Empty Creek did pose for *their* calendar, sans Cackling Ed, of course, although there was a movement afoot at Geezer World to publish their own calendar and to hell with those young whippersnappers who didn't appreciate the beauty of graceful aging.

A presentation copy of the Official Sixteen-Month Men of Empty Creek Calendar was mailed to Her Royal Majesty Queen Elizabeth II. Sometime later, a brief reply was received on Buckingham Palace letterhead. "What a splendid idea," the note read, "and for such a worthy cause too."

True to his word, Hiroshi Ishii gave up fossils and opened the Samurai Sushi Bar.

The Library Board, after a little persuasion, voted unanimously to abide by the First Amendment.

A Jacuzzi was installed and inaugurated by Penelope and Andy, who took the opportunity to further refine the rules of Olympic necking. They also hit another twelve on the kiss-o-meter at 1,200 feet above the desert floor.

A fund-raising drive was started to greatly expand the Empty Creek Museum in order to accommodate the nearly intact dinosaur that slowly emerged from the excavation. Until the money was raised, however, Corny-Milly resided in a huge tent behind the museum.

At the ribbon-cutting ceremonies, Cricket uncovered the plaque that read simply IN MEMORY OF CORNELIUS HACKER AND MILLICENT DEFOREST. She also caught the eye of one Juan-Carlos Estavilla, who bowed and kissed her hand both before and after inviting her to dinner. It is not known at this time if Mistress Juliana has come out of retirement, but Noogy is totally devoted to the woman with one name.

Cornelius Hacker was buried in his truck, which he would have liked. They never did find all his remains, and Cricket thought he would also like being a fossil himself, discovered a hundred million years from now.

Cricket received a doll from Dutch and it now stands on her mantel.

Speaking of retirement, Red the Rat hung up his spurs to help his beloved research fitness centers and mud baths. He also spends a lot of time practicing with the garden hose just in case they actually pull it off.

After much delay, Albert J. McCory broke ground on the Lonesome Bend Development, but with a much-reduced density, thereby preserving a great deal more of the desert. He also has a gaggle of paleontologists looking over his shoulder every time a bulldozer cranks up.

Stormy was undecided whether to take the lead role in an off-Broadway production or to star in a new film with the working title *The Erotic Adventures of Joan of Arc*. She left the choice to Big Mike, who gave both scripts two paws down.

As Penelope's hair grew longer and longer, Andy took great delight in brushing it each evening for the full one hundred strokes that the literature decrees.

And, of course, Penelope gave full credit to Big Mike for providing the clue that led to the arrest and conviction of the two bad dudes, resulting in a city proclamation and a medal on a red ribbon presented by Mayor Nicole Pagliero.

But, to tell the truth, Big Mike probably would have preferred a lima-bean-flavored frozen yogurt.

About the Author

Garrison Allen has been a Peace Corps volunteer in Malawi, an English instructor in Ethiopia, creative director for a public affairs and advertising agency, and a tank commander in the Marine Corps Reserve. He now lives quietly in Long Beach, California with his placid black cat, Oliver, and is at work on his fifth mystery in his acclaimed "Big Mike" series.